"Dammit, Rot, have you heard a word we've said?"

President Robert Owen Trayson glared over the top of his glasses at the chief of his political security staff. "Stop calling me Rot. It's B.T., or just Bob, even in private. Do I have any hope of turning this around?"

"Sure you do, but it's gonna cost you. It's time to strip the Federal Bureau of Environment of its direct law enforcement authority, or at least its power to levy fines for violations of it's own administrative laws. You know that, Bob. You've been promising to do it for months. Frankly I'm surprised you haven't done it sooner. Is it the money?"

"Of course it's the money. You know how hard I've been working to cut back the social entitlement programs, and so far I haven't saved a nickel. If I shut Eldon down the funding is gone and we run in deficit. I've already scaled back the military you know."

"You've obviously given this a lot of thought, Bob. Do you have a plan?"

"Yes I do, but you're not gonna like it."

The Restitution

By
Martin Wendell
Author of *The Forfeiture*

INFINITY
PUBLISHING.COM

Copyright © 2010 by Martin Wendell

ISBN 0-7414-5783-0

Published by:

PUBLISHING.COM

1094 New DeHaven Street, Suite 100
West Conshohocken, PA 19428-2713
Info@buybooksontheweb.com
www.buybooksontheweb.com
Toll-free (877) BUY BOOK
Local Phone (610) 941-9999
Fax (610) 941-9959

Printed in the United States of America
Published January 2010

Also by Martin Wendell
In Infinity paperback

"The Forfeiture"
ISBN 0-7414-3269-2

"The Forfeiture" took place a few hundred miles east of most of the action in this book, several years earlier. While there is no current connection between the two, a third novel is planned. "The People" will feature characters and backstories drawn from both of its predecessors.

For Nancy

My one and only Sweetie

THE RESTITUTION

PROLOG

The thing didn't look like it could ruin your life. Just a dark green metal box chained and padlocked to the post of a sign that said "Do Not Pass When Opposing Traffic Present". Good advice. A black rubber hose ran from it across the road. Knowledgeable drivers who ran over it assumed it was a traffic counter, used to justify the cost of repaving a road. A very few noticed the road didn't need repaving and wondered.

The developer of the Passive Emissions Sampling Vehicle Identifier, or "P.E.S.V.I". had been intensely proud of it. It would improve the nation's air quality by detecting the work of unscrupulous mechanics who would charge for federally required emissions system service but not actually perform it. Air was constantly drawn in through pores in the hose. When a vehicle passed over it a small sample of its exhaust entered and went through a test chamber where unburned hydrocarbon, nitrous oxide, carbon monoxide and a dozen other real and imagined pollutants were measured in a fraction of a second. If any were over limits, the license number was read by machine vision so its maintenance records could be checked and the culprit mechanic identified.

Only about a hundred PESVIs were made before tax irregularities were discovered that put the manufacturer out of business. None of the fourteen employees of the small company had any idea how the things were actually being used. Two of them had died. One of them had been the owner of the company. The other was the engineer who said from the start that the government only wants money, and unscrupulous mechanics don't have any.

THE RESTITUTION

CHAPTER ONE *Simple Pleasures*

"I'm sorry, it's not you. I'm just worried, and I'm not comfortable here. You're nice though." Alison was truly worried, and not only for Shelley, drunk out of her mind and upstairs alone with one of the guys who were "hosting" this party. She was concerned about the car she was driving. It wasn't hers – or even Shelley's. It belonged to Shelley's brother, and it was a rolling deathtrap, a little subcompact, rusty and sagging in back even when it was empty. When you let go of the wheel for a second it would start turning toward the middle of the road all by itself. It was more than twenty years old, and smelled funny. Shelley had made them keep all the windows partway down all the way to Fort Miller, a good hundred miles from home. The night was a lot colder now and staying over was out of the question. Carole and Lynne were scared to death, and Shelley was out of control.

Coming to this party of total strangers had been Shelley's idea. Her school was in Fort Miller and she knew some of the people, though evidently not well.

Alison realized she would be as terrified as Carole and Lynne if it weren't for Greg, the young man she shared a loveseat with. He was big, muscular, and in a similar situation. He'd been invited only because he didn't drink, making him an ideal designated driver. He'd accepted only for the chance to drive a car, a rare pleasure for a college student. Alison had been "designated" by Carole and Lynne after Shelley started drinking and obviously wouldn't be able to drive at all. She'd driven part of the way down to give Shelley a break. That's how she knew about the steering problem.

Women were outnumbered three to one by eleven o'clock, and the guys were in a drunken frenzy. Thank goodness there didn't seem to be any drugs. She was safe, sitting with Greg, but the other girls were vulnerable.

Greg said it first. "I'll be fine, but you three need to get out of here quick." He didn't know about Shelley upstairs. Alison had been ashamed to tell him. Her grandfather had an expression for times when you need someone's help; "Climb, confess and comply." She never understood it, but it meant if you need to summon help, tell them the whole story. Then trust them. This was such a time.

Greg's face froze as she described the fellow Shelley had gone upstairs with. He stood up, looked around and caught the eye of another man standing alone in the kitchen doorway holding a glass. Greg gestured and the smaller man started across the noisy room. His blue satin jacket said "John Walgren" in embroidered script over the right breast. The back said "Walgren Racing". Much smaller than Greg's six foot three, he was still impressive looking, with an in control look that was refreshing among the drunks.

After a quick buzz of discussion with Greg, the new guy leaned down to Alison and asked, "Did you get the name of the person your friend is with?"

"Yes, but I don't remember."

"First name Ross?"

"Yes, I think so!"

"Damn, how long have they been up there? Does she know him?"

"About half an hour. I don't think she knew him before."

"Want us to help get her out of here? This party is going to turn ugly real soon. I'm John. Greg is driving my car so I could drink, but I'm not drinking in this crowd. Only stayed because Greg seemed to have found a decent girl. Just couldn't break you two up."

It started out organized. Greg and Alison, holding hands, started up the stairs with John, left arm around Lynne, right around Carole following behind. John knew Ross Gofman, by reputation anyway. He'd just been released after serving four years in prison for burglary and home invasion. He'd spent the afternoon bragging about what he was going to do to some college bitch tonight. John said he was dangerous, and if it went badly, to give him room.

At the end of the hall a couple of guys were leering through a door that wasn't quite closed. Shelley could be heard pleading to be let go. She'd apparently sobered up a bit, and whatever had been intended hadn't happened yet. Seeing the big man and the racing guy coming with the other three babes Ross' bitch came with, the two creeps made way and Greg sort of pushed Alison through the doorway, entering right behind her, followed by the others. John shoved the door closed as Lynne found the light switch.

Ross Gofman was not happy with the girl he'd singled out. She was too willing. He didn't want to make love, or even have sex with her. He wanted to humiliate her, destroy her, make her want to die. She didn't seem to understand that. She was just drunk and horny. She seemed to think this was foreplay.

The bedroom filled up and the lights came on. The first thing she noticed was Greg. Smiling a little with her split lip, she took a bit too long covering herself with her arm and hand.

Ross stood dumbfounded while his buddy pulled a knife on Greg, who backed away making room for John the racing guy. Then something happened that horrified Alison more than everything else she had just seen. Suddenly John was holding a gun. She had never seen one before, except in police holsters. This way, it was naked, *obscene,* and in an unimaginable way, on her side. The goon's eyes went wide and he stopped in his tracks. Ross recovered and his hand went for his pocket, which wasn't there because his pants were on the floor. He dove for them, but Greg got there first, snatching up the pants as he kicked Ross in the ribs. Gingerly, he took the gun from the pocket and handed it to John Walgren.

"Well well, a stainless three eighty. Nice, didn't know they sold them anymore – to anybody, let alone someone just out of prison. You steal it? I'm going to try it out if your friend here doesn't drop that nasty looking knife."

Greg reached out and took the medieval looking 'fantasy' type knife.

"Alison, invite Ross' two friends in. Make them feel welcome." She was still in shock from the sight of the guns. Lynne went to the door as John got behind it. She opened it wide, smiling. "You guys want in on this?" The leering fools bumbled in, seeing only Shelley with hardly anything on. The door closed behind them. The first saw a blur of motion and the floor seemed to come up and hit him. The second turned to where his pal had been and found the muzzle of a .380 under his eye. "Have a seat."

One at a time, John made the four creeps lean against the wall while the girls searched them for more weapons. Lynne had to do most of it. Alison still didn't have her composure back and Carole was busy getting Shelley dressed. Greg held the knife and

4

guarded the door as best he could. John didn't offer him one of the guns. Just as well, he'd never seen one before either.

The bed provided plenty of material to tie up the thugs well enough to give them enough time to leave the house. Still shaken, but OK to drive, Alison followed John and Greg through the city to a huge shopping center on the north side where they all went into a restaurant for coffee. None had any appetite for food. Shelley, still drunk, didn't even feel violated yet. Alison couldn't stop thinking about the guns.

Knowing not to talk about them in public, she remained silent while Shelley tried without success to be cute with Greg. After a nervous half-hour calming down and exchanging names and phone numbers the two cars went separate ways.

Cold sober, John Walgren drove his own car. Greg sat silently in the passenger seat. John figured he was either already missing Alison Loch, which would be understandable, or disappointed because he didn't get to drive. "Want to drive, Greg? I forgot all about it."

"Naw, you go ahead. Do you have some sort of license for that pistol? I've known you since first term last year and had no idea you carried one of those."

"Oh Lord no. Nobody but government officers can carry one now, and even they can't own one. Not legally at least. My dad gave it to me a month before he died. He got it the same way from his father long before they started licensing them at all; much less taking them away from folks who already had them. Mine was missed 'cause it'd never been registered. No one but dad and me knew about it. Dad said the bad guys would always have guns 'cause they have no respect for the law. I love and respect the law, but choose to violate the ones that make us unarmed and helpless and let creeps like Gofman assault, rob and rape us. You saw a perfect example of that tonight, Greg."

"But what if you get caught with it?"

"I'll go to prison, probably five or six years. Tonight will make it worth it. Those girls would have all been raped, beaten, very likely killed. Without my .38 Special, we wouldn't have been able to stop it. We would've died too if we'd tried."

"Will you teach me to shoot one?"

Each lost in her own thoughts, the three conscious girls in the northbound clunker rode in silence. Shelley was sound asleep in the back seat with her head on Carole's lap. She'd started out that way and been made to turn around after throwing up on Carole's feet. Then she started passing gas. Carole decided it would be better to be barfed on.

The old car was running even worse than before and Alison was beginning to wonder if they were going to make it home. Whenever she needed to stop or slow down it took forever to get back up to speed again. She had to hold the gas pedal fully to the floor to go up hills. The exhaust smelled worse even with all the windows fully down and they were burning up gas like crazy. How could such a small car get such bad mileage?

This hill had a curve near the top. Going around it, Alison noticed a black line on the road surface, crossing it. She smiled, remembering how happy her dad had been when one of those appeared on the pothole filled road out to Loch Tool and Die. It meant the road might get fixed soon. Thump thump. Idly, Alison wondered what they had in mind for this highway, widen it? Even in the junker, the roadway seemed smooth as a baby's bottom. Still out cold, Shelley farted again. Carole was starting to get really annoyed.

Eldon Stewart Morris, section chief of the smallest division in the Federal Bureau of Environment, felt he had the most thankless job in government and was intensely proud to have it. Under the last President, he had *founded* the FBE, and served as it's first director. The bureau was monstrously unpopular with the public, and the new President had used that fact to discredit his predecessor with the voters. With the election won, he made a show of pruning it down to a more moderate size and cutting its budget. The banner headlines said something like "FBE Director Morris dismissed by President Trayson". No mention was made of his re-hiring - at the same pay - as chief of the Passive Random Sampling Division, the section the new President considered the Bureau's whole reason for being, one of the very few things he and Eldon Morris agreed upon.

The statements about cutting the Bureau's budget were lies. It had no budget in the usual governmental sense. The FBE was very much a profit making entity, mostly due to the efforts of the PRSD.

Eldon had a true hand picked team. One hundred people, fifty men and fifty women. The youngest was 23, the oldest, other than himself at 51, had just turned twenty-nine. The only agency of the federal government to take in more money the previous year was the Revenue Service, with over 145,000 agents and employees. Eldon's kids considered themselves an elite group of secret operatives in the business of saving the world.

Starting from scratch, Eldon had made an unusual request of the government hiring offices. He wanted resumes only from new college graduates who had grade point averages below 2.0 (C or lower) in the environmental sciences, and records of involvement with environmental, animal rights or anti-military activist organizations on campus. He got about a thousand resumes, interviewed ten and immediately hired six, assigning them to select 94 more with an even 50/50 gender split.

Once the team was assembled Eldon spent a couple weeks training them himself, making a handful of staff changes to weed out a few he wasn't sure he could trust completely. Trust and compliance were the qualities he required. Skill and knowledge were secondary. He considered any sense of justice to be an unacceptable weakness.

The main FBE headquarters on the East Coast employed several hundred people, most of them engaged in the business of selling permits and licenses to industry and conducting on-site inspections. The real work was done by the Passive Random Sampling Division operating out of a relatively tiny former Border Patrol office now identified only as "FBE West Coast Operations". Eldon's people constantly monitored data from a thousand or so secret automatic air sampling devices set up to sniff the air around major industrial, trade and shipping centers nationwide. When they got a hit, a field team was sent there to isolate the guilty polluter or polluters. To protect their anonymity, they seldom confronted a polluter themselves. Headquarters did that, using their own data collected after the fact so PRSD would never be challenged for evidence. In fact, the courts generally didn't know PRSD existed at all.

At any given time, 25 people staffed FBE west. Three shifts required 75 of Eldon's force. The other 25 were 'Field Operatives' – the gravy job. Everyone rotated through a yearly cycle. Three months on first shift, then three months on second, then third, then field. Since fieldwork was considered dangerous, all that wanted to be were armed. Given two weeks of part time weapons training and issued 9mm semiautomatics with nationwide unrestricted carry permits, they would really feel like secret agents. Every single one of them opted for it.

Eldon retained a couple important jobs for himself. Every time his field teams identified a violator, he made the decision whether to forward the hit to headquarters. The field team was to e-mail him and then encrypt all their files on it. One other kind of information passed through him alone. The computer pre-qualified hits from something called PESVIs. Only a small handful of Eldon's staff knew anything about them. The rest saw them as an undesirable potential source of extra duty. Eldon received prequalified PESVI hits automatically from the PRSD computer that processed them. He then verbally gave the names involved to President Trayson's political security staff who gave him a simple one-word response a few hours later: 'Go'. No response at all was to be interpreted as 'Stop'.

Eldon would then call FBE west and ask for one of the 'few' by name, making it sound personal. The recipient was always delighted, but couldn't say so out loud. It always meant extra "field" time his or her co-workers wouldn't be allowed to know about. A very special kind of field time. The kind where they would interact directly with local, county and state law enforcement – and carry the command authority of the federal government. Heady stuff for a twenty-something greenie activist with a low C in environmental studies.

The crippled car made it as far as Lake Osborne. Alison tried to time it, but the town's only traffic light turned red and caught her. The car stalled as it lurched to a stop and wouldn't restart. The girls were just deciding to get out and push it back into a parking space when the town cop pulled up behind them. The light turned green, the cop honked his horn. Alison leaned out and mouthed "It won't start!"

The town cop was nice and polite, but efficient. He could plainly smell alcohol, and figured the windows were all down to air it out. After calling in all the driver licenses and the vehicle documents to Central Dispatch he administered a field sobriety test to the driver. She passed it easily, but he gave her a preliminary breath test just to be sure. The young woman blew a zero-zero.

"Are you the designated diver, miss?"

"Yes sir. I never drink – never."

"Are you all from Dunningsville? It's only eight miles, can I call you a wrecker?"

"This isn't my car, sir. I don't know if it has that kind of insurance. How much does it cost?"

"Probably not much, maybe a hundred bucks. Not as much as a ticket for obstructing traffic. I'd do it if I were you." He was smiling pleasantly.

The tow truck driver turned out to be Shelley's cousin. He knew the car well. Shelley's brother was always trying to get him to fix it for nothing. This time, the thing was dead. It'd cost a lot more to fix it than it was worth, and with the police report on file it would have to be re-certified as passing safety and emissions. Not likely. He just delivered it to its owner's apartment and took all the girls home. An undignified end to a very bad night.

More than two thousand miles away one of the many computers at FBE West Coast Operations made the connection it was always looking for. Using the same fiber optic and satellite communications link used by the industrial effluent sniffers, PESVI number 76 had reported the license number of a car producing over-limits on nine identified pollutants. That part ordinarily happened several thousand times in an average day. Less than an hour later a police contact was recorded through the traffic information network identifying a driver of the same vehicle who was not a member of the registered owner's family, an occurrence that only popped up once or twice a week. That driver's household, comprising two individuals, had paid taxes on a combined income of between $150,000 and $225,000a year for the last ten years. They were presumably father and daughter. The range was not arbitrary. With less than one-fifty, they wouldn't be able to pay. Above two-twenty-five would enable them to assemble a legal dream team. The computer estimated a net worth of two point two million dollars, very close to the self-imposed upper limit of two point five. It hadn't made a hit this good in more than a month.

THE RESTITUTION

CHAPTER TWO   The Victim

Gary Loch ordinarily didn't keep secrets from his girls. He'd lost his wife to leukemia when Heather was sixteen and Alison had been only seven. Since then, he'd devoted his whole life to the girls and his small company, Loch Tool and Die. The girls were his reason for living. The company was his means of living.

He had one secret he kept from Alison. Two years after Bobbi had passed away, a high school acquaintance had tried to rape Heather. Another boy had intervened and stopped it. Heather was mortified, bruised and humiliated. Even though no actual rape had occurred, the emotional damage had been done. It crippled her for months and still affected her.

Gary knew the boy, or thought he did. Heather didn't want to report the attempt at first; it was just too embarrassing for her. Being a private person himself, Gary respected her wishes, but couldn't just let it go.

The next day he'd gone to pay the young man a visit at the local pool hall. He never intended it to become physical, but it did. Finding himself under attack by his daughter's would-be rapist and two of the guy's friends, all armed with broken off pool sticks, Gary had defended himself.

A weapon of sorts had found it's way to him. As one of the toughs broke off his pool-cue to make it a more effective club, the thin but longer end had gone flying. Gary caught it in mid-air. It had split off more or less lengthwise, leaving a long smooth point. The boys were brawling with clubs, three against one. Gary had been a fencing champion in college – almost made the Olympics. In just a couple seconds the almost-rapist had been disarmed and one of his buddies had ran. The other kid had been a little less lucky. He now had Gary's wooden 'foil' in his hand – the unpleasant way. It protruded through the back of his hand just above the wrist, dripping blood. He'd impaled himself with the force of his own club-stroke. The fight was over almost as soon as it started.

A legal battle had followed. It seemed the kid with the skewered right hand was seventeen. Gary Loch had committed an assault with a deadly weapon on a minor. Two nights in the Banworth County Jail, the limited disclosure of Heather's attempted rape and several thousand dollars in legal fees later he was sentenced to community service, a fine of ten thousand dollars and payment of the kid's medical expenses. The community service consisted of instituting an apprenticeship program at LT&D. Gary thought it was over, but every once in a while it would come back to haunt him.

This was one of those times. LT&D had applied for a loan of $85,000 to replace its oldest vertical machining center and been turned down – because the owner was a convicted felon. He would have to visit the bank – again – dragging in all the old court records. All these years and he still hadn't lived it down. The same sort of thing was always happening with insurance companies, suppliers, and even customers. Gary's biggest fear was that Alison would find out about the whole fiasco. He wanted to shelter her from it, keep her from suffering from it as Heather had.

"Morning sweetheart."

"Hi Daddy."

"You're up a bit late this morning, Al. You OK?"

"Yeah, I'm fine. We had a real bad night. Guess you were right, Daddy."

"Right? About what?"

"Everything, I guess."

"Want to talk about it, honey?"

"Yes I do, but it's a long story. Tonight maybe? You're late already, and I've got to talk to Shelley DuPont's brother. I was driving his car last night and it broke down. The wrecker guy says it can't be fixed."

"That old yellow junker? What on Earth were you doing with that thing?"

"Like I said, it's a long, dumb story."

"I hope not too dumb. I know the girls think Paul DuPont is good looking, but –"

"Oh, Lord no! Shelley had his car last night – borrowed it from him for a little, ah, trip."

"OK, tonight it is. I gotta go – I'll be back early, Al." If Gary was concerned, he didn't show it.

Pulling into his parking space, Gary wasn't surprised to see Dennis Davis' pickup in the lot. Like many of his employees, Dennis had keys to the place. Lately he'd been coming in on Saturdays to work on a personal project of some sort. Gary could understand that. He'd been working on a model steam engine off and on for two years himself. Dennis had done some of his detail drawings for it, off the clock of course. Dennis was honest, sometimes to a fault.

Entering through the side door to the shop on the way to his office, Gary saw what Dennis was working on, and it stopped him in his tracks. Always innovative on the job, Dennis was always coming up with labor saving ways for the machinists to use the equipment. His ideas almost always worked, but this was over the top. Gary couldn't begin to imagine what he was doing.

"What the hell?" Gary recognized the workpiece. A two-foot long piece of 4130 steel tubing, ¾ inch outside diameter, seven-sixteenths inside. Gary had ordered it for him, along with a bill of material for a progressive stamping die. The item had been marked 'Dennis Personal' on the requisition. But what on Earth was he doing with it?

The tube was clamped in a lathe chuck that was in turn attached facing upward to the cross slide of the large radial drill press. A strange looking apparatus was held in the machine's spindle chuck where Gary would expect to see a very long drill or reamer. A two-foot length of steel rod entered the upper end of the workpiece. Just below the spindle chuck, a drum or pulley that looked like part of an old-fashioned boat steering system was fixed to the rod. A length of 1/8th inch cable wrapped several turns around it passed through a simple block pulley attached by a bracket to the non-rotating spindle body, then upward to where it was clamped to the machine head. As Dennis ran the spindle down, the cable would pay off the drum causing the spindle to rotate – very slowly – all the way to the bottom of the tube. When he raised it back up with the handwheel, a large clock spring wound it back, keeping the cable tight. Up – down – up – down. Gary watched, fascinated. His first thought had been for what would happen if the machine started up. The whole unbalanced thing would most likely fly apart causing untold damage, but the expensive machine wasn't turned on. It wasn't even plugged into its 440-volt power receptacle. A legally required lockout cap covered the plug itself, as if the machine was receiving maintenance. Whatever Dennis was doing was entirely manual.

"I hate to ask."

"Care to take a guess?"

"There must be some sort of cutter in there."

Dennis released the up travel limit and extracted the rod from his workpiece tube. The end of it was machined to hold four tiny tungsten carbide slotting blades equally spaced around it and set in a slight spiral, apparently to follow the same rotation the cable and pulley arrangement would impart. "Rifling?"

"Yup. Don't worry, it's a muzzleloader."

"You mean one of those Davy Crockett guns? A little short, isn't it?"

"It won't look much like anything Davy would recognize. Sort of a .45 caliber single shot carbine."

"Is that legal? You're not going to get us arrested are you?"

"As far as I know it's legal. When they wrote the Civilian Disarmament Act they specifically exempted "muzzle loading arms for historical and recreational purposes". They didn't describe what they should look like. They only define them as "single shot sporting arms of at least 20 inch barrel length, to be loaded through the muzzle with propellant, projectile and ignition source as separate components"".

"A projectile should be easy, but what will you use for propellant?"

"I'll have to make that, too. Nobody manufactures it anymore. I'm working on an electric ignition. Sort of a spark plug. Two size D not included."

"Davy Crockett wouldn't recognize that, I bet."

"Look, Gary – I'm sorry. I should have cleared this with you. I'm almost done with this barrel. I'll take the whole thing home today, I can finish it in my workshop."

"That's good. You can work on small parts here if you want, but I'd rather you didn't keep enough of it here to be recognizable as a weapon. Remember what happened to McCowell Tool and Gauge when they found a pistol on their custodian during a safety raid?"

Gary found he couldn't work effectively. He'd come in to write a letter to the bank explaining his old felony conviction and trying to convince them the new VMC would make him more profitable. He was just too preoccupied today. As soon as he willed himself to stop worrying about Dennis and his homemade gun, he started thinking about Alison and her friend's busted car. He didn't know how, but down deep he felt he was going to end up having to pay for it. He drove home shortly after noon worrying that he was becoming a worrier.

Not the most pleasant person in even the best of times, Paul DuPont was in a rage when Alison Loch came to his door. Four years older than his sister Shelley at twenty-three, he'd lived on his own since their parents had kicked him out at nineteen, despite his being more or less unemployable. His apartment consisted of two rooms in a single family house that had been crudely converted into a duplex, then subdivided again to make four barely legal units. Seeing his car was back, he'd tried to drive it to the party store for smokes. The only smoke he got came from the starter when it tried without success to turn over the seized engine. Furious, he called home for his sister, only to find out she was still asleep and no one could get her up. Then he called his cousin at Bannermann's garage in Lake Osborne.

"Yeah, Paul. I'm the one who towed it. I probably should have just taken it to the junkyard. Why don't you get your stuff out of it and I'll come by Monday and tow it for you. Save you a lot of trouble."

"Bullshit! I didn't ruin it! Somebody's gotta either fix it for me or buy me a new one! Come get me right now and take me to Shelley! That bitch is gonna get it this time."

"Paul, I'm sorry. That thing was shot long before Shel borrowed it. She did you a favor, Paul. If you'd gotten caught in a Roadside Safety Inspection you'd have had to pay a fortune just to stay out of smog jail. I can't help you this time. The cops in Lake Osborne took a report on it. You'd have to get a recertification. It'd cost thousands. Face it. Buy a decent car or start walking."

"Shelly's gonna –" His cousin hung up on him. Then Alison Loch knocked on his door downstairs.

Gary had just sat down in his big chair to read when his daughter came in with tears in her eyes.

"Paul and Shelley are both jerks, dad. I hope I never see either one of them again ever."

Her father closed his book. "If you still want to talk, I'm listening, honey."

14

"Shelley came home from school in Fort Miller last week. We don't think she's planning to go back. Lynne and Carole have been trying to talk her out of quitting, me too, I guess. Yesterday she asked us all if we wanted to go to a party some of her friends were having down there."

"It's a hundred mi -."

"I know. Anyway, everything went wrong right from the start. If I'd known she was driving Paul's car I wouldn't have gone. She picked us all up at Lynne's with it. We didn't have any chance to get out of going without insulting her. I had to drive it partway down. It was awful. It isn't safe at all, lots worse than just being illegal. I don't know how he ever got a license plate for it. Anyway, when we got there Shelley didn't know anybody after all, but she still wanted to stay. She was stone drunk in an hour and we were all stuck there."

"That explains why you came home at three in the morning. I was wondering about that. I know you're a big girl, but -."

"This is the worst part, I don't know where to start."

"The beginning would be good."

"Shelley went up to a bedroom with the host. The fellow seemed dangerous to me. Turned out he was just out of prison. The rest of us sort of panicked. I'd met a really nice guy and asked him to help us. He was there as a designated driver for someone else, so he wasn't drinking. Neither was his friend, the guy he was driving for – too put off by the crowd. Anyway, they both helped us get Shelley and get away."

Gary was getting uncomfortable. He was prepared for a discussion about the perils of unsafe cars, not the sordid sex lives of his daughter's friends. Alison, however, had just realized she'd skipped over the part she most needed to talk about. Out came the details of the 'rescue' and the nick of time nature of it. By the time she got to the part about the guns she was crying openly. Shocked as he was, Gary found the composure to get up from his recliner, sit on the couch with his daughter and put his arms around her. He'd dreaded something like this happening for years, and when it did happen he hadn't been there to stop it. Someone else had to. Strangers. People he didn't even know.

Then a new thought started to creep in. His little girl's good judgement had *attracted* her rescuers, or more correctly, Shelley's rescuers. Alison had in a very real way been one of the rescuers herself. He was also painfully aware that if he'd tried to do the same thing he'd have been killed. Gotten them all killed, probably. The day had been won because this Walgren gentleman was – carrying a gun? His daughter's friend. Gary started shaking. He tried to visualize this John Walgren and Greg whatever as being cast in the same mold as Dennis Davis. Too old for her, certainly. An undercover police officer? Yeah! Had to be. A bit of his color returned before Alison noticed it had left.

She was calming down a bit, having gotten some of it off her chest. "Shelley was drunk stupid, so I had to drive that jalopy all the way home. Well, actually as far as it got us. It stopped running at the red light in Lake Osborne. The cop there had to call us a wrecker. I went over to tell Paul what happened this noon. He says I owe him a car! A *new car!* He can't do that, can he?"

"Of course not. Just to make sure, I'll let Joe Winter know about it. He's the only lawyer in Dunningsville or Lake Osborne. If young Paul wants to hire one he'll have to go out of town. If he calls you about it, have him see me at the shop next week. Maybe his car has a little life left in it. Tell him I'll try to help fix it." He had no idea what he was getting into.

Ahmed Tafar, the commercial lending officer for the People's Community Bank of Lake Osborne had been busy on Monday. The soonest he could see Gary Loch of Loch Tool and Die was 2pm on Tuesday. He already knew what Gary wanted, why it had gotten complicated and how it would be resolved. Tafar liked Gary, and believed in his business, but he had superiors to please. He intended to just tell him this time. Next time, they could just skip over all the disclosures and rate increase negotiations. It was only going to cost him a half a percent anyway.

"Before we get started, Gary, do you have any idea why the Federal Bureau of Environment would be looking into your finances? They came in yesterday afternoon with orders from our regional manager to make all our records on you available to them. Are you under some sort of investigation?"

"No, not that I'm aware of. We're a machine shop. We just cut metal. We don't burn anything, all our equipment is electric including the heat pumps. We don't have any smokestacks or even furnace vents. Total electric all the way. Lots cheaper than buying stack permits. All our cutting oil is recycled on site and returned to service. Our only outputs are products and metal scrap, which is also recycled. Our sewer water is monitored by the city. We're completely clean. Let 'em check if they want."

"What bothered me is what do they want with your *financial* records. There were two of them, Young, one man, and one woman. They had guns. I've never seen FBE people going armed before."

Gary hadn't touched a gun in years and didn't miss them at all. Now he was beginning to feel surrounded by them.

Annamaria Albarran had been on a previous PESVI field mission. Reinhold Hahnemann had not. That made Annamaria the command officer of the two-person team. Reinhold had been the one to get the call from the boss. To his credit, he'd selected an experienced partner, knowing that by doing so he relinquished command. He'd had an eye on lovely Latin Annamaria for weeks and had grabbed at the opportunity to go off alone with her.

Like all FBE field operatives, they traveled long on authority and short on funding. The flight east had been hitched on a military transport plane, uncomfortable but thankfully fast. Landing in Fort Miller, the airport security service had been expecting them. They were under orders to provide the pair with transportation to Dunningsville. The local police department was required to supply them with a vehicle and suitable accommodations, along with anything else they required during their stay, including pocket money. The FBE only paid their wages. It would be in the local governments' interest to help them hurry along whatever they were doing. Call it cost containment. Tom DeLong, the City Manager in Dunningsville, called it an 'unfunded mandate'.

The town considered trying to put them up in someone's house, but no one wanted them. Wherever the FBE went, resentment followed. Nobody wanted to be associated with them in the public eye. DeLong suggested offering them a jail cell, and no one was sure he was kidding.

Reinhold and Annamaria ended up sharing a room with two double beds and a broadband jack in the Twilight Inn on State Route 15 between Dunningsville and Lake Osborne. Anna wasn't happy, but not because of the shared room. She would torture Reinhold with partial nudity for a couple days and then just let it happen. That wouldn't make her happy either. Annamaria was never happy, but worked hard to never let anyone else know it.

Hooking up the computer took only a minute. The information release on LT&D for the bank in Lake Osborne had been waiting for them so they had started immediately, right after they changed clothes. Facing her partner, Anna had asked, "turn around, please" as she pulled the sweater off over her head.

Gary Loch got a call from Joe Winter on Thursday morning. "Look, Gary, I don't have any details for you, but something's up. A couple of FBE agents have been snooping around this week. They had releases to access your financial records with both banks, the credit bureau and the chamber of commerce. They been driving around in D-ville's traffic slick. I saw it myself this morning at Bannerman's Garage in Lake Osborne on my way to the office. Seemed kinda weird, so I gave it a couple hours and called Jake Bannerman. He wouldn't tell me a thing, seemed to be scared to death. He has the only wrecker service in Lake Osborne. Do you happen to know if they hauled that junker for your daughter last Friday night?"

"Not for sure, but it's probably a safe bet."

"Are you still thinking about offering to help that DuPont kid fix the thing? That might be a bad idea with the FBE around, even if they weren't already looking at you."

"Too late, Joe. It's already done. Dennis and I stopped over there Monday afternoon. It wasn't actually seized at all, just Hydraulic locked. Injector stuck open and filled a cylinder. Gasoline won't compress in its liquid form, so the starter couldn't turn it over. The thing probably stalled from flooding in the first place."

"I didn't know you were a car mechanic, Gary. How do you know this stuff?"

"I don't. I'm just reciting what Dennis said. Dennis knows everything. Uh, Joe – Do you think there could be a connection? I mean, between that old car, the FBE and myself?"

"It might be possible, but I doubt it. Did you tell me that car is running again?"

"Yeah. Dennis pulled the wire off the stuck injector, so it runs on three cylinders now. Kid doesn't seem to care."

"Let's both keep an eye out for it. If the FBE is onto it, they'll pull it off the street quick. Yellow, right?"

The slam-dunk nature of their investigation was rapidly becoming a bore. Annamaria already had everything they really needed by mid-day Thursday. The evidence needed to assure a conviction was of course already in hand before they had started out. The true purpose for the discovery mission was to determine whether the 'offenders' had sufficient assets to justify pursuing it, and to devise the lowest effort approach to prosecution. Besides, Annamaria had an agenda of her own. She was convinced she could get all of Gary's holdings, but not simply as a fine. It would be tricky and possibly involve some risk, but the reward would be worth it. She and Reinhold would be spending another week or two in the Twilight Inn.

She was also getting a bit bored with Reinhold Hahnemann. Nothing she did broke through his gentleman's posture. Even when she enlisted his help with her breast self-examination, he did exactly as he was told, and no more. He'd actually asked if he should wear rubber gloves! Twice now, she'd undressed for the shower in front of him, and come back out unannounced, stark naked. Nothing. He only averted his eyes like the perfect gentleman. Was he gay? She knew he wasn't married – none of them were, and sexual liaisons between them were almost encouraged by the boss. Part of the 'happy family, us against the world' mentality he was so obviously building. Anna astounded herself by resolving something to herself. Tonight, it would be different.

"Chief, you gotta see this." Administrative Assistant Sharon McCaufle normally date stamped and photocopied any warrants she brought back from the courthouse on her daily coffee run. These she took directly to Dunningsville Police Chief Albert Adamson. Something was very wrong, and Sharon knew it.

There were four related warrants. The first was a state warrant for Paul DuPont, charging him with operating a vehicle without a valid Certificate of Environmental Compliance, a misdemeanor carrying a fifteen hundred-dollar fine and a maximum of ten days in jail. That one was no real surprise, but the others were. The remaining three were federal warrants. Alison Loch was charged with Malicious Destruction of the National Environment arising from the willful use of a criminally non-compliant motor vehicle. Chief Adamson had no idea what sort of penalty *that* would carry. Gary Loch and Dennis Davis were both charged with conspiring to violate the National Environment Act by aiding and abetting the repair of a non-compliant vehicle in an unlicensed repair facility. Loch Tool and Die was named on both as a Co-Respondent.

Chief Adamson's duty was clear. He must carry out the arrests without prejudice or malice and with all possible haste. No law said he had to delegate it, though. He let Sharon post the warrant on Paul DuPont for the duty officers. The others he retained for himself. Few officers relished the thought of serving an FBE warrant at all. And none would want to serve one on a friend, but if his friend was to be arrested by his department, the least he could do was serve it himself. And not do it on Friday afternoon, requiring them to sit in jail all weekend until Monday when bail could be set.

The Chief knew Alison Loch as Gary's younger daughter. He knew Gary as a pillar of the community, but was vaguely aware he had a blot on his record from a long time ago, long before his own time on the department. He also knew Gary as Dennis Davis' employer, and Dennis always spoke very highly of him. Dennis was possibly the Chief's best friend in town. When Adamson first came to town as the newly hired Police Chief, Dennis had been serving as a reserve officer. In fact, he'd been the president of the reserve organization. He and all the other reserves were volunteers who donated several shifts a month to the community as uniformed officers. At first, all the full-time people resented their new imported boss. Several thought the job should have been theirs, and all the others had their preferences. Dennis and his people, none of whom were qualified for the position, made his life bearable for those first difficult months. A lifelong friendship grew out of it that would survive Dennis' resignation three years later. Like most communities, Dunningsville had began practicing 'Revenue Enhancement', the policy of skewing the law enforcement effort toward maximizing the monetary benefit to the government. Dennis had resigned over a case where two teenagers were caught with a case of beer bound for a party. One was the child of a funeral director from Lake Osborne; the other belonged to a single mother living in a rented house trailer – no assets. The mortician's kid was tried as an adult, and hit with a hefty fine or fifteen consecutive weekends in jail. The trailer kids' paperwork became lost. Gary had gone to the prosecutor with his duplicate paperwork, requesting both kids serve two weekends each with no fine option, and been turned away. In resigning, he asked the question on everyone's mind. "How can you charge a teenager with minor in possession – as an adult?"

The Chief sat for a long time studying the warrants. He'd known all week the FBE was up to something, but this was his first inkling that it had anything to do with Dennis. This was not going to be easy.

Reinhold Hahnemann was excited and nervous. Performance anxiety? Anna had told him in the car on the way back from the courthouse. It was Friday, so the motel would be filling up. Hot water would be in demand, so, in an effort to be good neighbors and guests, they would be showering together. For the common good of course. Reinhold allowed himself to consider what she had in mind. Her story was not in character for her. All week she'd taken delight in setting up this Loch fellow for his date with ruin. Why would she care about her motel neighbors' hot water supply?

Where was she, anyway? He'd been left alone since mid afternoon and had no idea where she'd gone. He'd called her three times, and his voice messages had gone unanswered. The protocol was to call for backup if you become separated from your partner on a field operation for over six hours. She'd left without a word at 3 PM. It was now 8:45. Buying 'girl stuff'? Getting contraceptives? In fifteen minutes, he'd have to call HQ.

"I'm back, Reinhold. Ready for our shower?"

Getting undressed was torture for him. She disrobed slowly, but impersonally, as if he wasn't even in the room. Would he become aroused too soon and embarrass himself? What was she up to? For the first time he wished he'd have refused the shared shower. He stepped in first, consciously avoiding looking at her. He turned on the water anticipating the distraction it would bring. Anna gasped and clutched him tightly around the middle as the cold spray hit them. For his body heat? The water started to warm up a little. There wasn't room enough to move apart.

"Watch it, slippery floor. I'd better wash you, and then you do me."

As he balanced himself with his hands on the walls, Anna washed him all over with soap and a washcloth. Finished, she hung the towel on his hand and giggled. "My turn."

21

She stepped in front of him, facing away. He washed part of her back before reaching around her. She moaned a bit as he scrubbed one breast with the little white towel and mauled the other with his bare hand. The towel splashed to the shower stall floor as he moved one hand down. Her breathing became uneven, exciting him the more. She reached outside the curtain for a small tube of something. Lubricant? She unscrewed the cap, squeezed a bit into her hand and – started washing her hair with it! Shampoo! A very confused and excited Reinhold Hahnemann put down the soap, picked up the washcloth and began dutifully rinsing her. "Want this?" She asked, holding the tube over her left shoulder.

She left the stall first, drying herself. Reinhold, fighting all of his natural impulses, waited for her to leave the bathroom. By the time he turned it off, the water was running cold. He came out of the bath wearing a towel and found Annamaria lying nude on the nearest bed, the one he'd been using. It was too much for him. She made no protest. At point he knew he wouldn't be able to stop if she had.

"Hello."

"Gary, it's Joe Winter. They picked up the DuPont kid this noon. Seized his yellow car, charged him with operating with a revoked smog cert. The warrant was signed by the FBE like the others. Looks pretty scary to me."

"Do you think I've got anything to worry about, Joe?"

"I don't know. They seem to know you helped him fix it. One more thing. Any idea how they might have known for sure that yellow clunker wouldn't pass smog? Until DuPont's arrest, the only law enforcement contact with it was a week ago in Lake Osborne, when it didn't run at all. It can't very well pollute if you can't start it."

"I thought you said the charge was no certification."

"It was. The car was last certified when DuPont bought it two years ago. The cert's good for three years or until the vehicle is found to be out of compliance, so it must have been retested."

"So when did they do it?"

"That's my point."

Annamaria lay in bed, sleepless. She was ashamed of herself. She'd been almost aggressive in her encounter with Reinhold. She almost had to rape *him!* No wonder he hadn't satisfied her. By the time he finally resorted to his pitiful idea of force, he was too frustrated and confused to be of any use. It couldn't have been very enjoyable for him either, not that she cared. Except for the obvious, he had nothing to even be ashamed about. For the thousandth time Anna considered what her therapist had said, and for the thousandth time rejected it.

The chief stayed in his office till the end of first shift, and called Dennis at work just before leaving for the day. It was four PM on Friday.

THE RESTITUTION

CHAPTER THREE   The Trap

"Dennis, I don't know what to say. This is the most difficult thing I've had to do in my twenty-eight years in law." The warrants, the originals, not copies – were laid out on Gary Loch's desk. "I'm technically off duty right now, and no one but me has copies, but a handful of my people and probably at least a half dozen at the courthouse know about it. The DuPont kid is in jail raising holy hell. If you lay low, I can give you until Monday morning, and then you need to turn yourselves in. I'll try to arrange a sort of 'house arrest' so you can continue running this shop."

"What about my daughter, Chief? I don't like the sound of that charge at all – Malicious Destruction of the National Environment? Sounds pretty serious to me."

"I don't know anything about it. I asked Sharon to request a copy of the statute from the feds. They'll probably fax it Monday morning. That's my excuse if I get accused of dragging my feet."

"Look, Chief, I'm sure you hear this every day, but I don't want my daughter in jail. I don't want her arrested at all. Hell, I don't even want her to *know* about this garbage. What can I do?"

"I wish I knew, Mr. Loch. I wish I knew."

When Anna dropped him off at the Banworth County Sheriff Department, the shift change was just starting. No one from day shift wanted to be stuck with him, and the afternoon shift road patrol had to go to report first. Only the traffic cars overlapped it by 'shifting' early. Reinhold would have to wait a while. Sitting uneasily in the waiting room with a half-dozen jail visitors, he was thinking about his encounter with his partner. A week before it would have been a dream come true. Now, after the fact, it only made him feel dirty – and maybe a bit used. It was wrong, and he was ashamed of himself.

He was painfully aware that no one from the Sheriffs' office wanted anything to do with him. Did they know? Were they laughing at him in report? Hopefully it was just another manifestation of the well-known public distaste for the FBE, but the dark thoughts persisted. He was actually startled when Deputy

David McBride came out and introduced himself, asking if he'd care to stick around as a 'ride-along' for a couple hours after serving his arrest warrant. Interagency cooperation, and all that.

McBride was new, twenty-five or so, and not familiar with the area yet. He still kept a county map handy all the time. The shift Sergeant had assigned him because he didn't know the Loch family personally, and was a gung-ho, ask-no-questions kind of officer. A minimum of personal feelings would help him more than long experience in this case. He was a compact man, about five foot nine, with a forward sloping flattop haircut and a pencil moustache that looked out of place on so young a man. Reinhold noticed the man's weapon, a duplicate of his own, and for just a moment feared him.

Anamaria Albarran fairly tingled with pleasure. The semi-marked police car was perfect for this. Pulled off the road a quarter mile west of LT&D, it looked like it was running radar for speeders. The old Chief would know of course, but Anna outranked him. If he complained, she'd slap him down. The proceedings would take place in federal court anyway, nowhere near Dunningsville.

Anna wanted to watch. She wanted to see the look on Adamson's face as he transported his friend to jail. She had no other real reason to name Davis on the warrant. He played only a small part in it and had few assets to seize. She'd probably have him released on Monday, but now she waited to see the result of her little side action. After they drove past her, she planned to follow them to the Banworth County Jail and participate in the booking process. Hopefully Reinhold would arrive there with young Alison while Gary Loch was still in booking and could see her in handcuffs. That would be a nice touch. Why wasn't the actual polluter a male? They were never male. The Chief drove by her slowly, alone. He hadn't made the arrest! Anna knew both the accused men were present at the shop. She could see their cars, and had been watching since before quitting time. She knew both of their faces well. The old chief didn't even seem to recognize her, 'running radar' in his own traffic car. Doddering old fool.

Now Anna knew she couldn't count on the locals. She and Reinhold would probably have to make the arrests themselves, not really an unpleasant thought. Perhaps she should call off Reinhold? Not let him use a Banworth Deputy to pick up young Alison, serving himself as the Deputy's backup? No, just let it happen. Anna had no interest in the girl's actual arrest. Maybe it would stimulate Reinhold's soggy libido. Make him more interesting as a roommate.

Alison was cooking dinner, waiting for her dad to come home. Later, she planned to go to a movie with Lynne and Carole. She was beginning to forget about the Friday night a week earlier, beginning to enjoy life again. For the first time since 'it happened', she was thinking superficially about Greg, knowing she'd probably never see him again. She didn't even know his last name.

She turned down the front burners when the doorbell rang. Brushing back her hair as she opened the door, she was surprised to find a policeman and a nice looking man in a sport coat with a lock of blonde hair hanging down over one eye. "Are you Alison Maye Loch?"

"Yes, I am. Is anything wrong, Officer?"

"Miss Loch, I'm placing you under arrest for the crime of Malicious Destruction of the National Environment. Anything you say can be used against you in a court. You have the right to an attorney. Do you understand these rights as I have read them to you?"

"Malicious what?" Total confusion and helplessness. Alison wanted her dad more than ever before. The cop held handcuffs. She expected them to be shiny metal. They were dull black, like a nonstick frying pan. This must have something to do with the guns last week.

"Turn around please, place your hands behind your back, palms out."

The girl's look of terror affected Reinhold Hahnemann in a totally unexpected way. Instantly, his heart went out to her. He wanted to stop this. He had to stop it. The enormity of what he was doing to this innocent young woman crushed down on him, suffocating him. This was a travesty. His job was a travesty. *He* was a travesty. He hadn't said a word, letting the experienced deputy do it. Alison's eyes found him, pleading, her only hope.

"Excuse me, Deputy McBride, This is not the woman we want. I'm afraid I made a mistake." He had no idea what he'd say to Annamaria, realized he could never face her again. His dream job was gone and he was two thousand miles from home with less than a hundred bucks in his pocket. The girl stepped around the Deputy and took both his hands. Thank you, thank you so much. She came up on her toes and kissed him on the cheek, knowing what he'd done. She *was* guilty, and he knew it. He had traced her all the way from Fort Miller after the incident with the guns. Now that he could see she wasn't a threat to society, he was letting her go free. What a fine officer. She'd always had a high opinion of the police.

"What? She's the only Alison Maye Loch in the system. The warrant matches the address. Are you sure sir?"

"Yes, I am. Sorry to waste your time, deputy McBride. You can leave me here, I'll arrange my own transportation from this point."

McBride apologized for the mix-up and left. Everyone said FBE people were weird.

"Mr. Loch, this is Chief Adamson. Can you put Dennis on?"

"Al?"

"The FBE woman is watching you. She's off the side of the road maybe four hundred yards west of you right now. Probably intended to back me up but she stayed put after I went by empty. I don't know what she's up to but I wouldn't put much past her. You two better be careful. Maybe go out the long way."

Annamaria didn't recognize the car as it left the LT&D parking lot, and it's windows were too darkly tinted for her to see who was in it, going eastbound, away from her. The bright red Italian sportscar belonged to Gary's father-in-law Lucky O'Connor, Alison and Heather's grandfather. Bobbi's dad. Heading east, away from town through the Darton Curves, the traffic slick had no chance of catching them if she tried. Lucky stored it during winters in the unused spare loading dock along with Gary's boat. Dennis hadn't drained it for storage yet. Anna figured it was a customer, which might also explain why the Chief had failed to make the arrest. She stayed put, watching for Gary and Dennis to come out. By now she regretted playing with the arrests for her own amusement and was back on task. The girl was the first priority, Gary the second. Mr. Davis and the DuPont kid didn't matter at all.

The traffic car's radio caught her attention. "Central Dispatch, sixty one forty six. 10-8, one up, downtown D'ville."

"6146 – one up? You lose your rider, Dave?"

"Affirmative dispatch. His warrant was in error. I think he knew her and mixed the names up. He stayed behind with her. I hope I never have to work with that guy again, sorry."

Alison knew Agent Hahnemann was mincing words, not telling her everything. He'd already told her about how he and agent Albarran had been sent from the west coast to arrest her and force her family to pay a restitution for the damage she had done with her borrowed car; how they'd spent the past week looking into her family business and finances. Why didn't they just go after Paul DuPont? He drives that car all the time?

"He has no money."

Alison still had Reinhold's hand, was just inviting him inside. The dark blue Dunningsville police car with no overhead lights lurched into her driveway, blocking it. A very pretty Hispanic looking woman jumped out of it with a pistol in her hand, pointing it at them. "Reinhold!" She spat out the word, disgusted by it. "You bastard! You traitor! You're both under arrest! Both of you!"

Alison tried reason. "No, you don't understand. This was all a mistake. That car isn't mine, I was just being a designated driver. Tell her, agent Hahnemann!" She held both his hands again. He was pulling her close, getting between her and the irate policewoman, guiding her back inside the open front door while twisting to face the irrational officer. Suddenly three things happened at once. The man slammed back into her as the loudest noise she had ever heard pounded her ears, leaving her deafened for a moment. She saw a flame burst out at the end of the gun.

"This thing's a little flashy for playing cat and mouse with those FBE creeps all weekend, don'cha think?"

"Yeah, Dennis. That's why we're gonna hide it. We'll have to use Alison's car if it's here. They may not know about it at all".

"They seem to know everything else about us, Gary."

"About me at least, but everything they know seems to be financial. Alison's car's only worth a couple thousand bucks, and it's in her own name." Stopped in front of Gary's garage at the end of the driveway in back of the house, he had to get out and raise the door with the combination keypad. No remote control in this car. "Let's go in and see if Alison can stretch dinner enough for all of us."

"I'm not sure I'm hungry, Gary." They both lost their appetite when they opened the front door.

"911, what is your emergency?"

"There's someone in my house who's been injured. Shot maybe. My daughter's gone. Looks like she put up a fight. Please send paramedics. He might be alive."

"Slow down sir. You say you shot your daughter and she might be alive?"

"No, no. Someone – a man I don't know - has been shot. He is alive but hurt real bad. We're giving first aid. Looks like my daughter has been abducted or something. Please send help. Try to get Chief Adamson for us. Tell him it's Gary and Dennis." Since the 911 system identified the phone address to 'Gary', the dispatcher assumed the victim was 'Dennis' and reported it to Chief Adamson that way. Adamson was first on the scene and directed the ambulance in.

"Can you hear me? Can you understand me at all? Blink if you can." Shot high in the center of mass· like that, Adamson correctly suspected spinal cord injury. Even a new quadriplegic can blink. Reinhold Hahnemann blinked. Hard and deliberately. "Can you speak?" Reinhold made an unintelligible croaking sound then appeared to start over. Breathing but unable to control it, he matched syllables to his spasmodic breaths. "Part-ner shot-me. Tried to help girl. She took her. So sor-ry. Thought I was –". And Reinhold was gone.

Annamaria knew she couldn't stay long at the Twilight inn. Leaving Alison trussed up in the back of the traffic car, she went in, gathered her things and made the call to her boss Eldon Morris. A text message really. "Things went bump in the night" It meant "Mission damaged, partner compromised, need assistance. Will contact within hour." Then she left the motel without checking out. She headed south on State Road 15 and avoiding Downtown Lake Osborne, toward Fort Miller. When she called Eldon back thirty minutes later he answered on the first ring. "What's your status, Reinhold?"

"It's not Reinhold, sir. I'm Annamaria. Reinhold was a traitor. He went over to the polluters and tried to expose us. I had to shoot him like you said. I have Alison Loch, the polluter, under arrest. We're southbound on SR 15 about twenty miles south of

Lake Osborne now in a police car that was provided for us. I'll need extraction."

Annamaria? The Latin gal with the big - oh, yes. "Good lord, Agent Albarran, it sounds like you've been through Hell. We'll try to extract you directly from the highway. The initial contact will be by cell phone. Is your battery up?"

To the officers on the scene of the FBE shooting, 'my partner' was David McBride, the officer who had delivered him here and then reportedly just left him, presumably uninjured. He dutifully responded to the call and arrived at the Loch home in less than ten minutes. Not the acts of a guilty man, but he would be asked to explain how he was talked into abandoning a warrant service and leaving his interagency counterpart at the scene. "Because FBE creeps are weird" wouldn't do it. The chief was sure Reinhold had identified Alison's abductor as 'she'. That would be the female FBE agent Reinhold was sharing his room at the Twilight with. County checked, she was gone. So was the D'ville traffic slick that had been issued to them. Terrific. So FBE creeps really are weird.

Since his man was involved, Banworth County Sheriff Wayne Boyt called in the State Patrol, asking them to look for the Dunningsville traffic car, probably southbound between Lake Osborne and the State line on SR 15, and to consider the occupant armed, dangerous and most likely holding a hostage. The person would be a female, either an FBE agent or impersonating one.

"Armed?"

"Yes, Definitely."

Since the Civilian Disarmament Act, they weren't used to hearing that.

State Patrol Trooper Dan Bolling, northbound on 15 a few miles north of the state line saw the stolen traffic car as he was copying its description. His brother worked for the state across the line. The two had just met for coffee. Matt would still be at the truck stop. Maybe they could make the collar together! How cool! Hitting the switch to disable his brake lights, Dan pulled off the road, killed all his lights and flipped around, turning his headlights back on under a hill. Throttle to the floor, he began to close on the suspect police cruiser.

"Hello?"

"Agent Albarran?"

"Yes?"

"Key your radio microphone and hold it down for five seconds so we can lock on your signal, Ma'am." The same voice, much louder, came over the radio speaker as soon as she released the push-to-talk button. "We will intercept you in ninety seconds. Don't be startled. As we slow down, you slow down with us. Do you understand? We'll be extracting you by air."

Dan Bolling smiled smugly as he flipped the rocker switch for the cruiser's mars lights. His expression changed in disbelief as the red and blue strobe flashes of his overhead light bar illuminated a large metallic object that shouldn't be there. It was just above him, moving considerably faster than he was, in the same direction. A long olive drab shaft like a knight's jousting lance with a couple of funnel cones, concentric with it, out toward the front. What the – a heavy duty looking wheel and tire followed it into his view. The wheel, perhaps six feet above his car, was attached to the bottom of something that looked like the removed nose section of a large airplane, hanging in mid air. The lance protruded from the front of it. Some kind of aircraft? The noise was incredible, a pulsing roar that made him cringe down into his seat to get away from it. A man sat in a phone booth window, facing him from the back of the disembodied airplane nose. He was dressed in a military flight suit with a large helmet. The man took one hand off a set of controls that seemed to belong on earthmoving equipment and pulled down a green visor from the brim of the helmet, obviously to shield his eyes against the mars lights. After half a frozen moment, Dan slammed on his brakes, sliding back out from under the biggest helicopter he'd ever seen. Shaped like a praying mantis, the main body of the thing extended aft from above the airliner-nose shaped 'head'. A pair of huge jet engines flanked it on either side just forward of the rotor hub. The blades, viewed in stop-action from the flashing strobe lights spanned wider than the whole roadway easement – a lot wider. A pair of long landing gear legs hung from massive spreaders below and behind the engines. The machine was obviously made to land straddling something the size of a railroad boxcar, hook onto it, and carry it away. Centered under the rotor hub was a huge double claw hook. The man in the booth must operate the hook. He couldn't be the pilot, facing backward like that. It was going forward at over a hundred miles per hour.

Matt Bolling saw it too. The science-fiction monster appeared like an apparition directly above his brother's cruiser, still a mile away. Stopped across the roadway, blocking both lanes, he could only stare and blink at the thing as it closed on the stolen cruiser ahead of it.

Going down a long, shallow hill approaching the State line, Anna saw the roadblock car ahead of her before noticing the pursuing trooper's car. Boxed in from both ways, her hope of rescue faded away, despite the promised rescue in 90 seconds. Then she found herself surrounded by machinery. First a wheel maybe four feet in diameter dropped down beside her window and began to slow down. As she slowed to match it, a man wearing a space suit of some sort appeared behind a window suspended in mid air at the front of her car. Mesmerized, she was aware the voice from her radio was that of the man in the window. The lips and gestures matched it. "That's good, Agent Albarran. Stay with me, try not to fall behind, but don't hit me either. We'll be coming to a full stop tonight. Fun, isn't it? Don't you just love these interagency exercises?"

Anna somehow brought the car to a stop more or less even with the huge machine, the nature of which she was too shocked to even guess at. The man in the space suit told her to pull forward a little, just like the operator of a car wash. Anna never noticed the other wheel until they both dropped a foot or so to the road surface, followed a second later by a third wheel directly below the space suited man in the window. Riding a unicycle? She tried to blink away the surreal image. Then she noticed the claw. It closed rapidly around her, sharp looking forklift tines sliding under her vehicle. The man said something she couldn't hear and the claw thing came up hard under the car, jerking it upward. The car's front end dropped and she saw the road surface in her windshield along with the man in the window. He seemed to stand still as if attached to the car, but the road was rapidly falling away, taking the world with it. Instinctively she stomped on the brakes, which had no effect other than causing the man in the window to laugh. "Don't worry, Ma'am. I won't drop you." Anna relaxed a little as she caught a glimpse of the roadblock car four hundred feet below. "You can shut off the car now, Agent Albarran. Did you end your cell phone call?"

THE RESTITUTION

CHAPTER FOUR   Knowledge

"Are you certain, Mr. Davis?"

"Yep, I'd recognize one of those anywhere. I had a college roommate whose dad flew one in Viet Nam. They used 'em mostly to transport light tanks and construction machinery into unimproved sites. It can carry almost twenty three thousand pounds. Four or five police cars, easy. They called them Skycranes back then. It burns over five hundred gallons of jet fuel an hour."

"See the Marine Corps markings? They probably operate that one out of a Naval Air Station. Not many of those this far inland, I bet. Do any of your departments have a listing?"

Six people attended the Saturday morning meeting in the Dunningsville Police Department report room. It wasn't being conducted very formally. It had just sort of happened when State Patrol Commander Myron Trask showed up unannounced with the dash camera tape from Trooper Bolling's squad car. Actually, the tapes from both Trooper Bollings' cars – the other agency had provided him with a copy.

Sheriff Boyt asked the first question. "Are there any of them in private ownership that you know of?"

"Power companies and their contractors use them a lot for things like setting transmission towers in swamp land. They usually lease them complete with crews, pilots, liftreel operators and ground support personnel – generally military trained. One of those aircraft wouldn't have Marine Corps markings. They just have registration numbers and company logos. I'm sure other industries use them also, probably lease them from the same sources."

Gary Loch felt they were wasting precious time. Tracking down the helicopter would be an easy clerical task anyone could do. Dennis was just showing off. "Can we decide what to do please? There can't be more than a few dozen of those 'Skycranes' in the whole world. Finding that one should be easy, you have all it's numbers. Some basics here, please: Commander Trask, Sheriff Boyt, Chief Adamson? Which of you is in charge of this investigation? Do you consider my daughter abducted or arrested?

Do you intend to arrest Dennis or myself under these bogus warrants? Will you help me?" Dennis Davis looked at his shoes. The three police commanders looked at each other in silence. "Are Dennis and I free to go, gentlemen?"

"What could you do on your own?"

"Get Alison back. She's not being held for trial on federal charges, she's in the clutches of a nut case who murdered her own partner for disagreeing with her."

"But, the federal warrant!"

"If it's genuine I'd have to honor it. It's not. The crew of that thing was communicating with our friend Annamaria on the police traffic channel, the same as your car was using, Commander. Listen to the tape, you can hear it. They thought they were on a training mission, coordinating with your people! Those guys weren't in cahoots with the FBE, they'd been suckered in. Just like you were."

"We don't know that, sir."

"O, come on, Sheriff. Listen to it for pete's sake."

"No, I mean we don't know the arrest warrant isn't valid. For that matter, we aren't sure about the ones for you two, either".

"So arrest us, Sheriff. You have that authority. Can I make my one free phone call now?"

"Don't make this ugly, Mr. Loch. Who are you gonna call, anyway?

"The news department at TV 32."

Someone tapped on the door glass, pointing to Sharon McCaufle. She put her head out the door for a second and came back to the conference table. "The slick is back, Chief."

"What? Where is it?"

"Back at the Twilight Inn. The manager doesn't know how long it's been there or how it got there."

"Well I'll be damned. Send somebody out there to see if anybody stayed with it. Better send two, and tell them to be careful. They'll need a crime scene kit."

"Want me to send a full state crime lab unit, Al?"

The Chief looked at Gary. "Yeah, that's a good idea Myron. Thank you." "Gary, I don't think we should hold you under these circumstances even with the warrants, but none of us wants you to go off and get yourselves killed. Research all you want, make some calls, go online. But please don't try going after your daughter alone."

"Listen to me, please. If you people will pursue this, I'll assist in any way you want, even if that means only staying out of the way. But if you choose to ignore it I'll be forced to go it alone, and nothing short of deadly force will stop me. Not even you. I won't just let that crazy woman keep Alison. You know very well that she's not under arrest in the constitutional sense. She'd have called me by now. Now, do we have anything else to discuss?"

Sheriff Boyt asked the question on everyone's mind. "If you're on your own, what will you do next, Mr. Loch?"

"Get on the web. Find out how fast a 'Skycrane' goes, how much fuel it burns per hour and how much fuel it carries. From that I can determine it's round-trip range. Then I'll locate every Naval Air Station and Marine Guard facility within that distance of where SR 15 crosses the state line. I'll bet only one or two has Skycranes at all, let alone Marine Corps marked ones. Officially or otherwise, I'll find out where they took Alison and who, if anyone, signed her out of military custody and control. From there it all depends on what I find out."

"OK, I'm in. That is, as long as this stays 'official'. If this starts to become 'otherwise', you're on your own."

Gary worked the calculator. "The Vietnam era HS-64E Skycrane holds 1345 gallons of jet fuel and burns 551 gallons per hour at it's design cruising speed of 109 statute miles per hour. Let's see, 1345 divided by 551 – it can only stay up a little under 2 ½ hours. Times 109, divided by two for the round trip. 133 miles with no reserve? Only an idiot would fly a helicopter to dry tanks at night. We're looking for a base within a hundred miles."

"Unless the new ones have bigger tanks or better mileage" Dennis replied.

"It doesn't look as if there are any new ones, not to impugn your knowledge. How do you know all this stuff, Dennis? You nailed its fuel flow within 51 gallons per hour from watching the tape."

"Any Vietnam vets here?" The Veterans club bartender called out, grinning. Eight hands shot up. "Any helo crew?" Two hands stayed raised. "Any NG units around here still operating the HS-64 Skycrane?"

It had taken twelve minutes, including unlocking LT&D and booting up the Internet. Naval Air Guard Station Lowreyville, about seventy miles west of Lake Osborne on the Games River

Shipping Canal. The two-hour 'meeting' at the Dunningsville P.D. had produced nothing useful, apart from their freedom and the dash camera tape.

Roger 'Lucky' O'Connor had company when Gary called. His granddaughter Heather and her husband Brian Pike had dropped in, finding him out in his garden. If he hadn't taken them inside to visit he wouldn't have heard the phone ring. Carla was out shopping.

"Did you sell your airplane yet?"

"Yeah, well, sorta. I took a partner in it. Sold a half interest. We use it on alternate weekends. Makes scheduling easy. I was only flying maybe once a month as it was. Having a partner takes care of half the fixed costs. I'm actually flying more now. Enjoy it more, too. Sometimes we take it up together."

"Is this by any chance your weekend, Lucky?"

"As a matter of fact it is, what do you have in mind, Gary?"

"A bit of recon on the Lowreyville Air Guard Station."

There was a long silent pause.

"Why?"

"It's a long story. I'm afraid I've got some bad news. I'd better come and tell you about it in person. It'd be great if you could keep Heather and Brian there. See you in a couple hours, I'll have Dennis Davis with me. You remember him, don't you?"

"Sure. We'll expect to see you in an hour and a half or so then, eh?"

"Look, NAS Lowreyville is kind of a hot spot right now. It's located at the middle of the Shipping Canal, right between two primary locks. It provides security for both of them and more; land, water and air. That canal is part of the most important maritime transportation system in the country. There are forty one locks total in the whole river and canal system and if terrorists could blow out any one of them they'd shut down the economy of the entire mid-states area."

"Locks? Like on the Panama Canal? Forty-one of them?"

"Yep, and nobody talks about them. The shipping channel has to stay at least nine feet deep for its entire length. That's how they do it. The Army Corps of Engineers built them, the Coast Guard operates them and now the Marines defend them. These days, all those services are based at NAS Lowreyville. It's not just a Navy Guard training base anymore."

The Sectional Aeronautical Chart showed a rectangular Restricted Area extending from the surface to Flight Level 480. A 'no fly zone' ten miles wide and sixty miles long following the Games River northeast to southwest. Air traffic desiring to cross it would have to go around unless they were over forty eight thousand feet up. Lucky O'Connor's four seater couldn't reach anywhere near that altitude.

A railroad track paralleled the edge of the Prohibited area for several miles just northwest of NAS Lowreyville. Lucky was following it, staying just north of it. He knew they were being tracked by radar. They wouldn't be shot down if they entered restricted airspace, but would be identified and heavily fined, probably escorted out of the area and questioned. The tracks made a great marker.

Gary, in the right-front 'co-pilot' seat held his digital SLR camera with a 400-millimeter telephoto lens pointed at the base from five miles out and 12,000 feet up. The resulting photos wouldn't be perfect, but should do nicely. Dennis was spotting features with Lucky's binoculars. The massive HS-64E was clearly visible, even without magnification. It sat on a small blastpad near what were probably the maintenance hangars, outdoors. No effort was being made to conceal it at all. Lucky said, "Guess they don't have a building big enough for it. Dennis, with the binoculars, spotted the tail rotor of another one partially inside one of the hangars. "Must have the main rotor removed. The thing's 72 feet in diameter, sure as hell won't fit through those doors." He couldn't resist showing off again.

The sign over the closed door said "Naval Air Guard Station Lowreyville, Admiral Jason Norwood Sanders, Commanding. Hat in hand, but feeling very smug, Eldon Morris sat facing the very displeased Admiral.

"Sir, I understand why the military was asked to give all reasonable aid to operatives of the Federal Bureau of Environment, but that stunt last night was just way too much. My aircrew went out on what was supposed to be a routine surprise interagency training mission and ended up bringing a detainee into a secure area trussed up like a roping calf, concealed on the back floorboards of an obviously stolen local police traffic patrol vehicle. Then your people breeze in here like they own the base, take both the young woman and the car without so much as a signature and draw their weapons when the girl begged my Marine guards for their protection. Now you want to tell me this is all business as usual? My Marines tell me that girl was terrified out of her mind."

"Please understand, Admiral. That young woman is an admitted polluter. Special Agent Albarran arrested her in an altercation that left her partner dead. The polluter's family is involved also, and seems to enjoy the complicity of the local authorities. I'm sure you're aware of the public ill will we constantly work under."

"As a matter of fact, I am. And I have to say I'm not exactly sympathetic. When my command is called upon to assist any civil law enforcement agency in any capacity, we have and will continue to do so in the spirit of 'Protect and Serve'. Can you honestly make that claim, sir?"

"We pay your bills. Don't forget that."

"I am painfully aware of that. Ashamed of it actually. Now, I need to know a few things. Who is your detainee? What exactly is she accused of? Most importantly, where have you taken her? What did you do with the stolen traffic car? Our aircraft are distinctive, easily identified and traced. We were observed by and clearly offended the Highway Patrol forces of two states. They'll be here asking serious questions very soon. Believe me sir, I will have answers for them. You'll not blame any of this on my command, sir."

Eldon listened respectfully until the Admiral began making demands. "Are you finished, Admiral? You seem to be under the impression that you outrank me or something. Does the President return your calls? Do you call him at all? I speak with him every day. At least half the time he calls me. I earn the money that pays your salary, sailor. I pay the salary of your commander in chief as well. As I said before, don't forget that."

"You should be a lot more careful how you use the word 'earn'. You cheapen it. Now, my answers, if you please sir?"

"Her name is Alison Maye Loch, of Dunningsville. She is under arrest for Malicious Destruction of the National Environment and will be standing trial in Federal Court. The police cruiser has been returned to the Dunningsville Police

Department, which legally assigned it to our use. I cannot reveal Ms. Loch's present location to you or anyone else without a need to know consistent with the FBE mission."

When Dr. Melvin Urlich took the part time job as Banworth County Medical Examiner, he thought it was the ideal retirement gig. He'd only have to work a day or two a week and he'd make thirty grand a year for it. His medical credentials would stay active. The realities of it didn't measure up though. People always managed to die at the worst possible times, and dead bodies won't wait. He had no Deputy Medical Examiner and no hope of getting one. His contract, which had eighteen months yet to run, even forbid him to hire his own at his own expense. He intended to renegotiate that clause next time.

Last night's victim had been typical. The guy had been shot early in the evening on Friday, and 911 had beeped him up at the lake. By the time he'd driven the hundred and fifty miles back, the body had been transported to the hospital morgue and most of his paperwork had been done for him, one advantage at least.

The guy's cause of death had been easy enough to determine. One gunshot wound, entering two inches below the Adam's apple and one and a half inches right of center. The nine-millimeter bullet had separated two ribs from the sternum and destroyed the right branch of the windpipe just below the junction before coming to a stop in his spinal cord. The partially completed report indicated he had been conscious and actually talking for a short time after being discovered. Surprised at first, Dr. Urlich realized that while one of his lungs was probably filled with blood and cerebrospinal fluid and the other rapidly filling, the unfortunate young man wouldn't have been able to feel it. If the first responders had sat him up to slow the flow into the still connected lung and emergency surgery had begun at once, he might have lived – paralyzed but alive. At the age of seventy, Dr. Ulrich had begun to notice ways *he* might choose to die if given the choice. This, he decided, might be one of them.

Chief Adamson had stopped him just at the edge of town on his way back up to the lake that Saturday morning. "I'm sorry Melvin. We need you at the hospital before you leave. You can follow me over there now."

"You won't be able to get me to change the cause of death. The spine injury didn't do it. He slowly drowned in his own fluids. Took about fifteen minutes, but he probably didn't feel a thing."

Dr. Ulrich had half expected the cause of death to become an issue because it could impact the validity of the statements he had supposedly made to Chief Adamson right before he expired. Would he have been capable of understandable speech or coherent thought?

"Our problem is simpler that that. We don't know what to do with the body. We called the Maxwell Funeral Home for removal, but they don't want him until we identify his family or some other responsible entity. I can't blame them. No business of any sort wants to call the FBE under even the best of circumstances. Maxwell operates a crematorium. Imagine having the FBE snooping around *that*. Right now the remains of poor Mr. Hahnemann are still in our cooler. As Medical Examiner, do you have an answer for us?"

"I'd say we have three choices. Call the FBE ourselves as local law enforcement, force Maxwell to take him under his contract with the city, or bury him ourselves at public expense. I would suggest the first. If you want, I'll make the call myself, right now."

Tom DeLong, the City Manager made the decision, "OK, Melvin, let's make the call."

The phone listing for the FBE didn't show any branch offices. Dr. Ulrich called the headquarters number in the capital and talked with several department secretaries before finding anyone who would take his report. Them he drove back up to his lake home.

Flying back to Lucky's home in Carthage would only take an hour or so, but driving from there back to Lowreyville would take the rest of Saturday afternoon. Gary Loch was determined to speak with the base commander, and didn't want to wait until Monday. "Can I borrow your 328, Lucky? We had to use it to get home from the shop last night. It's in my garage now. My truck's out at the shop. The car we brought to your house is Alison's"

"Coming back here, are you?"

"That's my plan."

"I'm coming with you."

"Me too." Dennis said, from the back seat.

"Thanks, really, but that's not a good idea. If I'm gonna get detained, I'd better be alone. If all of us did there wouldn't be anyone to get us released."

"They'd seize my car and sell it. Sure wouldn't want to lose that one. I'd rather land here and rent you a clunker. I will, too. It'll save some time. There's a car lot almost next door to Lowreyville's public airport. He lets visiting flyers he's familiar with 'test drive' cars he can't sell for forty-five bucks a day. I've done it several times.

"That's a pretty good looking car, Mike. Or should I call you 'Honest Mike'?" How come you can't sell it?"

"I take in a lot of cars as trades, and they all gotta pass smog before I can sell them. I have my own tester, of course, and use it on every potential trade-in, but I still have to submit the vehicles to a federal test center. Once in a while I get stuck with one. Like this one for instance. Most dealers just raise the price of everything to spread out the risk. I let pilots test drive 'em to make back my investment. They seem to understand. I had two of 'em available till last Tuesday. The other one's three-year cert expired."

Lucky resisted the temptation to stay and discuss the state of the automobile business with someone who was making a living in it. He and Dennis walked back to the airport immediately after Gary left for his 'test drive'.

The sprawling inland Naval Air Station was even more impressive when viewed from the ground. Long and narrow, running parallel to the Games River on its south bank, it had only a single runway. Almost two miles in length, it was more than four hundred feet wide. The taxi strip that ran along most of its length was very nearly as wide. Gary watched a flight of ground attack fighters take off as he approached the main gate. "My name is Gary Loch. Would you ask your commander if he has a moment for me regarding my daughter Alison Loch of Dunningsville?" The wording was designed to get the guard's attention and hold his interest. It worked.

"Which commander, sir? My immediate superior? The Captain of Marines? The base commanding officer, Admiral Sanders?"

"Admiral Sanders, if you please, sailor."

"Welcome aboard, Mr. Loch. I know why you're here and hope I can help you. I didn't actually see your daughter last night, but I'm very aware of the incident." He slid a photograph across his desk. It showed Alison being helped out of the D'ville traffic car below one of the huge helicopters. Her face was more or less expressionless. "Is this her?"

"Yes. Why, how did you get involved with this, Admiral?"

"The military is under orders to provide assistance to FBE field operatives. This is not a popular order, as you might imagine, but we occasionally do joint training exercises with them. This is the second time a crew under my command has been called into a training mission and found itself in control of a civilian detainee in a situation outside the realm of legitimate crew training. I personally filed a formal complaint with the department of defense earlier today. Since I have not yet received a response I consider myself free to discuss this with you openly at this time. Do you mind if my Marine stays in the room sir?"

"Of course not. I half expected to be detained myself. I just want to know where Alison is. Where did you take her? Is she here? Can I see her?"

"I'm afraid she is no longer on my base, sir. We held both Ms. Loch and her arresting officer, FBE special agent Annamaria Albarran overnight, expecting an apology from FBE headquarters. Instead, the head of the department, a Mr. Eldon Stewart Morris, visited us. His name may be familiar to you if you follow politics, Mr. Loch. He founded the Bureau a few years ago. I always thought President Trayson fired him as soon as he was inaugurated. Guess I was wrong."

"You weren't mistaken, Admiral. Morris was fired. I saved the news clipping. Dumping him was the biggest blessing Trayson could have given to the manufacturing industry. You say he was here today?"

"He was, and carried orders releasing both women to his custody. I was obligated to comply, the orders checked out."

"Who signed the order?"

"He did, under the auspices of the Department of Justice, Environmental enforcement division. Look, Mr. Loch, I have his signature on a nonstandard custody transfer, but not much else. I can have my people review the gate security camera disks to find out which way they went if you think that would be helpful"

"You film all your gates?"

"Sure. We're a high security installation."

"A vehicle description and license number would be nice", Gary smiled.

The Admiral called his chief of security. "Give me a shot of the first FBE car to leave this morning. About 0530. Put it on my screen. Not sure, but try the South Gate first." About a minute later the Admiral's computer screen filled with four images, each occupying a quarter of it. The upper left showed the back of a police car, a pair of young women in the back seat, one of which sat leaning forward as if in handcuffs, the municipal registration plate showing clearly. The upper right panel showed a close-up of the plate. The lower left showed the same vehicle from the left side, the stylized lettering saying Lowreyville Police. Sanders identified the driver as one of the FBE team. The lower right image was a moving picture, jerky, but clear. The right turn signal was on. The car turned right as it entered traffic. The time stamp said 0541. Gary asked about the Dunningsville traffic car. The gate crew found it in seconds, leaving right behind Alison. Surprisingly, it went the other way, turning left out of the gate. So did Mr. Morris' car almost an hour later.

"Mr. Loch, I need to ask you a favor. I expect you to use this information to secure the release of your daughter, and I sincerely hope it's helpful. I stepped over a line with this, as you might imagine. I'm past my retirement date and am in the process of selecting my own replacement. Any consideration you can give me will be appreciated. I'm sure you understand."

Paul DuPont had ridden in police cars before, but never like this. He rode in the front seat, with no more restraints than the seat belt and shoulder harness. His knee leaned against a riot shotgun in a locking holder of some sort. A panel of switches and radio equipment filled the space between himself and the *Chief of Police!* He had plenty of legroom. Instead of hoping no one saw him, this time he hoped everyone he knew would. The Chief was actually being nice to him, treating him like a 'good guy'.

"I couldn't leave you locked up. I know your car was defective, but there's no valid proof. It passed smog for the dealer who sold it to you, and that certification should be good for another year almost. You haven't had it tested on your own, have you?"

"No, why would I?"

"Good question. I don't get mine tested either, it's not required. But if you do and it fails, the cert. is voided and the car can't be used until it's fixed. Yours was tested by Jake Bannermann on the order of the FBE, but that was *after* your arrest. It makes no sense. I don't think you were the target of this at all, Mr. DuPont. I believe they wanted Gary Loch, that young girl's dad."

"Why?"

"They think he has money they can grab. I think we can prove – I think my department and I can prove it."

"For just a sec there it sounded like maybe you wanted me to help."

"Maybe you can. Can you think of anything that happened or was said that might have given you any reason to think something like this was up?"

"Nothing at all."

"How well do you know Alison Loch?"

"Not hardly at all, but I'd sure like to. She's my Sister Shelley's friend, really."

"Why was she driving your car that night?"

"I let Shelley use it. Honest, sir, I had no idea she planned to take it out of town at all, let alone clear down to that school of hers. Shelley must have let her drive for some reason."

"Actually, Alison was driving because your sister was drunk. I just had to make sure you were being upfront with me, Paul. Can you think of any time since you bought the car that someone could have taken it long enough to give it a safety and emissions test?"

"No, I don't think so. I never loaned it to anybody except Shel, and her just that once. Never got it worked on in a real shop either. Do you think maybe the girls had to have somebody fix it that night?"

"Doubt it. Alison would have to be the one to do it. She would have told her dad and he would have told me. It is possible, though, and it had to happen sometime unless they just made it up. They showed test results on the paperwork. No date, though."

THE RESTITUTION

CHAPTER FIVE Power

Gary Loch had the Marine direct him through the base to the South gate. All three of the entrances were off the same street, but he simply wanted to see for himself why Alison's FBE driver would use the least convenient one, and then head southwest. The street map Honest Mike had loaned him showed the street approaching the base from the North, and simply ending there. The thing was an advertising map intended to show the locations of several motels, not a detailed travel aid. The Marine got out at the guard shack, leaving Gary facing the stop sign wondering if the security photo system would pick up his dealer plate attached inside the rear window.

Why were Alison and presumably Annamaria taken south, unlike the other cars? The answer came to him as he turned to follow her route. She had been in a Lowreyville police car. The Dunningsville traffic slick and Eldon's FBE car would have been leaving the area. The local car would need to be returned to the Lowreyville PD, most likely with Alison still in it. Would they still have her? Maybe she was being held in their lockup waiting for transport! Turning around in the parking lot of a small, grubby looking private marina half a mile south of NAS Lowreyville, Gary noticed a local cop car parked there. It bore the same stylized lettering he had seen in the base security photo. Much better looking than the plain block letters D'ville and Lake 'O used. By the looks of the place, Gary wasn't surprised to see a police complaint car there. He'd ask directions somewhere else.

"Are you holding a young lady named Alison Loch by any chance?"

The desk Sergeant checked his computer terminal. "No one by that name, sir. What would the charges be?"

"Some overblown FBE charge. The FBE detained her and brought her into Lowreyville through your naval base. She's my daughter. I was hoping you were holding her temporarily for them and would let me see her."

"We did have some FBE activity here last night, let me check the log. Yeah, they came in about two AM and demanded a vehicle. One of our officers had started the shift and then got sick, so his cruiser was fueled and available. They signed it out for today, and promised to have it back for first shift, but they never came back. We haven't seen it and it doesn't answer radio calls, but then, FBE guys never do. They seem to think they're a breed apart. We can't really act on it until 2AM tonight when their 'day' is up."

"I think I may have seen it parked at Games River Marine, just south of the base. Can I borrow a detail map of that area please? I promise not to take it away from your desk." The Sergeant checked dispatch. No officers were out of their vehicles anywhere near Games River Marine, and had not been during the last six shifts. "That little marina used to do a lot of business with the base back when it was just a Guard training station, kept their shore patrol boats there. Military put in their own docks with the buildup, and the marina got left high and dry. A few of the sailors keep private boats there now, and they do a bit of repair work. An off-course barge smashed their fuel dock a couple years ago and the Department of Water Resources won't let them rebuild it."

Gary studied the map. River Street did end at the base. The roadway continued Southwest past the Marina, becoming a residential subdivision looping back on itself and ultimately rejoining River Street directly across from the main gate, closing a sort of oversize cul-de-sac. The Navy owned the whole subdivision. Off base rental housing.

"They took her out of the Lowreyville area by water. They must have. The Precinct shift Sergeant was so pissed that he let me ride along on the investigation of their abandoned patrol car. The Marina operator was scared shitless when we dropped in on him with three uniforms and a crime scene unit. He clamed up when I started asking about his relationship with the FBE, and tried to claim federal protection from the military. He changed his tune when Admiral Sanders sent over a couple S.P's to assist us."

"It's just unbelievable how much you guys have gotten in one day. Just unbelievable. All this information, *evidence!* Photographs, the assistance and support of a major metropolitan police agency and the very military commander responsible for that huge helicopter. How do you know the boat carrying her went south? That's about the only thing I can't understand."

"Well, Chief, the current in the Games River flows that direction, and the FBE boat has a port engine that overheats. It was on the marinas' shop schedule for next week. It's not likely they'd try heading upstream on a single screw, especially amid that much southbound barge traffic. It gets better. The Games joins the Missacantata just eighty miles west of Lowreyville. The current there suggests they'll have to go south toward the Gulf."

"So now you know their entire route all the way to the national border, but not where they get off the water. What's your next step, if you don't mind my asking,"

"Well, we've got to determine where they got off the river system and figure it out from there. The web gave us an FBE field office and training center down in Holden, but that's more than six hundred miles south of Lowreyville if you measure it as a straight line. The way the rivers twist and turn it's really more than that. The marina told us the boat they used could only make twelve knots on the single engine. I can't believe they'd take it that far. I think we should take to the water and just start looking. Got any better ideas, Chief? Are you going to help us here?"

"We already are. You may be surprised to hear I've taken young Mr. DuPont under my wing. He's always been a suspicious sort of character, but he's never been convicted of anything so he has a clear record. I got him a job as a janitor over at the courthouse. If that works out I might invite him to start reserve training. He really seems to enjoy being one of the good guys for a change. We've been trying to figure out when and how the FBE got a test report to condemn his car. The official report is based on a test run after his arrest. It just makes no sense. Tonight we're going to take a little trip down 15 to the state line to look for any federally licensed test centers that might have had access to his vehicle when the girls took it down to Fort Miller and back. Jake Bannermann runs the only one I know of, but I can't be sure. He never tested it before the FBE had him tow it in after the arrest."

"Aren't those places listed as public record?"

"Yeah Dennis, they are. I'm doing it the hard way partly as an exercise for Paul. Test his observation skills. Besides, the feds may have a temporary shop set up somewhere."

"Why would they do that? The law says you can drive a car for three years following a test, then you need another test."

"You're part right. The law says an *owner* can drive a successfully tested vehicle for three years. It says nothing about a borrower. That's the fine print trap they used against Gary's daughter."

"But you have to, Dennis. Someone I can trust with the financial aspects of the business needs to stay and run it. As Engineering Manager, you're the obvious choice. If nobody stays here, the guys will all go file for unemployment while our customers listen to the inevitable rumors and go away. We'd be ruined. If we were gone more than a couple days the bank would take control of our assets, or maybe turn them over to the FBE. No, this time I go alone."

"What should I do if more FBE agents show up and try to take it over anyway?"

"Let 'em take it. Keep the customer and supplier lists handy. If that happens, call them all and tell the truth. Don't stand and fight them. You won't be much help to me in jail."

"Where do you plan to put in?"

"Deer River, twenty miles east of Lowreyville, just down from Lock 3. I want to fuel up and provision at Games River Marine. See if the FBE boat is back yet."

It just kept getting better and better. As an employee of the court, Paul DuPont was *driving* the police car this time. Chief Adamson rode in the passenger's seat. Driving south through Lake Osborne with his elbow out the open window, Paul had seen Patty what's-her-name, the cheerleader who'd snubbed him so cruelly in high school, and casually waved at her. The bitch had actually tripped and almost fell down.

"Bannermann's is coming up on the right, Paul. See the green Federal Inspection Center sign? That's what we're looking for."

"All the way to the state line?"

"Nope, all the way to Fort Miller. I'll drive back if you want."

"I'll be fine."

"Figured you would be. Just help keep an eye out for more of those green signs. Most likely on auto repair shops in small towns like Lake'O.

"Why is that, Chief Adamson? Why doesn't Dunningsville have one?"

"The government pays very well for shops that'll do inspections, but the public avoids 'em if any options exist. Generally, only shops without any local competition do it. Bigger cities have stand-alone Inspection Centers that don't do anything else. Fort Miller has two of them. I already checked. Neither of them saw your car that night, or ever, for that matter."

They didn't just stay on the main road. Every tiny town they came to got looked over closely. Driving up and down side streets, they'd stop at stores, restaurants, any kind of public service businesses they came to, and ask where the nearest inspection center was. Everyone in Ricketts, Magnolia and Redlyn said Lake Osborne. Just over the state line in Woodbine, the answer changed to Fort Miller.

Gary Loch was beginning to see the point Dennis Davis had been trying to make. 'Single Handing' a boat even as small as his in a busy international shipping channel was going to be tough, especially in this mid-autumn weather. His craft was far from ideal for making a long river and canal passage even in the best of conditions. It was a bass boat. Nineteen feet long, it had a two hundred horsepower two-stroke outboard motor in back and a small electric trolling motor with a front-mounted retraction bracket. Both were controlled from the helm on the right side, a bit closer to the back than the front end. The big motor had a lever control there for forward-reverse and throttle control, and a steering wheel like a car. The little electric had a foot control that could be placed anywhere. Gary ordinarily left it at the helm, where a gas pedal would be in a car. Set up for fishing, the boat was open. Not so much as a bimini sun shade to protect him from the elements. It was raining now, and the temp was just under fifty degrees Fahrenheit.

The little hand-held GPS receiver said he'd only covered four nautical miles. Already his clothing was soaked through and changing into dry ones wouldn't help for very long. Dennis was right. He'd be of no use to Alison or anyone else with a case of pneumonia. He had to rig a shelter for his helm, and a way to heat it. The Navy patrol boats in Viet Nam came to mind, with their thatched roofs made of jungle leaves. No leaves like that around here. He considered cutting up the dome tent he had intended to set up on the aft deck as a sleeping shelter, but he wouldn't be able to see out. He'd be a hazard to navigation and the purpose of the trip, watching the shoreline for a clue, would be lost.

Then he had it. He had the boat cover with him! Cutting up the expensive fitted canvas trailering and storage cover would be hard to do, but he'd be able to stay reasonably dry. He would set up the tent and nail it to the aft deck as originally planned. His gas lantern would keep the tent warm and dry enough at night, but being open front and back, the cover would only serve to keep the rain off him while underway.

"Ahoy the anchored fishing craft!" Gary was bent to the task of finding the widest part of the cover that would snap over the helm, intending to simply cut off the front and back sections. He'd use the fiberglass bows to hold it up, hopefully above his head. The loud hailer startled him. He looked up to see the white hull of a sailboat. About twice the length of his own boat, the thing had an unfinished look about it. It bore it's name in black script just below the bow rail; "Atropos". Its mast was short. Much too short for a boat its size, but it carried a much longer one lengthwise on some sort of rack above its cabin. Gary turned and sort of waved at the voice. "Could I maybe interest you in ten yards of .025 Vinyl window sheeting?"

Gary sat with Captain Dale Lucans in the salon of s/v Atropos watching a master at work. This man he didn't even know had taken him in tow, moved to a safer anchorage, side tied him and set about modifying his fitted cover with a raised center cockpit featuring all-around clear plastic windows! He'd helped snap the cover on all the way around Gary's boat and marked out a square opening with a laundry marker; match marked it and cut it out with the sharpest pocketknife Gary'd ever seen. Then he rolled it up and tossed it over into Atropos' cockpit. Both men clambered aboard her, taking the cutout portion into the salon. Capt. Lucans flipped over a hinged portion of his chart table and a sewing machine appeared! An hour later the finished article was back on the bass boat. Its new raised cockpit enclosure was held up by Atropos' spare bimini frame. It looked good, and sheltered the full length of the boat. The vessel now had a sort of rakish military gunboat look about it that Dennis would surely approve of. They'd also cut and hemmed two boarding access openings, one over the forward live well and the other aft over the fuel tank bay. Rainwater entering either would be ported overboard by the scuppers and bilge pumps. The Captain said Gary could cover them with tarps or something if the weather really got bad.

"I've been on the water all my life, I guess. This is the third ocean going vessel I've built. Well, I guess you'd have to say I'm still building it, actually. I'm trying to finish it on the way down to the Gulf. We'll step the mast after passing the last bridge and have a couple days to tune the standing rigging before hitting open water, hopefully under sail. This river passage seems cumbersome, but it's a lot cheaper than trucking her. Besides, I've always wanted to do it."

"I wondered about the short mast, Captain. Guess that explains it."

"Took it off a junked daysailor. It comes down easily for low bridges. Use it as a steadying sail. It lets me maintain steerage way without burning diesel most of the time. It's not much use here though. Wind is usually from the west here, the direction we're heading at the moment, and the channel is way too narrow for tacking upwind. I only need a half-knot or even less to steer, and the current gives me four for free, so I don't burn much diesel. Going all the way to the gulf shouldn't put much of a dent in the 180 gallons I left Hennison with."

"Did you build her in Hennison?"

"Yep, took two years so far. I cheated though. Bought a bare hull and most of the rig from a salvager down south. The guy buys and sells hurricane damaged boats down in the islands for a living."

"Won't it be tough being under your small sail farther south where the river starts to switch back on itself every few miles?"

"Yeah it will, but I think I'm up to it. You know, I hate to sound judgmental, but you seem pretty heads up for a guy who hits the water unprepared this time of the year. What's your story anyway"?

Gary fought off caution and told Dale Lucans the whole story, even the names and places. The Captain listened carefully until Gary was finished, and then asked his only question. "Why didn't you use the airplane to search the first couple hundred miles on the first day? You might have caught up with them."

"Most of the access points are near the locks. All but a couple of the locks have restricted or prohibited airspace areas over them. No fly zones."

"Oh."

For the life of her, Annamaria Albarran couldn't imagine why Eldon was so pissed. Reinhold had been a traitor. He'd turned his back on his country and his profession. He'd also turned his back on her, not that she wanted him. He was a crummy lover anyway. The guy had been useless. She wasn't exactly pleased with herself for putting an end to his disgusting life but she certainly wasn't sorry for it

Eldon had ordered her back to FBE West, where she found herself under a sort of house arrest. Administrative Sequestration, he called it. She was to work the terminals doing double shifts, and was not allowed to leave the facility without being escorted by another agent. The only thing that made the arrangement tolerable was that she was allowed to choose her own escort. She picked Bud O'Brien, a much better lover. When he wanted her, he just took her. No games, no talk, and no visible bruises. Tonight would be fun, but first she needed to get through this ridiculous double shift. Anna was beginning to dislike Eldon Morris. What sort of lover had *he* been, back when he was young enough to be one at all?

Putting in at the Games River Marina had presented two related dilemmas of seamanship. First, with the entire deck covered, Gary couldn't manage the boat from its helm station and handle his own docklines. Realizing this, he'd moved the foot control for the trolling motor forward to the boarding opening Dale had made there. Controlling the boat while standing in the empty live well proved surprisingly easy, except that the little electric motor didn't have enough power to overcome the river current. Docking would be a one-shot effort. If he got in trouble he'd have to crawl on his hands and knees back ten feet to the helm, tilt down and start the big motor and get control without bow thrust before hitting anything solid or expensive. About two miles short of the Naval Air Station Gary approached the bank in an area with a few overhanging branches for a bit of practice. The current was slower near shore, which heartened him. After a couple successful tries he felt confident enough to do it for real.

Twenty feet from the dock it dawned on him. He'd been so preoccupied with docking control he'd done it without a rope in his hand – or anyplace to tie it off! All his lines, and for that matter all his cleats, were now under the canvas cover. Too late to abort, all he could do was grab hold of a dock piling and hope someone came to help him. Someone did. Laughing out loud, the same man he'd helped the local police question on Saturday came running out on the dock. He caught the bow eye with a boat hook and guided the boat to rest against the upcurrent side of the dock without recognizing Gary, who immediately asked him to install four new cleats, just below the canvas snaps, within reach of the two boarding cutouts. Singlehanding was going to be even more difficult now, but he was going to stay warm and dry.

The FBE boat had not returned, and Gary now realized he'd originally docked in its usual spot. The man had hauled him out with a travel lift to make the cleat installation, re-launched it and placed it on the downcurrent side when he was done. Were they coming back soon? Gary spent the night aboard. He put up the little dome tent on the aft deck, under the cover. It made a four-inch high bump in the cover and wouldn't need to be nailed down. Leaving the tents' tiny rear vent window open, he could see the new aft boarding opening from inside. The helm station, foredeck and bow opening were all visible through the entrance flap. It was like the tent had been made special for the boat and Captain Lucans' modified canvas cover.

Warm and dry, Gary fell asleep appreciating how fortunate he'd been to meet Dale and s/v Atropos. The fuel and the new cleats had cost him a hundred and fifty bucks. The enclosed cockpit with all-around windows had cost him nothing. He'd expected to pay seventy-five a night for motel rooms. Surely the FBE boat would wake him docking at night five feet away. His batteries were being charged from shore power.

He woke up four hours later when his air mattress went flat. The rain had come back and the temp was down to forty, but he was still reasonably comfortable. After blowing the mattress back up with the plastic bellows foot pump he urinated in a plastic bottle and closed the tents' vent and flap windows. It was harder to go to sleep this time. He started worrying again, first about breathing the fumes from the gas lantern, then about keeping his batteries charged after leaving the marina. Then he started thinking about Alison again.

"Uh. Hello? – Good morning."

"Mr. Loch? Sorry to wake you. It's Dale of Atropos. Is yours a picture phone?"

"Uh, Yeah."

"I'm sending you a pix. Where are you now, Gary?"

"Lowreyville. Spent the night at the marina."

"I spent the night underway. The wind was favorable. Got your chart handy? The one that shows the confluence where the Games channel meets the main river about 80 miles down. There's a sizeable island there. I saw a government helicopter leaving it in the dark and checked it out a bit for you. I found a boat tied up in a cut channel about three hundred feet past it's eastern tip. Looks like it could be the one you described yesterday. Do you have my photo?"

"Good lord, yes." Gary stared at the tiny picture in the phone's display. It was the same kind of boat all right. "Can you see any reason to think one of its engines might be ailing? A black exhaust port maybe?"

"I'm afraid I've moved on. Gotta pick up my son this morning in Walker. He'll be spending the rest of the month with me while his school is shut down. It's a little bible college, all in one building. Its heating plant failed an inspection and it'll take at least three weeks to replace it. With a little luck my wife can fly down and meet us before Greg has to go back. It would be great to have them both aboard for a few days."

"Sorry to sound so presumptuous, Captain. I can't begin to thank you for all you've done for us as it is. If you ever need anything made by a machine shop, be sure to call on me, OK?"

"You can depend on it. Sailboats are full of machined parts. Do you by chance have a CNC laser? Maybe we can make some money together. I've got some ideas. By the way, does your boat have a name? Now that you're a "liveaboard", you could start going by your first name and your boat name like I do. It'd give you some anonymity without sounding suspicious."

"My Engineering Manager sometimes refers to this boat as *November Alpha,* the last two characters of her registration number, does that help?"

"Unusual for a boat, but it works, doesn't it? So be it. Henceforth you shall be known as 'Gary of November Alpha', by me at least. See ya later, Gary. You have my phone numbers, right?"

Anxious to get going, Gary settled with Games River Marine, bought a portable toilet for eighty dollars and asked if the river had a speed limit. "25 knots in the marked channel, 55MPH outside the channel, but watch for bouys that mark the wing dams, lots of them are partly submerged. No wake speed within 100 feet of shore. Vessels traveling downstream have the right of way. Have a nice day, sir."

Knowing the marked channel was a minimum of nine feet deep and 'November Alpha' drew under two feet at rest, Gary stayed fifty feet or so left of the green can buoys marking the north side of the channel. Making about 35 MPH to keep from blowing in his new vinyl windows, he was passing all the commercial barge traffic easily, the big outboard humming along at a conservative 3200-RPM. At this rate, he'd make the confluence before 10 AM.

Shivering uncontrollably in the dark concrete room, terrified out of her mind, Alison Maye Loch despaired. She had no idea where she was, and little idea how long she'd been here. Life as she knew it had ended when she'd answered the door for the deputy and the nice looking young man who – who had been killed for trying to help her? The woman from the second police car had clubbed her across her face with the gun as she tried to explain the obvious mistake she was making. The next thing she was aware of was being face down on the back seat floor of a car that didn't sound like a car at all, and seemed to move strangely, as if it were somehow flying. They hit a bump and all motion had stopped instantly as the noise subsided. She had been dragged out of the car – police car? – by the same woman, onto a large empty parking lot with several soldiers of some sort. Running to them in handcuffs, begging for their help, she'd been struck again. At some point in all that she remembered seeing a huge tire attached to some kind of enormous machinery. The only other things she recalled were bright lights. The next time she came to she was soaking wet, on her back in a boat. She heard two people talking. The evil policewoman and a man she couldn't place. Not wanting to be struck again she had played dead, lying motionless despite her discomfort. The two were seated one on each side of her, facing each other. The man rested his foot on her chest as if she were a footstool, the woman was clearly irritated and defensive.

She had heard it. The two were discussing what to do with her. The woman wanted to drown her then and there. The man didn't agree. The driver of the boat would have to be eliminated as well. Perhaps he could find a way to trick a state or local officer into doing it. He spoke as if the evil policewoman were no longer involved, although he was speaking directly to her. Alison noticed the woman tense up as she evidently began to realize that herself. Deep in shock, Alison had passed out again, waking up in this cell. Enough time had passed for her clothes to dry on her body. Filthy, torn, but dry. An indistinct recollection of a small but clean restroom with metal walls haunted her memory, but she couldn't place it.

She began to notice things in the dark space. The surface she lay on was much more comfortable than the boat bottom or the floor of the car. It was an actual bunk bed, the lower one. In the dim light she could see the upper mattress through its wire spring mesh. A perimeter of short coil springs surrounded it. Where had she seen this kind of bed before? Girl scout camp! The similarity to a pleasant memory calmed her a little. Enough to take stock, to plan. Maybe to save herself. The handcuffs were gone.

Alison sat, then stood up. Turning, she expected to find she had a cellmate in the upper bunk. Finding no one there demoralized her a little but didn't destroy her. She searched the room for her purse, momentarily hoping to have her cell phone. No such luck. Unless the evil woman had thoughtfully gotten it for her it would be back in Dunningsville, useless. The rooms' only source of light was a window less than a foot wide and half that high set so far up the wall she had to sit on the top bunk to see out of it. All she could see was woods. Once in a while she heard a horn. Not like car horns, some deeper than even train whistles. Ships? Couldn't be. They hadn't time to take her to the coast. At least she didn't think so.

THE RESTITUTION

CHAPTER SIX *Observation*

The map Dale had made with the chart plotter aboard Atropos showed the island, identifying it only as 'government owned'. The sectional aeronautical chart he'd borrowed from Lucky showed no restricted airspace over it.

Gary Loch stood in his vinyl and canvas pilothouse studying it as he approached, floating with the current. He bumped the trolling motor from time to time, using it as a bow thruster to stay on course and bow forward. From a mile out, no buildings were evident at all; it appeared to be entirely forested. Most of the leaves had fallen already so he could see well inland. Looking carefully as he drifted slowly past the island's eastern tip he could make out the outline of a boat about where Dale had described. Filled with hope, he had his picture phone ready as he crossed the channel mouth. The boat was the same kind all right, and its port exhaust outlet was shiny black and wet.

Now Gary knew how a dog feels when he catches up to a car. You've caught it, now what are you gonna do with it?

"What? In two days? No way, Gary!"

"Well, I actually didn't cast off from Deer River until mid afternoon yesterday. Technically it's one day. I was fortunate enough to get some really good help. How are things at your end, Dennis?"

"Could be better. Alice heard a rumor about one of your girls being arrested. She's telling everyone who comes in the office about it. There's been a guy here all morning from the FBE. He's a real creep. Says he's IRS but I don't believe it. He hasn't looked at the books. He seems to be taking an inventory of the place. Where are you, anyway?"

"Fairport. About 15 miles south of the island I was telling you about. Place called the West Harbor Resort. It's a bar, really. Great three dollar burgers. Try to be nice to the FBE guy, but get the customer list and accounts receivable out of there. Try to secure the supplier list too, and make copies of all the payables. If anything bad happens let me know as soon as you're alone, OK? I've gotta call Lucky. I need his plane again."

"There's got to be more I can do to help, Gary. I'm going nuts here. Has anyone brought back your truck and trailer from Deer River yet?"

"Good idea. Why don't you call Lucky for me? The public access site at Deer River is right across the street from the airport there. My Sectional shows the 'Fairport Air Park' about three miles west of where I am now. I'll walk it if I don't hear from you. Tell Alice all of the truth you dare, and leave the place in her hands for the rest of the day. She just runs her mouth to feel important anyway. Hide the trailer in the loading dock after your creep goes away, hopefully tomorrow."

"What time should we pick you up?"

"We?"

"Don't start"

"As soon as possible. Let me know so I have time to walk three miles."

With the boat securely tied up at the tavern's dock and its freshly altered cover back on for security, Gary went back inside, ordered a beer and prepared to nurse it for an hour or two keeping his ears open for any local knowledge of the 'government owned' island. He didn't have to wait long.

A drunken discussion between a pair of bar patrons pitched up into a loud argument. One of their sons had been arrested for trespassing while hunting on 'The Island'. Pop's point was that the government couldn't declare private property rights. "Go'mints land is our land!"

His friend Bubba thought the kid had it coming. Gary had noticed several small signs on it that said "No hunting or trespassing. Violators will be prosecuted". His ears picked up. So apparently did the ears of a troubled looking woman seated near the end of the bar. "What does the government do on that island that's such a big secret, anyway?"

"Dam 'if'n I know", said Pop. "Shur's hell ain't shootin' no squirrels. No squirrels to shoot." Both men stopped arguing as she stood up.

"Do they use it as a prison of some sort?"

The lady, whom Gary had exchanged involuntary flirting glances with a time or two over the past half hour now had his full attention. She only noticed Pop and Bubba staring at her while trying hard not to say 'I dunno'. She had approached within five or six stools of them before she saw the mistake she was making. "Oh forget it," she said, turning on her heel. Bubba lurched after her, caught his feet in the barstool ring and fell, but somehow managed to grab both her ankles as he hit the floor. Down she went, with Bubba climbing her left leg, groping with his free hand inside her skirt. The bartender, a young fellow of about 25, came around the end of the bar. "Ya better stay outta this, son". Pop wasn't about to see his buddy interrupted. Gary suddenly saw how dangerous the two drunks were, and how vulnerable the lady was.

The young bartender retreated behind the bar and returned with a billy club. "Get your hands off that woman, sir." Bubba stopped groping. Fighting was more fun anyway, and this punk was half his size. Pop roused himself to join the fun. One of the woman's feet connected hard with bubba's face as she scrambled to her feet. She turned to face the idiots, finding herself flanked between the youthful bartender and Gary. Outnumbered two to three, the drunks retreated, muttering something about another bar.

"Thank you both. I should never have tried to speak to those two, but I'm desperate. I – We –"

"My name is Gary Loch, ma'am. You mentioned something about an island and a prison. It sounded a lot like what I'm here about. Maybe we could help each other. Can we talk a minute?"

"Right here, OK?"

"Of course. Although 'right here' doesn't seem as safe now as it did a minute ago. The island you want to know about – is it the one at the confluence of the two rivers just north of here?"

"Ah, maybe. What do you know?" The two were both too suspicious to speak openly. The wide-eyed bartender listening intently wasn't helping matters either.

"My daughter Alison was kidnapped by a woman claiming to be an FBE agent. I tracked them there."

The lady offered to shake Gary's hand. Doing so she grasped his wrist with her left hand. "I'm Andrea Sturm. My daughter's name is Diane." Tears streamed down her cheeks.

After the leaves have all fallen, a lightly forested area shows an unexpected appearance when viewed from directly above; the trees hardly show at all. The denuded branches aren't any more noticeable than the shadows they cast on the forest floor below them. "Are you sure this is the island? It looks so bare."

"It's the one alright, Andrea. From up here you see the ground through just one tree at a time. We're used to seeing a forest sideways, looking through all of them."

'Government Island', as they'd come to call it, was definitely not home to a prison. It had no significant buildings at all, but it did hold a few surprises. Right at the center, at its highest point, stood a triangle of three concrete foundation pillars, each about five feet in diameter and maybe three feet high. Three cleared paths radiated outward from this center, each ending almost a quarter mile away in small clearings cut around larger foundation blocks, rectangular, maybe eight feet wide and twenty feet long. Oriented lengthwise to the center of the pattern, each had three short steel girders protruding from its top surface, angled back away from the center pylons. Dennis recognized it first. "They're just building an antenna tower."

"A damn big one" Lucky added. "Those guy wire anchors make a half-mile circle. I'll bet it's over two thousand feet tall when they're finished. See the helipad? That's where your new friend Dale's chopper came from."

"Why would a helicopter be leaving an antenna construction site in the wee hours?"

"Dropping off the work crew?"

"Could be, but you'd think they could find a cheaper way to do it. Besides, if they only wanted access by air they wouldn't need those boat channels." The island had three of them, one near each point. Footpaths connected them to each of the guy wire anchor clearings. The path from the eastern boat channel, the only one on the Games River, had what appeared to be an outhouse or porta-potty near the anchor end. The FBE boat was gone. Gary studied the outhouse with the powerful binoculars. It wasn't an outhouse at all. It was just equipment housing of some sort with no doors or windows. All four sides had louvered vent panels with padlocks. It's single pitch, south-facing roof was a solar panel.

"I've been telling myself Diane's being held here." The tears were coming back.

"I know exactly how you feel, Andrea. I've felt Alison was here since Dale first told me about the place this morning. I can imagine how you feel after two weeks in this area asking questions that all seemed to lead here."

"Listen, both of you. You've got good reason to be disappointed, but you can't afford to give up on this island. All the evidence points to it. Your girls may not be here now, but Alison most certainly was and Diane probably was as well. We've got to check this place out at ground level. Find out who's working on it and learn all we can from them. Go through their trash if needs be. Dennis and I can go check out the taverns in Fairport without being noticed. Your drunks won't be that hard to spot in a town that small. We'll find out who caught their kid and how they did it. Lower our chances of getting caught out there ourselves. You two'll just have to lay low for a few hours. Think you can handle it?"

Andrea Sturm was suddenly anxious to be back on the ground. She'd never been up in a small plane before, and under any other circumstances wouldn't have been comfortable sharing such a small space with three men she didn't know. On another level though, spending some time alone with Gary Loch, this resourceful and fascinating widower of about her own age who was facing the same nightmare situation and getting to know him better, wasn't unappealing at all. "Yes, sure we can. You can take my van and we'll just sit in Gary's boat. We can watch for the FBE boat. It might still be around here."

Gary passed on his chance to point out that the FBE boat had most likely been towed back to Lowreyville, and even if it had gone south under it's own diminished power, it would probably be far beyond Fairport by now. Lucky and Dennis would be watching for it from the front seats on the five-minute flight back to the Airpark anyway. He had a good feeling about Andrea and wanted to be alone with her.

"You really want to sit in November Alpha? It's under forty degrees out there!" Dennis tapped on the windshield-mounted Outside Air Temperature gauge, or 'OAT', for emphasis.

"You haven't seen her lately, have you? Remember when I mentioned getting some really good help?"

Heath Roper was the drunk both Gary and Andrea had come to call 'Pop'. Not an especially intelligent fellow, he compensated with unfounded pridefulness. His buddy, actually called Bubba by his family and friends, hadn't taken the altercation in the tavern seriously. He'd just gone home to sleep it off. Heath Ropers' manhood had been insulted and his damaged pride demanded revenge. He'd gathered up his sons and dug up the old .22 rifle he'd buried under the dirt floor of his woodshed ten years before.

In his own mind, everyone in and around Fairport was afraid of him, cops included. He'd backed down from a stranger, a scrawny barkeep and a bitch because Bubba weren't no help in a fight. If he didn't put it right before folks found out they'd laugh at him. He could deal with Bubba later.

Heath knew the van the bitch drove. She'd been in town with it a couple weeks. It passed by them as they sat in Heaths' truck, parked on the main drag. Heath pulled in behind it to follow as Billy loaded the gun. They could see two men in the van. The stranger and the barkeep? Going from bar to bar telling folks how they'd bested Heath Roper? The oaf snorted like a bull as the van turned into the side lot of the Flatboat Saloon.

The two men confused Heath as they climbed out of the van. One was definitely older than the other, but seemed maybe too old. The barkeep was bigger than he remembered, and somehow more confident. He would have to be careful with that one. He parked behind the van, blocking it in. He and Billy, the older boy, jumped out. "Stop where you are, you pussies!" Heath seethed over the barrel of the .22. The younger man turned slowly, saw the gun.

"Oldest one's armed, .22 semiauto." Both men put their hands out to their sides.

"Shut up. We're gonna take a walk out back now. Lyle! Get them tire irons!"

Walking toward the back of the small parking lot, Dennis was to the left of Lucky. Heath held the muzzle to his back. Dennis could feel it there, centered. Hands raised like in an old cowboy movie, Dennis moved his left hand to scratch hard at the top of his head as if he had lice, probably a familiar condition to the likes of these three.

As Heath stepped over a parking curb, his captive spun left, dropping his left arm to trap the barrel between his body and elbow. As his sudden turn continued his right hand grasped the weapon just ahead of the receiver and his left wrapped around its forearm. The .22 levered easily out of Heath's sloppy, drunken grip. Half a second later the buttstock connected with his forehead, straight on. Stunned, he tripped backwards over the concrete curb. As his senses cleared he found the barrel of his own gun in his mouth almost far enough to gag him. The man was smiling. He pulled back the gun, removed its magazine tube, racked the unfired shell out of the chamber and offered his hand to pull him up.

"The name's Dennis. This is Lucky. You don't want to know our last names. I bet you thought we were the ones you had a run in with this afternoon. We have business with them too. Maybe we can help each other. Let's go inside. I'm buying." Billy and Lyle just stood there with their mouths open.

"I'm not going to tell you more than you need to know. We represent a group of families who have certain business interests that are not ordinarily discussed with outsiders. Lately we've become aware that another far less honorable organization is operating under our noses with the protection of a particularly vile government agency that's building a base of some sort on the island. Naturally we need to learn all we can about it. You and your people have run afoul of these individuals at least twice and escaped with your lives. You have our attention, gentlemen."

Lyle, leaning so far over the tavern table that his butt was off his chair said "the Mafia" under his breath.

Lucky got into it. Speaking for the first time, in his best Italian accent he said, "Never speak that word my son, never."

Billy, in a posture similar to that of his little brother breathed "Wow".

Heath beamed with pride and omnipotence.

"Now what can you tell us about the island and the activities on it? By the way, you must never mention this meeting to anyone, ever." The three morons spent the next hour and a half cheerfully telling them the details of every local rumor and observation about 'Snake Island' they'd ever heard or seen. Lucky took notes. The boys were better at it than their old man was. Slightly smarter and not nearly so drunk, both of them had been on the island recently.

Gary and Andrea sat in the 'pilothouse' of Gary's boat. The two comfortable bucket seats were swiveled astern so they could watch the river, ostensibly for the FBE vessel. The lantern was more effective as a heater with its glass globe replaced with a coffee can with both ends removed. Only a small amount of light escaped through the vent holes in the chimney top. It had smelled pretty bad for the first few minutes while the paint burned off. Placing it outside on the dock for a while had stopped the smell but allowed the tentlike shelter to go cold. Now the interior was warm again, but both remained sitting in sleeping bags. It was cozy, for want of a better word. The boat rocked slightly in it's moorings, little waves lapping at the hull. Their conversation was quiet, hushed. They didn't want anyone to notice the vessel was occupied. The open entrance to the tent at their feet was a constant reminder to both of where this could lead them. The surroundings were intimate, but the seats were bolted to the deck four feet apart.

"How did they take your daughter?"

"Well, it was her own fault, sorta. She was speeding in a church bus. Fifty miles per hour in a forty-five zone. She got a ticket and paid it two days later. A week after she paid, they came and arrested her for what they called 'Malicious Destruction of the National Environment' because the bus failed a smog test. The fine was only a thousand dollars, but they told me I'd have to make a restitution payment of $180,000 to cover the damage done or Diane would be taken to a prison farm to work it off. They gave me fourteen days to pay. I don't have that kind of money myself, but my name is on my deceased father's trust account as the executor. The money will be divided up among the family after it goes through probate. I told them that, and haven't heard from them since. That was six weeks ago. I've called every FBE number I can find. All the police agencies, even my Senators. They all say they never heard of her. Three weeks ago I got a call from a man with a message from her. She was being held on an island at the end of the Games River Canal, but would probably be moved before it got cold out. That's all I have. He said he was a construction worker and she slipped him a note."

"How did the FBE find out the bus was out of compliance? Did they test it?"

"Yes, and that's the weird part. The test was done the day before they took her. My lawyer said they couldn't do that. They couldn't prove it was out of compliance at the time she drove it. I told them that, too. They just laughed at me."

The romance of their surroundings was gone, leaving only the cold, hard frustration of their dilemma.
They sat in silence and individual despair.

Dennis and Lucky drove Andrea's van back to the West Harbor Resort. Lucky headed for the restroom and Dennis ordered coffee for them both. Dennis had had a few beers on their round of bars, Lucky had not. Not only was he driving, he was 'driving' an airplane. The rule is eight hours 'from bottle to throttle'. It had been a long day, though, and coffee seemed to be a good idea. Dennis stood looking out the windows facing the river when Lucky joined him. "Where are they? Gary said they'd stay tied up here till we got back. Maybe all night."

"See the big one out at the end on the North side? The registration number ends with 'NA'. Is that why you call it November Alpha?"

"Can't be. No way." They walked out the dock and slapped on top of the new pilothouse roof.

"Damn! This is perfect!" Dennis was astounded at the transformation. Gary and Andrea had come forward to meet them and were now standing together in the empty live well below the opening in the canvas cover. Andrea held Gary's arm for balance, having no foot room to speak of. It was like trying to stand on the gently rocking boat with all their feet tied together. A team effort that made it impossible to look dignified. Not knowing about the footing problem, the two men on the dock assumed they were lovers now. Slightly tipsy lovers, and treated them accordingly. After all, they were both single adults. Lucky thought he'd better not mention this to Carla.

On the drive out to the air park Dennis filled Gary and Andrea in on what they'd learned. Two local contractors were involved in whatever was being built on Snake Island, and were sworn to silence about it. Rumor had it that the Federal Bureau of Environment was building an automatic communications hub of some sort there. Work was only done on Wednesday, Thursday and Friday. Construction crews would be there for three days starting tomorrow. Once a week a 50-foot trawler that appeared to be a converted pleasure boat visited the island. It usually came up from the South late on Wednesday evening and left again in the wee hours of Thursday morning. One of Heath Roper's sons had seen it up close when he was arrested. It's name was *m/v Secant.* It's hailing port was *Holden.*

There were two other ways the girls might have been moved off Snake Island. The grubby, crippled 22-ft. launch docked in Lowreyville, or by helicopter. M/v Secant looked pretty good, and Holden had an FBE facility. 600 miles South of Snake Island, Holden would be an easy two-day sail for a fully crewed 15-knot trawler like Secant. Andrea found the courage to say it as they sat in the parked van watching Lucky's plane take off for home. "You've been so good to me, Gary. It's like a dream. We've accomplished so much today. I'm afraid if you go back to your boat you'll be gone tomorrow and I'll never see you again. Stay with me tonight? We can stay in the van – or get a motel?"

Gary turned in his seat to face her fully. "I do plan to leave tonight – and I want very much for you to go with me. We have maybe six hours until the first work crews land on the island, so we gotta work fast. You with me?"

"You know I am."

"Can you drive my boat? At night?"

"I think so."

It took Gary fifteen minutes to cut openings for the navigation lights in the fitted cover. This was an important point of intersection in a major international shipping channel. No point getting arrested for failure to display required signals. They ran up the channel with Andrea at the helm, getting the feel for November Alpha. They went past the island, cutting the lights as they turned into the narrow shallows at its north shore. Gary jumped out as they touched land fifty feet short of the recently cut docking channel there. Andrea backed away from shore and headed out the way they had come in. Reaching the main flow, she dropped anchor outside the marked shipping channel and turned on the white anchoring light. A casual observer would suppose she became confused in the dark, made a wrong turn, suspected her error and retreated to check her position and bearing. She was hiding in plain sight.

Gary made his way overland to the footpath and followed it rapidly to the northwest anchor block. The distance was less than he expected. The path was littered with food wrappers, cigarette butts and foam coffee cups. Nothing useful, just ordinary construction site garbage. A forgotten lined nylon jacket hung from a broken off tree branch near the first anchor. It bore an FBE logo embroidered below an American flag on the left sleeve. An inside, zippered pocket held a tiny handgun. At first Gary thought it was a toy. He pulled back the slide and a small bullet cartridge appeared. More were visible in the bright moonlight, down inside the magazine. He picked out the top one. On the flat back end it said '. 32 ACP'. The presence of the weapon made Gary angry. What kind of idiot leaves a loaded pistol lying around? The same kind of animals that abducted Alison – and Andrea's Diane. In a fit of righteous indignation, he took it. In another pocket he found paydirt – almost literally. A paycheck stub. The imprint said "Federal Bureau of Environment, Holden Facility, education and employment training division."

The cleared path to the center was cleaner. Far less trash was visible than along the winding footpath. Feeling exposed, Gary walked more carefully, and along the right edge where he was shaded a bit from the moonlight. A surprise awaited him at the center. Looking down the length of the clearing to the southwest anchor he saw a large construction crane and several fifty-foot tower segments stored flat along the edges. How could they have missed that from the air? He decided it was possible. Both the crane boom and the tower were steel latticeworks. The shadows cast by all those tree branches would have hidden them quite effectively. The crane cab? Well, that was another question. Probably just poor observation. Nothing had been moved for a long time. Grass and weeds had grown through the lattice before it had died off for the winter. The crane cab had been mowed around.

Gary's real objective was the east path, where the girls had most likely been brought ashore. The small building, an equipment enclosure actually, had FBE logos placed over black lettered stenciling saying 'Army Engineering Corps.' The Crane cab had been similarly marked. Everything, even the tower segments, was painted in military olive drab. From the air, the tiny building had appeared black or dark gray. Gary found no litter on the east and southwest paths at all, but the one he came in on was filthy. He could think of only two explanations; the FBE supervisors might insist on cleanliness, but never used the less convenient route themselves. It was also possible that no one connected with the project ever used the northwest approach at all, and local curiosity seekers were littering it while doing the same thing he was, but for recreation. Billy Roper had just been stupid enough to get caught at it. If that were the case though, why had they dug the docking channel there? Either way, the route in that he'd chosen was very lightly used.

Satisfied, Gary hiked back to the spot where Andrea had dropped him off an hour earlier. The pre-arranged signal for pickup was one ring of her vibrating cell phone. As soon as he did it he saw his boat move upstream slightly as she pulled in the single 12-pound mushroom anchor. Within moments she was approaching him at no-wake speed. Smooth.

THE RESTITUTION

CHAPTER SEVEN   New and Old

Andrea Sturm was still at the wheel as the big bass boat turned cruiser approached the dock at the West Harbor Resort. Gary was at the bow, painter in hand, ready to lasso a dock Bollard with it. He had the controller for the trolling motor, but wouldn't need to use it. Andrea was doing fine.

"Last call is in twenty minutes, folks. You the couple from the big outboard convertible?" The bartender was a portly woman about their own age. Her voice sounded like she'd been planning to close up early.

'Convertible' – There was the word Gary had been searching for. "Can we have just one draft beer and some carry-out?"

"Need ice?"

Gary started to say yes, but Andrea stopped him. "I've got a 12-volt fridge in the back of the van. Bunch of other stuff we might want to take along. Food, my clothes, another tent heating lantern, half a dozen more propane tanks like you use. You have lots of room, and an extra mouth to feed. Come to think of it, the ice might come in handy for your big picnic cooler, assuming you use it for food."

The two of them sat at a table at the back while their waitress started cleaning up, occasionally giving them a well-practiced hurry-up glance. The lady had brought the draft beers, the twelve-pack and the bag of ice all at once, so the beer would start warming and the ice would start melting. She had obviously done this before. Gary and Andrea got the message and were gone in five minutes, telling her the van would be picked up in a couple days.

The quick look through Andrea's van produced a bonus. Heath Ropers' .22 rifle, wrapped in a blanket, lay behind the fold-down rear seat. Mentioned only in passing earlier, it didn't surprise Gary very much to find it there, though he hadn't expected it. Dennis and Lucky probably wouldn't want to leave it with those unstable knotheads, and would presume Gary and Andrea would have more need for it than they did, not to mention a perfect way to get rid of it instantly if needed – just put it overboard. What the hell, they needed the blanket anyway. It took two trips to move everything to the boat. Gary crawled under the vehicle and hooked the keys securely over a muffler clamp after locking it up.

Thank goodness for the lantern heater. The boat was fairly warm and comfortable by the time they got settled in. They were docked facing out this time, the better to see m/v Secant when it passed. Andrea popped a beer and handed it to Gary. Their fingers touched in the passing, something both of them noticed. "Oh look! It's snowing!" It really was, if only a little. As soon as a flake would settle on the canvas outside the window it melted. "It's going to get cold tonight. We should get some sleep. We're both beat and we need to head south to Holden tomorrow. It'll be warmer down there."

"Wouldn't it be faster to just drive my van down to Holden? We'd be there by tomorrow night."

"Yeah, it would. It would be quicker for them too, but for some reason they do it by boat. Finding out why seems like a good idea to me. I want to follow them down, maybe sneak into the FBE facility with Secants' crew."

"You really do have this all figured out, don't you?"

"I sure wish I did. Drink up, my friend, we should be asleep by now. Is it OK with you if we both sleep in the tent? It'll be warmer that way. We don't have to-"

Her eyes smiled, and her lower lip jutted out in a mock pout. Two beers didn't make Andrea Sturm lose any control, but did make her just a little playful. Gary was sure now. This woman was an absolute delight to be with.

Untold thousands of years ago an ice-age glacier picked up a large rock from a mountain range sixteen hundred miles to the north and carried it here. A really large rock. Roughly cubical in shape and about eighty feet per side, it weighed over a hundred thousand tons. The ice pack dropped it smack in the middle of what was to become the Missacantata River. For the first few thousand years the torrent of water from the melting of a million cubic miles of ice crashed into the face of it, exploding over the top of the rock and flushing away the sand river bottom in front of it. Every few hundred years the rock would tip and roll slightly upstream into the hole all that sand had been washed out of. As it inched upstream, a deep furrow formed behind it as sand ridges formed to flank it, deposited there by the slowing of the water as it trailed out behind the obstruction. A few thousand more years passed as the two sandy spits grew and eventually emerged from the waters' surface forming tails on the island that had been a rock on a mountainside far away. Plant life appeared. Weeds were replaced by grasses, which were replaced by brush, which was in turn replaced by trees. Evergreen trees, like on the mountains far to the north, undoubtedly planted on the island by Indians or the early white settlers. Few people paid any attention to this particular island. It was too small to build anything on, and too steep for camping. The Army gave it a number once, a hundred and fifty years ago during a survey. Island 215 was noted on the original survey map with the words "Pine Trees".

By mid-morning Gary and Andrea had decided to find a place to conceal themselves and keep a watch for *Secant*. The farther south they went before sighting her, the longer they would have to wait for them to return from the island worksite. It would be a waste of observation time. Besides, if Secant didn't show up at all they would need to return to find out why, wasting both time and fuel. The high, heavily pine forested island offered something to hide behind. The green can buoy just off the east side of the island indicated the shipping channel narrowed down to clear the island, passing to the east of it. They approached the northwest shore intending to find an anchorage that would allow them a view of the northbound traffic from a position of concealment. No suitable spot presented itself, so they circled the island looking for a nook of some sort to tie up in, and thus found the entrance to a fine little bay, maybe thirty feet wide. From halfway back in it's 90-foot length they would be able to see the entire width of the river for five miles. After sighting Secant, they could move a bit east and have total concealment.

Gary didn't trust the appearance of the diminutive bay. It looked like clear, deep water but he knew that structures like this are usually shallow. He couldn't risk his prop, but wanted to back in so they could get out fast if they needed to. He shut down and had Andrea back in with the electric motor while he stabilized with a canoe paddle from the stern. He was pleased to see his paddle never touched bottom, despite his being able to see it clearly.

The day was getting a lot warmer. Up to sixty by noon with bright sunshine, they removed the cover to improve their ability to see and to regain the appearance of a fishing boat. The tent was left up and Andrea went in to get some more sleep while Gary took 'Afternoon Watch'. She would be taking the 'First Dog Watch' from 4 to 6 PM, while Gary rested. Both would be up for 'Last Dog Watch' from 6 to 8 PM. Gary would have 'First Watch' from 8 to midnight, and Andrea would sleep again so she would be fresh for 'Middle Watch' from midnight to 4 am. The four hours from 4 to 8 am, the 'Morning Watch' would be Gary's, and she would have 'Forenoon Watch' from 8 to noon.

"Where on Earth did that come from, Gary?"

"This little card Dale Lucans gave me. He said the British Navy came up with it three hundred years ago and nobody's ever been able to improve on it. I thought I'd be alternating watches with Dennis Davis. You're a lot better looking."

Gary spent most of his 'Afternoon Watch' inspecting and familiarizing himself with the two guns. He unloaded the small handgun and checked it over first. He had no idea how to take it apart, but felt no real need to. The thing seemed new. The magazine could only hold six cartridges, but the weapon had been loaded with seven. The owner must have loaded six in the clip, then put it in the gun and worked the slide to chamber the top one, then removed the magazine to top it up with the seventh. Gary didn't think that was prudent. He didn't want a pistol in his pocket with a round already chambered, completely trusting the safety catch. He'd heard Dennis refer to that condition as 'cocked and locked'. As if that weren't enough to convince him, working the safety seemed to fire the gun. When he pulled back the slide and released it, it cocked the hammer. Dropping the safety snapped the hammer back down. He decided to carry it with six cartridges in the magazine and the chamber empty. It would be a simple matter to pull slide back and release it to chamber the first round just before firing the gun. That way he wouldn't have to deal with the apparently useless safety at all. Down deep he knew he just didn't understand the safety and its correct operation, but this was no time to experiment. With only seven bullets available he couldn't even afford to test fire it.

The .22 rifle was familiar to him already. He'd owned one almost exactly like it as a child. He'd gotten it as a thirteenth birthday present and kept it as a prized possession until he had to turn it in at the National Guard Armory in Lake Osborne a few years ago. This one was loaded with fourteen long rifle hollow points. Two more plastic boxes with sliding lids held 186 more. The full box of 100 and the opened one the gun had obviously been loaded from had been wrapped up in the blanket with the weapon. Everything was in fine condition considering it had been buried and hidden by a family of nitwits for a decade. Here was a gun he could test fire, but he would have to wait until 4 PM. It would be a good way to wake up Andrea for her 'Dog Watch'. He wanted her to fire it too, if she would.

Gary sat in the helm seat glassing every northbound vessel with his binoculars for the last hour and a half of his watch, looking for m/v Secant. By 4 PM the inactivity and boredom had made him tired and listless. He decided to hold off on the target practice and catch a couple hours of much needed sleep.

As the English Navy set it up in the seventeenth century, The 'Dog Watch' is divided into two parts. 'First Dog', from 4 to 6 PM is resting time for those not on duty, but during 'Last Dog', from 6 to 8 PM, everyone is awake to have an evening meal and some social time with the entire crew. Gary would be getting up after two hours, helping Andrea prepare a meal, and then standing 'First Watch' from 8 to midnight. That was when Secant would most likely come into sight, during darkness. He'd have to stay sharp then. Andrea would be staying awake with him for part of it. His first real opportunity for a full four hour break would be 'Middle Watch' from midnight to 4 AM.

The Army survey crew that had numbered all the islands in the navigable southern three-quarters of the Missacantata River had started with number one, situated less than a mile from the rivers' mouth on the Gulf. Gary and Andreas hiding place was number 215. Snake Island, where the huge antenna was being erected had been given the number 223. All but the first few numbers had soon become meaningless as smaller islands, sand bars actually, sank and raised as the river swelled and receded, and sand shifted. The numbering system had been abandoned in the year 1877 as unworkable. Island number 81 was special, for a number of reasons.

Eighty-one had a name. Holden's Island was the largest island in the river. Over two miles wide and 12 miles long, it was almost flat. The Indians had used it as a neutral meeting ground for thousands of years, agreeing by tradition that no battle would ever be fought there. The white men found a new use for it. The manufacture of explosives. Black powder for the military and the westward expansion – and later for the South during the Civil War. Smokeless powder followed, and was joined by trinitrotaluolene, or 'TNT' for bombs and mines. Rocket propellants, smoke markers and incendiaries were made there and tested there, safely in the middle of the nation and safely out of the public eye. The place was off limits to the public. Named for General Buford Nathaniel Holden, an Army ordnance officer of the early nineteenth century, the city of Holden, five miles north of its northern tip on the West bank of the river, had grown up to support it and provide homes for the families of its men. Military personnel assigned there were almost always required to live there, but their families were usually not allowed on the island at all. With all the explosives it was considered too dangerous.

The Holden Arsenal was decommissioned in 1956 after a freak accident caused a nerve gas discharge that killed six soldiers and four civilian employees. In 1960 it was declared safe for human inhabitation and turned into a federal penitentiary. That use ended in 1970 when a prisoner found an unexploded experimental claymore mine on the grounds and used it to blow out the side of his cellblock, dying in the explosion himself along with several others. The public outcry over the housing of prisoners on an ordnance dump was over. The weeds and insects then reclaimed it until President Trayson decided to give it to Eldon Stewart Morris for what the public came to call a smog jail. Trayson assigned Morris to it as superintendent, giving him a plausible title and job description. After all, the general public wasn't supposed to know about his true function at all. Trayson had expected another benefit from the arrangement. He thought it would keep Morris out of the capitol. With the image of a conservative to project, he certainly didn't want to be seen or photographed with someone widely thought of as a leftist greenie. It didn't work out that way though. With the Federal Bureau of Environment raking in billions upon billions in seizures, Eldon managed a nearly unlimited travel fund. An airstrip appeared on the open south tip of his island within weeks, followed by a pair of docking facilities capable of handling anything from rowboats to freighters, all funded by payoffs and bribes. Boats and planes were purchased, or simply seized directly, usually without supporting paperwork. His private jet whisked him back and forth to the Capitol at least once a week. Eldon was always discreet, calling the President from area hotels and restaurants, never showing up publicly. The unspoken threat was sufficient. Take my toys away and I'll reveal you for what you really are.

The planes were nice, but Eldon's pride and joy were the boats. Air travel is fast, efficient, but to his way of thinking, flamboyant, too visible. An airplane made Eldon Morris feel like a fish in a bowl, like everyone was staring and pointing at him. Far from shore, a man can relax on a boat. You can live on one, safe from the eyes of others. Your secrets are safe on the open water.

The FBE hadn't seized her themselves. M/v Dream Lover had been nabbed for running drugs by the Coast Guard the same year the FBE had been founded. She'd been stored for a couple years before Eldon acquired her in an interagency exchange and had her refitted, painted white and renamed 'Secant' intending to live aboard her himself. When he was given the task of supervising Holden's island he'd ordered her brought there from the gulf. The hired captain arrived with her a week early, before the dock was finished. Not wanting to draw attention with a sixty seven-foot trawler anchored off his island, Eldon solved a minor logistics problem by offering to transport a load of water pollution detection equipment north to the island at the confluence with the Games River himself. The Engineer corps had already built three docking channels there, one of which was big enough to hold and conceal Secant from casual view. That trivial decision would have a great effect on Eldon Stewart Morris and the FBE.

While Secant was tied up at the Comm center site on Snake Island, an arrest went badly wrong. An overzealous field team arrested the Chief Financial Officer of an international corporation that owned a fabrication plant found to emit several parts per billion of Beryllium copper as welding fume. The corporation happened to be a major defense contractor and was almost immediately cleared by the President's political security staff. Almost. The arrest should not have been made. Livid, the President called Mr. Morris intending to fire him again, meaning it this time. Facing the end of his career, Eldon had lied to the President, blaming the incident on a private environmental extremist group and claiming the unfortunate CFO had been kidnapped from under their noses. That had left him with the serious problem of what to do with the prisoner and the two agents that had arrested him. With little choice, he took control of the situation himself.

Ordering the field team to lay low with their detainee, he sent one of his helicopters to bring them directly to him aboard Secant using the Army's construction site helipad. After interviewing the team he decided he could risk leaving them on duty doing inside work at FBE West. Using a windowless restroom on Secants' lower level as a brig, he held the executive on board while a special cell was prepared for him in what had formerly been office space on the uppermost floor of the old Administration building on Holden's Island. A special cell block, actually. The entire building was in the process of being converted into a small prison. Building a single cell on the third floor would raise eyebrows among the workers. Twelve relatively large, comfortable cells were eventually built there, with two beds each. From the beginning, Eldon knew it wouldn't work out to house two 'special inmates' in the same cell. He couldn't have them comparing notes with each other. His ability to let them live might one day depend upon their complete lack of knowledge. Another problem loomed. This last special inmate, the girl from Dunningsville, made twelve specials. He had run out of room to hold them alive.

Eight of the twelve had been brought in on Secant through Snake Island. Two had been brought in directly to Holden's island by air, infuriating Eldon. Two others had been the arrest team of a thirteenth, who had been killed attempting to escape, not knowing she was on a relatively tiny island, from which no escape would be possible without a boat. That ones' body was cast into the huge antenna's east guy anchor block and presented no further problem so long as the arresting field team never spoke out. Eldon originally planned to accumulate enough money in his own accounts to be able to flee aboard m/v Secant a few weeks before Trayson's next election and sail to a third world country where he could await his prisoners' discovery safe from prosecution. By now he was heavily considering just eliminating them along with their arrest teams and everyone involved with imprisoning them.

Thump. The sound and motion of the boat awakened Gary Loch from his light sleep. The indistinct slapping sound that followed brought him to a sitting position. What the -. He unzipped the tent flap and did not see Andrea. Scrambling out, he didn't see her aft either. He was definitely alone in the vessel. There was no sign of her on the shore of the bay either. The slapping sound repeated, behind him. He spun and saw a hand clawing at the side of the boat from overboard and jumped for it. She was in the water, and injured, drowning or both, unable to stand up. Wearing nothing but his undershorts so he could sleep more comfortably, he jumped over feet first to help her. He could see bottom, had his knees flexed a bit to take the shock, but never touched it. Expecting the cold water to be waist deep, he was shocked to find himself in over his head. Disoriented, he tried to swim to the surface and became tangled in Andreas' flailing arms and legs. Surfacing at last, he spotted a small floating object and tried to grab onto it. It was a shampoo bottle. Andrea grabbed onto him, one arm going around his neck. Both of them managed to get a hand on the gunwale, sputtering water, trying to catch their breath.

"What happened?"

"I wanted to clean up while you were asleep."

"So you jumped overboard?"

"I hit my head pretty hard coming up. Musta hit the bottom of the boat. This water is deep!"

"Cold, too. We better get back in the boat. You go first." Andrea got both hands on the gunwale and tried 'float-bouncing' herself a couple times to get a start on pulling herself in. From inches away, Gary saw she wasn't wearing a top. Cleaning up? The shampoo bottle?

She couldn't do it. "Let me help." As she braced herself for another try, Gary hooked his left arm under her butt to try giving her a boost. No bottom either.

"I'll give you just an hour and a half to stop that." He saw that pixie smile again.

She couldn't do it that way either, and neither could he, even with Andrea pushing on his nearly bare backside. He worked his way around the boat to the cleat where the painter was tied off "We'll have to go to shore and pull the boat up. The anchor shouldn't be that hard to drag."

Andrea was still a little disoriented. She held the bow line in her free hand as Gary swam the ten feet to shore in a lifesavers' sidestroke. "You don't really have to get out of the water before I can get you some clothes or a towel."

"If you were a gentleman, you'd give me your shorts." He saw that smile again. Gary Loch seldom did anything on whim, but this time he couldn't stop himself. He stood up in the foot deep water and peeled them off.

"Nice and warm?" Both laughed as she stood up, handing him the painter, helping to pull the anchored boat to shore.

"It's good to have that out of the way, Gary. We're living together on a nineteen-foot boat and there's so much chemistry between us it's a wonder the water isn't fizzing. Hope you don't think I'm being forward." As the boat neared them, she tossed his shorts on the deck.

"You're bleeding! Lets have a look at that." Gary carefully started parting her wet hair, trying to inspect the scalp wound.

"You may as well, you've seen everything else." She said with mock sarcasm.

Andrea had quite a bump on the left side of her head just above the temple area. She'd come up hard into the chine of the hull, knocking herself senseless and opening a gash two inches long. Gary held a compression bandage on it while she wrapped herself up in the blanket the rifle had been in. Gary had her keep it away from the open wound. "It belonged to the Ropers. Might have cooties."

"We'd better not sit on it naked, either!"

"I think you're going to be fine." I few minutes later, he wasn't so sure. As the bleeding subsided she started to feel weak and faint. A second dry blanket didn't seem to help either; she started to shiver and complained of being cold. Fearing she might be going into shock, Gary started planning to get her to a hospital. Andrea didn't agree.

"I'll be OK, You'll see. Just let me rest a few minutes to warm up and clear my head. I've bumped my head worse before. I hate to admit it, but I think the sight of all that blood got to me." It's still my watch, but I'd sure like to go in for a while. Is that OK?"

"Of course it is. I'll be in to check on you in a few minutes."

"Can we put the cover back on when I get back up? I really do think it's getting colder already."

Gary looked at the air thermometer readout on his fish finder. "You're right, it's down to fifty. I can put it up myself if you don't mind the boat bouncing and rocking a little."

"Woo – Hoo!"

Yep, she'd be just fine.

In no real hurry, Gary started putting the top up. The first step was to set up the bimini frame Captain Lucans had provided to hold up the 'pilothouse' roof. The light aluminum structure folded in a manner similar to a car's convertible top framework, but without the automatic power assist. Folded down as it was, it rested on the top of the two snowmobile-like windshields mounted to the consoles in front of the two fixed seats. Gary turned as he stood to erect it.

There it was, not a quarter mile away, approaching almost head on at a good fifteen knots. He was sure even as he reached for the binoculars. At seven-power magnification the name was still too distant to read, but definitely had six letters. The description the Ropers had given Dennis and Lucky was dead on except Gary thought she was well over fifty feet long. Could the dimwits have estimated the waterline length? As she approached she turned slightly eastward, but not enough to clear the island. She slowed, then stopped dead in the water maybe four hundred yards out. The name 'Secant' was now plainly visible on her port bow flank.

From behind him, North of the small island, Gary heard a powerful ship's horn sound two quick, sharp blasts. Almost immediately, Secant sounded the same signal. Secant and another much larger vessel were preparing to pass each other head on, starboard to starboard. Ordinarily, a 'left sides facing' approach is preferred, like cars passing in opposite directions on the highway. Why would Secant be hugging the wrong side of the channel?

Something was moving just beyond the trees to Gary's left, something very large. The ship's horn sounded five short rapid blasts, the universal danger signal, warning Secant to hold her position or back away. The larger vessel appeared. A huge barge, it's blunt bow plowing the water. Then another and another. Gary and Andrea had seen a rig like this earlier. A sort of oversize tugboat at the rear pushed dozens of these enormous barges, tied together in a double or triple row almost half a mile long. Dale had warned him to stay clear of them. "They don't want to run over you, they just can't help it." He'd said. The tow boat crews were good, but their job seemed impossible. They were steering what amounted to a triple freight train from the back end, with the current behind them. A lookout on the front barge could warn the helm if an obstruction appeared, but they probably couldn't stop without the cables breaking and the barges all getting loose. Why on Earth would Secant want to do this the hard way?

Andrea emerged from the tent, awakened by the noise. "What's the hose for?"

Gary had noticed the four-inch black rubber hose that passed under Secant's rail and into the water amidships as the vessel had started and aborted its slight right turn. He had paid no attention to it. Now the end of it was snaking around in the water as if something was being pumped out of it under pressure. Of course. Secant wanted to pass the barge tow on the wrong side to conceal what it was doing. The flagship of the Federal Bureau of Environment was dumping its sewage holding tanks directly into the shipping channel. "And then there's us, peeing in a jar."

"That's the one we're looking for, isn't it?"

THE RESTITUTION

CHAPTER EIGHT   Thieves

Agent Bud O'Brien loved fieldwork and only tolerated working the terminals at FBE West. It bored him almost to the edge of sanity.

Always on the lookout for things to occupy his mind while sitting in front of the damned things, he'd long since started pulling up personal data on his co-workers, especially the attractive female ones. The jacket on Annamaria Albarran had been interesting to say the least, and since hers was the first entry in the alphabetical listing, he'd learned about her early on.

Annamaria had been under psychiatric evaluation her entire adult life. It was a wonder she'd been hired at all, much less issued a weapons permit. A name was given to the condition she suffered from and was receiving counseling for, but Bud couldn't pronounce it. He recognized it though, from its presentation. Anna had a rape fetish. She could only be aroused or achieve sexual gratification as a rape victim.

Born and raised in a third world country along with two younger brothers, her sex life had began at the age of eight as a little prostitute. Her drug addicted, desperately poor mother served as her coach, co-worker and madam. The woman would dress her up in short skirts, garter belts and halter tops over an empty padded bra and then leave her at home tending Juan and Ernesto while she went to the waterfront bars. Some of the men she brought back were clean and well dressed, some were filthy. Some had teeth or eyes missing. All of them were drunk, and none of them would stop, even if little Anna begged them. Sometimes they wanted her mother first. Some only wanted her. Mother would help them, with her hands. She seemed to enjoy it, and tried very hard to get her daughter to enjoy it as well.

It was worse when she brought home two men at once. The shack only had one bed, and by the time the night was finally over it would be a mess. Mother would put Juan and Ernesto to sleep in it to stop their crying.

Eventually Annamaria did learn to enjoy it, sort of, but the rage against the men and her mother remained. The end came when she was fifteen. He hadn't removed his pants, just pushed them down. A folding citrus knife fell out of the pocket neatly into her hand. She acted without thinking about it, as she always did in bed. Seconds later, instead of enjoying commercial sex with a child, he was bleeding to death. Her own mother was already gone; the thin four-inch long blade sank to its full length in her neck, just below the right ear. Anna washed up, sent the boys to a neighbor and walked 30 kilometers to San Paso Elama, where the rescue mission took her in and sent her north. The seaport men had taught her fluency in three languages and tavern obscenities in several more.

She had told none of this to her doctors and therapists because she had no memory of it herself. They only knew what they were able to ascertain: she had a violent early life filled with forced sex, and several languages had been spoken in the home.

"Do you recognize this guy?"

"Yes Bud, I do – His name is Paul DuPont. He owns the car we caught Mr. Loch's daughter driving. How did you get this?"

"Something I do in my own PESVI collars. Sometimes I just do it for fun. When a PESVI sniffs a hit, it takes a picture of the back of the car to get the license plate number. It's not a still shot. It starts immediately and films for ten seconds, sending the footage to our computer along with the emissions data. The machine vision alphanumeric determination is done in house, reading out the number and the state name as spreadsheet data, so we don't ordinarily need to see this. All these picture files get automatically deleted when the system cleanout runs anyway. I wanted to see the car you told me about. No reason really, just curiosity. You have to scroll back from the most recent hit. Most of the entries show a car passing at speed, and the file ends right after they go over that hill, so this one kind of stood out. Since this guy is involved in your case I think you need to see the whole ten second show."

The full-face image of Paul DuPont was the very last frame. Buds' laptop blurred for a second as it reversed at 16x speed to black, then Bud started it from the beginning in slow motion. "The vehicle is moving very slowly as it comes into view. Watch. It's parking on the berm just past us." Anna gasped as the passenger side door came into view bearing a "Dunningsville Police" shield. The police cruiser stopped and two men got out.

"That's Chief Adamson, the one I sent out to Arrest Mr. Loch." Anna was starting to turn ashen. The Chief left his door open. Paul DuPont closed the driver's side door and walked back, moving out of the cameras' field of view. The chief dropped to one knee directly in front of it. The camera tilted up, showing Adamson's face. He was moving the box, presumably to examine it better. He looked up and his mouth began to move, talking soundlessly. Paul's face appeared, looking intently straight into the lens. The image went black again.

"I sent a copy of just the moving mouth to my sister at the deaf school. He's saying "You're right, Paul. It's not a traffic counter." "

"What does this mean, Bud?"

"Don't you get it Anna? The owner of your target car is a cop, a plainclothes detective. This is no coincidence. That thing is fifty miles South of Dunningsville, and they found it. That's never happened before. We've never seen a noncompliant vehicle owned by a cop before either, you do the math."

A flash of denial struck her. "Why did the PESVI hit on the cop car? Is it out of compliance too?"

PESVI's almost always hit on cop cars, but the computer sorts most of them out. They have big engines and no emissions controls to speak of. Military vehicles and fire equipment's the same way. They're government owned, exempt."

Bud O'Brien knew nothing of Rienhold Hahnemann's death. It had not been announced or even mentioned to the staff at FBE West. A few had heard the news short about a Federal Agent being killed in the line of duty but never guessed it was one of their own. He saw the intense crazed flare in Anna's eyes and took it as an invitation. They were alone in her one-room apartment. Physically strong, he picked her up by the waist under her skirt and roughly tossed her on the bed face up, catching her panties with both his thumbs and index fingers, pulling them down below her knees in the same fluid motion. The rest passed in slow motion. Instead of bouncing on the bed and bracing herself for him, her feet came up in a backward somersault that ended with her out of sight off the far side of the bed. Her purse appeared on top of the bed with her hand in it, and as she came up to her knees the purse flipped away leaving her 9MM aimed squarely at his face. Her other hand joined it for a two handed grip. Bud's last thought before the flash came was that her panties must still be down.

If President Robert Owen Trayson could have made it so by himself, there would be no government services beyond the Post Office and the military. The schools might get a stipend, but would be fundamentally private. There would be no regulations placed on industry and commerce, no government licensing of professionals. There would certainly be no Federal Bureau of Environment. Minimum wage laws would not exist, nor would limits on loan interest rates. The income tax would be capped at about 5%.

Trayson was way beyond what most folks would consider conservative, but practiced the fine art of keeping that to himself. He hadn't prevailed in every election he'd ever entered by practicing total disclosure. He despised little bloodsuckers like Eldon Morris, but had a purpose for him nonetheless. Eldon and others like him were useful for extracting money from other liberals to fund all the wasteful social programs they had enacted and he, as President, couldn't get rid of. It was Trayson's world view that most of the population were liberals, and deserved to be taxed, fined and surcharged into oblivion to pay for their own giveaway programs. He had no desire to see his conservative faithful suffer under the load. His temporary intent was to keep taxes low by giving goofball bureaucrats like Morris a free rein while protecting his own supporters from them. His leading concern was that the public would discover his complicity in the continued use of their disgusting tactics.

Lately, something was going on that threatened to cause that to happen. Some jerkwater town in the Midwest was calling FBE offices in the capitol trying to get them to remove the dead body of an agent. The dead guy had been carrying credentials connecting him with Eldon Morris, and had reportedly been killed by his own partner. The matter was being investigated by local, county and state police agencies in conjunction with the disappearance of the daughter of an area industrialist.

Another problem had popped up that involved Mr. Morris. One of the Navy's most highly regarded officers, a Rear Admiral Jason Sanders, had started complaining about the FBE abusing interagency cooperation standards. He actually mentioned Morris by name, calling him 'self aggrandizing', and criticizing his professional judgement. The complaint involved the use of military equipment and personnel for the transport of civilians on short notice by combining that activity with routine interdepartmental training missions. Fortunately, the Navy complaint had been delivered directly to FBE headquarters in the Capitol and the Director had forwarded it to Trayson's own political security staff. Thank goodness both problems didn't originate from the same area. If his memory served, NAS Lowreyville was on the southwest coast, near FBE West. The young punks Eldon called Agents were probably taking their dates up in helicopters. Eldon Stewart Morris had better have some pretty darned good explanations ready real soon, but right now the little turd wasn't even returning his phone calls.

Seven thirty on Thursday morning. Almost through Gary's morning watch. Andrea had gotten up and joined him a half-hour earlier. Following the motor vessel *Secant* discreetly wasn't going to be as easy as they had hoped. Unless obstructions or conditions demanded slowing down, she held rock steady at 14.2 knots. Heading South now after waiting all night, the 4 knot current gave her a speed over the ground of just over eighteen knots. November Alpha wasn't capable of matching it. The big two-stroke outboard couldn't go that slowly for more than a few minutes without fouling its spark plugs. It needed at least 20 knots to breathe right, and could easily produce over seventy-five, though only with the top down to save the windows. The little electric trolling motor could only give them three knots or so, diminishing as the batteries discharged. His plan was to power up to within a quarter mile or so of Secant, then slow down and switch to the electric until they almost lost sight of her or the batteries became dangerously low, whichever came first, then repeat. Gary intended to pass Secant at speed a couple times per day, proceed out of sight as his batteries charged fully and then anchor outside of the marked channel to let them go by. That would serve two purposes: They would have a chance to look Secant over in close-up, personal detail. Also, if they made a show of fishing, swimming or maybe loving while anchored, it might just dispel any suspicions about the small boat that almost always seemed to be staying in sight.

Andrea was rummaging around in the provisions for something for breakfast when Gary's phone rang, startling them both.

"Gary Loch."

"Morning boss. Where are ya?"

"Maybe forty miles South of Walker. We have the boat we talked about in sight. We first spotted them last evening when they were still headed north. How's it going there on your end?"

"Better than before. The FBE's auditor left us with an apology! Says he's off the case and not being replaced. I was skeptical of course, but then I got a call from the Chief. Remember Commander Myron Trask from the State Patrol? The President called him!"

"The President? President Robert Trayson?"

"The one and only! He told Trask that Annamaria Albarran and Reinhold were both fraudulently impersonating FBE agents. He's sending the Marshals to remove Hahnemann's body from the morgue here. When Trask asked about Alison, he said he'd put some Federal investigators on it. Said he didn't know the two incidents were related."

"How the hell could he know about both and not know they were related?"

"Now that you mention it, I don't know. I assumed he didn't know about your daughter at all until Trask asked him about her."

"And that could still be the case I guess. Stay on it for me, will you? We're committed to following Secant all the way down to Holden. I don't know who to believe anymore, and we also have to find Diane."

"Is Andrea still with you, Gary?"

"Yes, Ms. Sturm is very definitely still with me, Dennis. We're starting to became, well, kinda inseparable." He twisted to smile back at her as she approached to join him on the phone, walking on her knees to stay below the window level, still all unbuttoned and jiggling.

"Hi Dennis."

"Morning Andrea, wha'cha wearin?"

"Ya don't want to know."

"Then don't let him point his phone at you anymore." Dennis heard laughter and mock screaming "Glad to see you two are having some fun. You both deserve it."

James S. Riad had been born Selim Sherif Al Riad. He had adopted the more western sounding version when he decided he really never wanted to return to his homeland and it's strict fundamentalist rule. The west had been good to him. After college, he'd gone to work for a medium sized aerospace company and grown with it, rising over eighteen years to the position of Chief Financial Officer. Prior to his 'arrest', he'd been in charge of the finances of his chosen country's third largest defense contractor. Every year he was investigated, and welcomed the annual opportunity to demonstrate his loyalty each time. Very well paid, he always offered to pay his investigator's hotel bills, and bought them lunch whenever he could. He had lots of friends in the FBI, Department of State and the Defense Department. He'd been known to date the ex-wife of a former Chairman of the Joint Chiefs of Staff. Everyone seemed to like him. He had no idea why he was being held incommunicado in this obviously political prison, not believing any of the arresting agents' ranting about beryllium copper and the national environment. If he hadn't honestly believed his country had no facilities like this he'd never have settled here. Without really knowing why, he was sure he hadn't been abducted by a foreign power or a terrorist organization and spirited out of the country.

Having been here for seventeen months, he'd made a few observations. While he was quite sure he was the first one to be incarcerated here, he was aware of the others. He could often *hear* them, though faintly in the soundproofed structure. Most were young women. They were probably lifelong citizens, because they were all terrified out of their minds. None of them seemed to have any background for this sort of persecution. He most certainly did. His own parents had suffered worse. There were far worse things than solitary confinement. The food was actually quite good.

His cell was a lot like a hospital room. That had caused him some worry early on, but no medical experimentation had been done on him, and he never heard anything remotely like screams of pain from the others. That of course didn't eliminate the possibility that such was being done elsewhere and he and his unknown companions were only being held here while awaiting their turns. That possibility had driven his decision to escape. He fully intended to rescue as many of the others as possible when he did it. And the time was fast approaching.

The room had a set of bunk beds, a toilet, sink and shower made of stainless steel. Nothing else. For about three hours on most afternoons, enough light came in through the single barred window to allow reading. The door, directly facing the bunk beds, had a slot in it through which a meal was passed three times a day. Sometimes, maybe three times a week, a book was passed through. He often saw the hands that did the passing, his only human contact. He never was answered in any way when he spoke to them.

His plan involved moving his bed out of the line of sight through the door slot. He correctly surmised that his jailers wouldn't allow that without some sort of confrontation, and steeled himself for a severe beating or worse in order to get the small amount of information he needed at the same time. He wanted to know if his jailers all carried keys, whether they were armed, and if so, how. Were they male, female or a mix of both? Do they speak English, or some other language? Generally, how vicious are they? Would they try to conceal their identities? Would supervisors accompany them? With these questions in mind, James Riad moved the bunk bed to the far end of the unusually shaped, long narrow cell and waited. It didn't take long. The evening meal arrived and instead of staying balanced in the slot it was jerked back out when the jailer saw the change. James heard the person running back the way they'd came. The footfalls came five minutes or so later. The door burst open for the first time since he'd been brought here and half a dozen hooded guards rushed in. The first aimed a small spray can at him as he lay in his bed. Prepared for that, he covered his head with the thin sheet just as the blinding liquid struck. He could see through the sheet well enough. He peeked out from behind the sheet as if he didn't know what was happening, and was instantly sprayed, but did not care at that point. He did not cry out. No sense further traumatizing his fellow prisoners. He concentrated on breathing - and listening. Every word, though few were spoken, were in English. A supervisor of some sort did most of the talking, mostly issuing orders not to injure him unnecessarily. He was dragged out of bed face down and held there in an armlock while his bunk was moved back where it had been. No one addressed him personally at all. Two of them picked him up and placed him back on the lower bunk and he was alone again. The whole thing had taken just seconds. Three weeks later he did it again with the same result.

He had given this next step a lot of thought before committing to his plan. The same guard brought his breakfast and midday meal each day, no doubt the result of a shift arrangement. The second-shift guard brought the Evening meal and occasional book to him. He'd studied the hands for many weeks, often contorting himself to be able to view them from only inches away without being detected. The hands he had chosen delivered the second shift meal and a book on Saturday and Sunday. They belonged to the only guard among the five he'd counted that he was sure was female, probably single, and still in possession of some remnant of human decency. He regretted the need to so terrify his favorite among the unseen guards, and was resolved to do her no more physical harm than necessary to prevent her from being accused of complicity by her superiors.

James Riad had made the pivotal preparatory move on Saturday evening almost four weeks ago. Judging time by using the match mark he'd made on the wall showing where the rectangle of sunlight had been when dinner had been last served, he lay on the upper bunk and began acting out the appearance of abusing himself. At the sound of the door slot cover opening, he turned to face it in mock surprise and embarrassment. "I'm so sorry," he said to the pair of eyes transfixed there. "I didn't mean for - I'm not allowed any privacy." The brass cover slammed shut. A few seconds later it opened just enough to admit his food tray. "Please – You're the first person I've seen in seventeen months! I'm James."

"My name is Dorothy. You can –" The cover closed again.

James lay back, pleased with the outcome. He'd be busy the next few weekends. The next day he moved the bunk beds out of sight just before the evening meal and nothing happened. He spent the next twelve hours taking the beds apart and putting them back together again, inspecting each part in minute detail. It wouldn't be long now. He had no way of knowing he was preparing to escape into a government compound on an island in the middle of a major shipping channel. He only knew that a river large enough to support shipping traffic ran nearby. The only direction he could see by climbing up to the small barred window was west. Sometimes he could see the sunset.

Andrea Sturm had chosen a good spot to pass m/v Secant. The river was moderately wide and almost straight for over fifteen miles here. She'd have room to get well ahead and still keep Secant in sight while her crew would surely lose sight of the much smaller boat. They'd have plenty of time to 'put the top down' without being seen doing it. At thirty knots, she had little fear of damaging the windows. Gary had awakened when she throttled up.

Gary found his binoculars and trained them on something along the shore ahead. "Slow down and try to come up on that big sailboat without alarming it, Andrea. There's someone I want you to meet."

She saw the white vessel, not immediately recognizing it as a sailboat because it's mast was missing. Two men were on her deck and pilothouse roof, securing something in a rack there – the missing mast, or at least parts of it.

"Ahoy the sailing vessel Atropos!" Gary was standing in the bow opening, Andrea still at the helm.

"Why, it's Gary of November Alpha! I see you got yourself some new cleats and a good lookin' crew."

"I sure did! Why'd you take down your mast, Dale?"

"We've got a low bridge up ahead. It's a railroad swinging bridge. They say they can't open it until Monday. Even with the little mast, we're about eight feet too tall and we didn't want to wait".

"Will a sixty or seventy some foot trawler clear it?"

"Hard to tell. Does it have a tall funnel or a fixed derrick?"

"That one right there." Secant was now about a half a mile upstream, and slowing. Dale turned up his VHF marine radio, intending to caution the big trawler about the possible obstruction. The bridge authority beat him to it.

"FBE motor vessel Secant, this is lock and dam operator thirty six. Be advised our co-located railroad bridge is disabled in the extended position. We expect repairs will be completed next Monday morning. Our closed clearance is twenty-six feet. Can you clear? Over."

"Lock 36, Secant. Negative, we require 30 feet. Secant requests interagency cooperation in the form of workers to remove and reinstall our antennas and foremast. We'll tie up in the lock approach to take your crew aboard."

"Secant, Lock 36 negative, our people are all busy with the bridge work and the lock approach is full of barge traffic. Suggest you anchor where you are. Sorry". The radio operator didn't sound sorry at all.

Dale Lucans laughed out loud. "Typical FBE jerks. Thought they'd force some butt kissing out of the Coast Guard by parking in their way. Wait a minute, Gary. The FBE is who you believe has your daughter. Do you think she might be on that trawler?"

"Not at present, but we're pretty sure she was recently. We're tailing it to see where it goes. Both Alison and Andrea's daughter Diane were transported off that island you spotted for me on m/v Secant. We believe it goes somewhere down near Holden but may have other stops."

"I know where it goes. John and I saw it lots of times last summer. There's a special dock built just for it on Holden's Island. They take it up and down the river all the time. John says her captain's an idiot. I didn't know it had anything to do with the FBE though." It was the first the big guy helping out on Atropos' deck had spoken.

"Excuse me, Gary Loch, I'd like you to meet my son Greg Lucans. He's with me while the furnace in his one-room school gets fixed. I told you about that earlier."

"Gary – Loch? Like Coke? You mentioned a daughter Alison?" Young Mr. Lucans rummaged through his wallet with a shaking hand and passed Gary a scrap of paper, part of a placemat from a restaurant in Fort Miller. It had Gary's home phone number on it.

Gary already knew, but he couldn't keep himself from asking. "Where did you get that?"

The comparing of stories and the amazement at the coincidence would have to wait. M/v Secant was stopping directly alongside them. She looked even larger from twenty feet abeam. "Do you want to get aboard her, Mr. Loch? I sort of know Secant's captain Morris. We helped him get off a sand bar he'd grounded himself on last July. He was grateful enough to invite us on for a dinner and drinks. We went aboard of course but didn't drink. Captain Morris acted like we should have been honored to be in his presence or something. It was kinda creepy. We could offer to help him get that stuff down. I'll bet he'd let us."

The details of Alison's Fort Miller story were coming back. He wanted to know about the guns. Would Captain Lucans, Greg's father, know about them? "Ah, yeah. We could try that."

"Can we dad?"

"Sure, I guess so. We're sort of involved now anyway." He handed his son the VHF mike.

"Trawler Secant, sailing vessel Atropos, immediately to your starboard. We just finished our dismasting; can we offer assistance with your rigging? You may remember me from the sandbar incident last summer. Greg of Rat Racer?"

"A Topo, this is Secant. Young Greg from the amazing little outboard that helped rescue us from the uncharted shallows? Good to see you again. Sailing now are we? Is Mr. Walgren with you?"

"The same, Secant. We're delivering Atropos to the Gulf Islands. John's sick, he'll be joining us later. You caught short handed again Captain?"

"Yes I am. I appreciate your help. I just can't depend on my other agencies anymore. I'll open my transom hatch to bring you and your work crew aboard."

"Slow down a second, Greg. These people can't use their own names, and your friend runs the most despised agency in the whole government. He'll check any names you give him."

Gary took over, "Andrea will be staying here with Atropos and November Alpha. No offense, but you wouldn't be convincing as a shipfitter. You two can use your own first names. Call me 'Harry'. I'll fake a German accent so you can pass me off as an undocumented deck ape. That won't be too surprising on a cruiser headed for the islands. If I get caught sneaking around, it's 'Spricken ze English? Nein'. He won't want an international incident. This Captain is really Eldon Stewart Morris?"

"That's the name he gave us last summer, sir. I sure wish we had some time – I've got a million questions."

Gary thought 'you and me both'.

Gary Loch knew he was running an enormous risk in actually boarding the FBE trawler. It probably carried at least a half-dozen crewmen as well as the former head of the agency, a man Gary now knew still headed its most diabolical department. As if that weren't enough, He'd only known the young man controlling the situation for a few minutes. The fellow knew both Alison and Eldon Morris personally, though by his own account not particularly well. It was just too convenient to fully accept at face value. Was he being set up? He felt he could trust Dale Lucans, but would he be willing to oppose his own son? He was depending on Andrea for his very life. If things went wrong enough for him to jump overboard she would use November Alpha to pick him up.

Like Atropos, the much larger Secant had anchored bow upstream. The three men used Dale's inflatable to cover the twenty-odd feet and tied it by its painter to Secant's stern boarding ladder. Mr. Morris was waiting for them at the aft companionway. Captain Lucans had wondered what he meant by 'Transom Hatch". As he started down the steep stairway leading below, Gary spotted Andrea returning to the bass boat. Good girl. She was already getting prepared.

The narrow passageway ran forward past two identical closed doors to each side before widening to pass on either side of what appeared to be another companionway hatch. Gary assumed its stairs descended into the engine spaces, probably landing on a catwalk between two low-RPM diesels. Mr. Morris took the port passage, followed by Dale and young Greg Lucans. Gary, bringing up the rear, asserted his independence by turning right. He could plainly see the two routes around the engine room header converged again a dozen feet forward. He reached that point first and waited politely for the others to pass before rejoining the little procession at the rear again. Morris looked at him in mild disdain but said nothing. So far, so good. Slightly wider here, the main passage passed two more facing doors. The one to starboard bore a 'male' symbol. A small circle with an arrow projecting from it. The port door had once carried a corresponding female circle with a suspended cross. Gone now, its outline was still visible in the paint. The door had a sturdy but hastily applied hasp and a large padlock. It also had a new brass food tray slot, like an old-fashioned prison solitary cell. How clever. Make a brig out of a restroom. A prisoner could be left inside for the whole trip. Gary could almost hear Alison and Diane begging to be let out. For the first time Gary had to put down a powerful urge to just throttle Eldon Morris and simply beat the truth out of him.

Just beyond the brig the passage opened up into a lavish salon. The comfortable seating and little tray tables gave it the appearance of a VIP room in a swank restaurant. Potted plants graced the corners. The draperies must have cost thousands. The walls were hung with original art. Two young women sat facing each other over drinks at one of the tables. They wore bikinis that wouldn't fill a matchbox. It was obvious these girls didn't get out much, it was 40 degrees outside.

A rather steep stairway led up to a landing at eye level opposite the central passage. The landing gave access to another steep ladder-like stairway up to the bridge and the open doorway into what appeared to be a large red and gold bedroom. The

Captain's quarters? Possible other rooms, probably another head or two. Morris led them to the bridge, and out through a side doorway onto the wide foredeck.

All three men could see that taking down the several antennae would be easy, but the foremast was another matter. The six-inch diameter aluminum tube was really a self-supporting jib crane derrick. Its gaff, mounted high above the pilothouse and almost as long as the mast itself, trailed aft and upward, supported by a hydraulic cylinder. Spreaders flanked the boom hinge joint with standing cables that ran out to almost the end of the boom.

"That crane boom can't swing out over the side, Dad."

"Not unless the whole mast rotates with it."

Gary surprised himself by noticing the long scratches running up the mast vertically. "Guys – that mast telescopes! It retracts straight down into the deck."

"No shit. And he doesn't even know it."

"Oh, he knows all right, Greg. He uses that rig a lot. See the dirty lines on the teak deck? Pallets for tower parts he delivers up to the Games River. I'll fill you in later. I think this screwball just gets off on soliciting free help and watching them struggle with it. Let's milk it. We have the run of this ship while we mess with this thing. When we're ready, we'll just ask him where the fuse is for the retraction motor."

"What are we looking for, anyway, Mr. Loch?"

"Anything that makes you think this boat stops anywhere but Holden long enough to unload a prisoner quietly. Maybe we can find out how they're armed, if they have a weapons locker somewhere. I don't expect to have to fight them physically, but if it has to happen I'd sure like to know what I'm up against."

THE RESTITUTION

CHAPTER NINE   Opportunity

"Good afternoon, Ms. McCaufle. This is the Office of the President. President Robert Owen Trayson would like to speak with Chief of Police Albert Adamson. Will you connect us please?"

Sharon McCaufle had began her law enforcement career as a dispatcher, and had a well deserved reputation for being able to stay cool under pressure. Now she couldn't even keep her voice from cracking.

"Al! – It's the Pres – it's the – It's President *Trayson!* He's on the line right now! Line one I think. Yeah. He wants *you!"*

The Chief was almost as starstruck as his Administrative Assistant. "Dunningsville Chief of Police Adamson here. How can I help you, Sir?"

"Will you hold for the President sir?"

"Yes, of course."

"Good afternoon, Chief. I trust I didn't interrupt your crucial work. I need to ask your help in a matter of national importance. A law enforcement matter. Can I depend on you sir?"

"Certainly, Mister President. Permit me to risk a guess. Does it involve our own Alison Loch and the recently deceased FBE operative Mr. Reinhold Hahnemann?"

"I see you're already up to speed, Chief. It also involves at least one other criminal posing as an FBE agent, a woman using the name Annamaria Albarran. She and Mister Hahnemann evidently conspired to kidnap Ms. Loch for the purpose of extorting money from her family. They had a falling out and Ms. Albarran killed Hahnemann. My Marshals suspect the conspiracy may extend into the actual FBE hierarchy. It might take some time to complete the investigation. That's where you come in. I need you to help keep this under wraps. It could undermine the people's trust in our public servants."

"I'm afraid it's too late, Mr. President. This mess hit the local papers last Monday. All the networks have camera crews here. When the Marshals Service picked up Agent Hahnemann's body it started a media circus. They're interviewing everyone in sight. About all I can do is keep this call a secret."

"Oh, my. This is bad news. How is the young woman, Alison Loch? She must have been terribly traumatized by all this."

"You really don't know, do you sir? Alison was taken. Arrested or abducted by Agent Albarran at the same time she murdered her own partner. Alison must have witnessed the killing."

"I – I don't know what to say. Are you making any progress at recovering the young woman?"

"No, we haven't. Look, may I be open with you sir? I'm on your side politically and mean you no harm, but please. The Federal Bureau of Environment is just plain rotten to the very core. I have all the warrants they used against the Loch family. It's all in order, everything, to the letter. And there's more. We have indisputable evidence that leads all the way up to Eldon Stewart Morris, the director you fired as soon as you took office. He's back, and placed highly enough to demand and receive assistance from the military. We have proof of that as well. Photographic evidence, some pretty dramatic stuff. Dash camera footage of a Marine helicopter taken from patrol cars in two states. If you really want to eliminate the FBE like you promised during the campaign, we have exactly what you need, sir."

The President listened to the rest of it in a cold sweat, missing most of the details while coming to the only conclusion that made any sense. Eldon Morris was out of control and had to be stopped.

Eldon sat watching his volunteer work crew from the comfort of his master's seat. Centered in *Secant's* wheelhouse, well aft of the controls, the oversize swivel seat had originally been mounted on a high pedestal of chrome tubing with a foot ring, allowing good all around visibility. It was the single feature Eldon found most appealing in Secant's design. Throne like, it gave him a feeling of total control. He'd had it re-installed on a raised floor section to maximize the visual effect, eliminating the ring. Now it gave the impression of a battleship, or maybe a Starship.

Ann Winslow sat at the helm, forward of Eldon a few feet and to his right, wearing a bikini top and a wrap skirt. With the ship standing at anchor she had little to do other than help her boss keep an eye on the free help. That was turning out to be pleasant enough. The young one seemed to be in charge, freely bossing around the two older men who had come aboard with him.

"Where have I seen the tall one before, Eldon? He's familiar but I can't place him."

"Remember last summer? John Walgren? We all thought you were going to rape him or something."

"Oh, no. That isn't John Walgren, no way."

"That's his partner. The other guy from the little outboard boat that pulled us off the sand bar down by Springport. It seems he's gone on his own, doing sailboat deliveries."

"Oh, yeah! He's looking good now!"

"If you want to give him a try I'll stay off the bridge for a while. I gotta find out what the one who doesn't speak English is up to anyway. He keeps going below. I never could trust foreigners."

The guy with the guttural accent was disappearing down the forward stairway again as Eldon came out of the port wheelhouse exit door. The fellow was quick, and way too independent, having found the port deck stairs to the salon entrance seemingly by instinct. He'd be working away one minute and seem to vanish a moment later. Who could possibly need to use the head that often? Eldon had intended for the three to have to pass through his wheelhouse on the way to the head. Still, he imagined this slacker just wanted to get an eyeful of Sheila and Monique in the salon. Eldon would enjoy this. Watching him watching them. It must be torture for him, a sweaty European deck ape among nubile young FBE agents in training. His agents in training.

The wheelhouse phone rang with Eldon's hand just inches from it. He answered it instinctively, forgetting for an instant that Ann was screening his calls today.

"Eldon Morris." He also forgot the wheelhouse took the outside calls while underway.

"Dammit Eldon, I've been trying to catch you all day. I need some answers, and I need 'em now. Your dummies really screwed up this time. How are you going to fix this mess, Eldon? My phone is ringing off the hook."

"What mess, Bob?"

"You know very well what mess! Loch Tool and Die, Dunningsville, Gary and Alison Loch. A dead operative by the name of Hahnemann. Surely these ring a bell. There's more. I've seen pictures of a giant helicopter carrying off a police car with one of your morons and the Loch woman in it. The base commander responsible for it is throwing a fit! If he goes public I'm doomed. Listen to me. You have to fix this. I'll try to give you twenty-four hours, but don't count on it. If this gets too hot I'll have to remove you from office along with the rest of FBE management. That might give me a few days to work out disbanding the whole bureau. Do you understand what I'm telling you Eldon?"

"Oh, come on Bob. Aren't you overreacting a bit? We've been on the spot before. We're good at it."

"Bullshit. You idiots aren't going to explain this away on my watch. Either fix it or get rammed for it yourself. By the way, Gary Loch is tracking you. He's following you downriver in something called a 'Bass Boat'. Its registration number is 4535NA. Don't bother trying to outrun him. His police chief says it'll do eighty miles per hour."

"Can you stop him for me Bob?"

"No, I can't. You just don't get it, do you? If this blows up I'm on his side, not yours. *You* have to take care of it, you idiot. And stop calling me Bob."

Practically no one called it the "Federal Bureau of Environment, Holden Education and Employment Training Division". Almost all of it's employees called it what the public called it; the Smog Jail. Dorothy Spence knew first hand they didn't pay their cooks very well. They made eight bucks an hour flat, without any real possibility of advancement. Her bi-weekly check for four hundred forty eight dollars met Dot's obligations and put some food on the table, but didn't allow her a life worth living. The only thing her boss could offer was more hours. Two options were suggested. She could simply work seven days a week in the kitchens, giving her an additional $134 a week, but eliminating her spare time, or she could work weekends as a part-time server. That would involve working two mini-shifts of two hours each on every Saturday and Sunday for six bucks per hour. Seventy-two extra dollars a week. Getting almost six hundred every two weeks would allow her to go out on Saturday nights. Maybe find a man who would be decent to her. She took it, and had done it now for quite a while.

Shortly after she started, a new wing had been opened. The Special Detainees Section, or 'G-Block' was supposed to be for short-term confinement of environmental terrorists under military jurisdiction. She was forbidden any sort of personal interaction with these people under any circumstances. The cells were individually soundproofed, as was the long single hallway. As an hourly employee, Dot questioned the wisdom of placing all the cells on the same side of the hall. The same number of them would fit along half the length if they were on both sides. Also, why were the rooms made so long and skinny? Not much wider than the hall itself, each cell must be forty feet long judging from the spacing between the doors. They were arranged end to end. Looking in through the meal slots, she only saw the bunk beds. Seldom did she see the prisoners unless they were in bed. She had no way to know it, but there was a reason. Originally, G-Block had been administration offices. Each one of them ten by fifteen feet, they had seemed larger because of the two picture windows offering a commanding view of the river and its west shore. The windows had been sealed up and covered with soundproofing material inside, tin siding outside. Surely the prisoners would never notice. The soundproof brick looked and felt real enough. Two out of every three doors had been covered as well. The flimsy partitions had been removed, leaving only the load bearing walls, every third one.

Dot was losing sleep. The incident in G-Block last weekend had left her shaken. She wasn't shocked by what she'd seen. Her own source of pleasure ran on batteries - her 'current lover'. The sight had been a changing moment for her. Long ago she'd willed herself not to wonder why these 'short term detainees' never left. Why were most of them young women? Do terrorists in captivity all spend most of their time crying softly? She felt a connection to the man in G-1, had seen his eyes in a moment of shame. He wasn't a terrorist, couldn't be. This Saturday she was going to break a rule. So what if she got fired, she had a few dollars saved up. His name was James. She had to know if he deserved a year and a half of solitary confinement. If not, the others probably didn't either.

There wasn't much to see. Taking them below and routing them to the foredeck area through the lower level probably hadn't been a way of keeping secrets. Mr. Morris probably just liked to keep people a little off balance. The beautiful teak deck, wide as a sidewalk, ran uninterrupted from stem to stern on both sides of the ship. Doorways on both sides entered two luxurious staterooms, a second salon even more impressive than the one below, and another pair of heads marked with male and female symbols. Gary peeked into one of the darkened staterooms. A sleeping couple occupied the queen-size bed. Behind it was the door to yet another restroom. Small wonder Secant had such big holding tanks for black water.

Walking aft, Gary descended the companionway to return to the foredeck work area the way they had been led in the first time. He encountered Eldon Stewart Morris in the lower salon. The two girls were gone.

"Wiegates, Herr Kapitan!"

"Drop it, Mr. Loch. I know who you are." A gun appeared in the man's hand. Another man came up behind Morris holding a shotgun, one of the stainless ones made especially for use at sea. "Let's go rejoin your accomplices, shall we?"

One of the bikini-clad girls ran in. "The bass boat got away, Eldon! It's headed back to the North. That thing is fast!"

"Damn, we'll never catch it. I'll have to trust the Coast Guard to do it with a chopper. Now go take over that blasted sailboat."

They heard the diesel start on Atropos, saw her moving slowly forward. "Ann! Get started up! Catch that sailboat." Atropos could make nine knots under power, Secant about fifteen, but the slower vessel had other advantages, it would take a few minutes to get Secant running, up to speed and her anchors hoisted. The railroad bridge could be managed. Captain Morris still had a couple antennas up, the radar and the satellite TV. All his two-way communications antennas were down and disconnected. "Ann! Retract the crane mast!"

"I already tried! It's not responding, Sir."

Eldon sent the shotgunner to get ready to fire on the sailboat. He already suspected the crane controls had been disconnected. "All right, Mister Loch, back up to the wheelhouse. I want you to see this."

Secants entire crew, with the exception of Eldon Morris and Ann Winslow, were at the starboard railing, guns at the ready, watching s/v Atropos as she moved away heading for the disabled bridge while going further into the shallows. Captain Lucans knew his lead ballasted fin keel drew five feet nine inches. He was hoping Secant drew nearly the nine-foot channel limit.

Entering the wheelhouse, Gary saw his boat approaching fast on the opposite side. Eldon did not. He pompously settled into his master's chair and started barking orders at Ann Winslow. The splash followed by the roar of the big outboard were his first indications that Gary Loch was no longer his prisoner. Furious, he bodily shoved the attractive 39-year-old woman out of the helm seat and took over. Spinning the oversize wheel hard to port while shoving both throttles forward to their stops sent Secant clumsily in pursuit of a vessel capable of more than five times its speed – and into the path of a small tourist excursion boat. HonkHonk-HonkHonkHonk. The warning blast made him chop his power and stop dead in the water with reverse thrust.

The engines starting had followed the anchor winch racket. Then the ship had lurched forward, come up to full throttle and turned abruptly left. Then it had jerked to a stop just before the gunfire started. Bent over the crane motor wiring in the compartment under the master stateroom floor, Greg Lucans knew this didn't bode well. For just an instant his soul told him to rush to the defense of his dad, but his common sense stopped him. All the shots came from the right side of the ship. All seemed to be directed overboard. None of them had brought guns on board that he was aware of, so it must be FBE people doing the shooting. One or both of the older men must have jumped ship for some reason. If one of them had been identified they all would have been. One escaped from each side? That would explain the turn to the left and shots to the right. As silently as possible Greg reached up and closed the floor hatch. It wouldn't save him for very long unless he re-connected the crane controls. One of the crew would be coming to fix it.

Greg sat still for a few seconds, listening and letting his eyes adjust to the near-total darkness. He wished he'd brought a flashlight from Secants toolbox. The high current traction motor had only two wires, red for positive and black for negative. Reversing them would make the control work backwards. Up would be down and vice-versa. That would bring a crewman just as surely as leaving it disconnected. In the dark, Greg couldn't tell red from black.

Greg was wearing Gary Loch's lined nylon jacket. Faking work outside had made him cold, and Gary had left it behind on the foredeck. He'd been comfortable in his shirtsleeves while really working to remove Atropos' mast. Gary had something heavy in his pocket, a flashlight? No, a gun! His first thought was the fear of being caught with it by federal government agents. Then he remembered hearing them shoot, probably at his dad, just seconds ago. The feeling of combined guilt, protection and self reliance was a lot like when he and John had saved Alison's friend three weeks ago. Not only was the feeling the same, the gun itself was almost exactly like the one John had taken from the would-be rapist. The one John had been teaching him to use. The only gun he'd ever fired or even touched. Greg Lucans realized how lucky he was as he pinched back the slide in the dark just enough to feel the slightly smaller chambered .32ACP round held to the breechface by the extractor claw without ejecting it. John Walgren had taught him well. M/v Secant was moving again.

With Andrea at the wheel, Gary frantically scanned the water around and behind the FBE trawler for either of his people. There were none. Dale and Greg must have made it to Atropos together. "Want me to take over, Andrea?"

"No. I can do it. I saved your sorry butt didn't I?"

"Yes you did. And thanks, by the way. We gotta get to the sailboat before they shoot Dale and his son. Try to stay out ahead of the trawler by seven or eight hundred feet or so. Come up on the sailboat on her far side. We'll have to take them aboard quick. I'll uncover the aft deck so they've got a big open space to jump into." Gary could see Captain Lucans at the wheel in his cockpit. He saw no sign of young Greg.

Dale Lucans was aware that his boy was still aboard *Secant*. The pretty lady had stepped out from the right side wheelhouse door and read the numbers from Gary's boat aloud to the trawler's master. The second she went back inside, Dale had gone over the side expecting Greg to follow. Just as he hit the water eight feet below, Dale remembered that Greg had been about to go below to disable the crane motor. The splash would have been heard, so going back aboard the trawler was out of the question. As he clambered up the three steps built into his transom he saw Andrea cut the side ties between Atropos and the bass boat and pull up her anchor by its' ridiculously short nylon rope. She fired up and disappeared before he could even start his own little diesel. Gary had been the only one of the three carrying a gun. He'd get Greg and escape from the far side of the large vessel while he drew away their attention with his own retreat. He could hear the bass boat over his own exhaust and the rumble of the trawler. Andrea was doing exactly as he surmised she would, but his heart sank when he saw Greg wasn't with them.

"You don't have my son, do you?"

"No, we thought you had him. Can you hold your own for a minute while we go back and look for him? He may be in the water."

"I think so. I might even make the bridge. Please find him for me Gary!"

Gary took over and flipped around, matching the sailboat's speed. "You won't slow him down much. I've gotta do this alone. Please don't argue with me Andrea. Get on that sailboat right now."

Dale had said the windows would blow in if he went over about 35 knots. They went at forty, along with the entire canvas cover turned shelter. Unsnapped at the back, the whole thing fluttered violently and shook off into the river as Gary accelerated away from Atropos in a wide circle, looping back to face the guns on the trawler. November Alpha was herself again. Light, agile and fast as hell, Gary skipped across the water, jinking back and forth to throw off their aim, seeming determined to pass close to Secants' starboard side directly under their muzzles at over eighty MPH. At the last second, Gary flicked his wheel, disappearing along the trawlers gunless port side, circling wide to miss Greg if he were swimming there. Gary already knew he wasn't in the water west of the vessel. He wasn't here either. Nor was he on the surface behind it. Gary could see the flattened water marking Secant's most recent moves. It looked like an enormous cursive letter 'V'. Greg Lucans was not in it or near it. He was still on the ship.

Simultaneously in terror at what the President had said and a purple rage at the incompetence of his people, Eldon Morris sat uneasily in his command chair watching Ann slowly gain on the white sailboat. The speedboat, or 'bass boat', as Trayson had called it, had rejoined it about a quarter mile ahead in the shallows west of the marked channel. It appeared the small fast outboard intended to take the much larger sailboat in tow. The idea seemed ludicrous at first, but if they could manage just 20 knots that way they could outrun him easily.

As much as he wanted this Loch fellow and his cohorts eliminated, Morris had something more important to consider. No more than 24 hours from now FBE Holden would be crawling with Marshals and other law enforcement officers. It wouldn't take them long to discover G block and his 'special detainees'. He had two choices; make them all disappear along with everyone who knew about them, or disappear himself. It didn't take him long to realize he'd have to do both, and at fifteen knots m/v Secant wasn't going to be much help.

"I got the crane coming down sir! It works backwards, did you know that?" Ann Winslow had been trying the crane switch every few seconds. She suspected the mast was strong enough to split the hull if it hit the bridge at speed and was sure the boss would order her to do just that.

"Finally, something goes right. We don't need the radar or the TV. We got em' now, Ann".

Just as they hit the bridge, sending bits and pieces of the two expensive antennas raining down on Secants' superstructure and the surrounding river, the powerboat took up the towline slack and began pulling away just as they came into scattergun and pistol range.

"Ann, call Holden's Island on your cell phone. Have them send our fastest helicopter down to pick me up right away. While you're at it, have them send for Agent Annamaria Albarran from FBE West. Disarm her and bring her to Holden under guard."

Towing the big sailboat was a lot harder than Gary had imagined. Almost twice as long as *November Alphas'* nineteen feet, the sleek looking craft was heavy. The 5600 pounds of lead keel ballast alone was more than twice the weight of Gary's whole boat. Gary's propeller was wrong also. The 23-pitch wheel he had fitted was made for speed, not slow-speed power. Feeling like driving a car from a standing start in third gear, the thing ventilated or cavitated if Gary gave it much throttle, but they were making almost 20 knots. Atropos' 7-pitch auxiliary prop quickly overreved and had to be throttled back, but was helping a little, if only by making the sailboat easier to steer.

Burning gas like mad and unable to use Dale's ample supply of diesel fuel, Gary knew he couldn't keep this up for long even if his motor didn't overheat. He also knew they were terribly outgunned. The FBE boat had at least eight handguns and a couple shotguns. At least they hadn't mustered any long-range rifles or lord forbid a deck gun. All he and Andrea had were two – he felt for his pockets – one .22 rifle. He'd managed to lose the captured pistol while on the trawler, along with his jacket.

THE RESTITUTION

CHAPTER TEN   Shortfall

"Sailing Vessel Atropos, Lock Operator number 36, over."

"Lock 36, this is Atropos, go ahead."

"Please drop back from the fishing boat. You'll have to wait, the lock is full. Please anchor above the guide wall and expect to lock through with M/v Secant and the lock tour boat with a small barge tow aft. It'll be about an hour."

"Lock 36, Atropos can't comply. We're under tow at this time, dismasted for the bridge. Looks to me like there's plenty of room, I'll take responsibility for it."

The lock operator didn't want a dismasted sailing yacht adrift in her traffic. She had to respect the guy's initiative in securing his own Good Samaritan. Best to let them through together before her supervisor got back. "Alright, Atropos. You can lock through together. Hope you have a lot of fenders."

Finally, a bit of luck. Gary watched in relief as the huge lock doors closed behind them and Dale stopped both boats with a jolt of reverse from his little diesel. Andrea hauled in the towrope as Gary reversed away from the screws of the towboat ahead of him. Secant was stuck behind the tour boat she'd almost collided with. He could see her Captain seething in his wheelhouse as the lock slowly lowered him out of sight. This was going to give them an hour's head start at least.

Andrea seemed to want to stay aboard Atropos. Was she upset over being left out of the high-speed rescue effort? Gary Loch didn't really care. It had been his decision and a good call. His boat had at least two bullet holes in it, one of which was letting in enough water to keep the bilge pumps running almost full time. The other had pierced the seat where Andrea would have been.

Dark thoughts filled his mind. Who was Greg Lucans? How did he really know Alison? Was he really what he claimed, or was he with the other side? Why did he stay on the trawler, and how? What about his dad? He and Andrea had been working a good plan before meeting up with the Lucans family today. Now, he was running for his life while towing something that outweighed him ten to one and rapidly running low on fuel. The canvas top Dale had made for him was gone as was the dome tent and his heater. He'd lost the best of his guns and worst of all, Andrea wasn't with him. He still didn't know where Alison had been taken, though Holden's Island seemed likely. When something seems too good to be true, it probably isn't true.

The time in the lock had been wasted. With the two boats crowded into actual contact with each other they should have been talking, deciding what to do next. Instead, each of the three were lost in their own worlds.

Gary Loch had spun an amazing story. A little paranoid, but still amazing. Captain Lucans had heard a lot of sea stories over the years and thoroughly enjoyed them. Gary's had taken the cake. For a few days at least. Now it was horribly real and had sucked in his own son.

Maybe Gary didn't know where his daughter was, but he knew exactly where to find Greg, and how. Running away wouldn't do for long. To Captain Dale Lucans, Gary Loch had gone from a skilled storyteller to a spineless pussy. It was his *daughter* those worthless shitheads had taken, and Gary was sneaking around in the weeds looking for tiny bits of information to use against them. His way would be faster and a lot more effective, but he needed a little time and privacy to get prepared for it. He really didn't want to alienate Gary; in fact he'd probably find Alison in the process. If anyone aboard that trawler knew, they'd tell him - one way or the other. For now he'd play along, but in the morning he'd be on his way alone. He would definitely not be running downstream away from Secant and her rail full of unskilled pistol punks. Gary's pretty girlfriend could do as she wished, just not on his boat. All she wanted was the comfort it provided. He needed to think and plan. Having an airhead woman aboard was almost too much already. Absently, he realized his dinghy was still tied to the trawler's stern and had probably been swamped.

Andrea Sturm had known that inviting themselves aboard the FBE boat was a terrible mistake and had said so out loud. Men. They just had to do everything the hard way. Just look at them now, tied together with a thirty-foot rope and being dragged southward by the one with the biggest engine. What was Gary thinking? Try as she might, Andrea couldn't remember one time in the last three days when Gary had even mentioned Diane. It was always Alison Alison Alison. She had overlooked it because the two girls were probably together. Now Mister Lucans' son was danger and Gary seemed oblivious to it, even though they all knew where he was. Sitting on the sailboats' low coach roof, leaning back against the coaming, she was the first to notice the big helicopter, five or six hundred feet up, streaking straight up the river at them. As it passed overhead she could feel the sound of it change.

Real sailors are a tradition bound lot. Not everyone can handle an offshore vessel, and those who can tend to share a rather high standard of moral character. But Ann Winslow had come with the boat, and M/v Secant had been confiscated from drug runners. When Eldon Morris took over the seized vessel he made a deal to retain her chief pilot. As long as Ann did as he said, she stayed out of prison. She acted as First Mate and frequently shared the master's stateroom. Being a realistic man, Eldon had never made her an agent or armed her. She was one of the oldest women employed by the FBE in any capacity, but showed no real loyalty to anyone but herself.

Eldon would be leaving for Holden on the chopper, and she'd be in command. She knew two things Eldon did not. While he and the rest of the crew were below rounding up the slippery German guy, she had been at the wheel watching the foredeck. The old guy went over the starboard bow rail, the German from the port side abeam of the pilothouse door. The tasty looking young one was still aboard, probably in the crane motor compartment under the stateroom sole. Of course she knew about it. She'd lived on this tub for seven years now. She would do as Eldon would want, but she was going to have some fun first.

The Helicopter pilot wouldn't land on Secants' fantail. He said the weight would either crush it or capsize the boat. The offer to take Eldon off in a rescue harness had been declined. "Why did you call for this particular aircraft, anyway? Do you want me to take off your entire crew?"

"No, just myself and one other. I asked for the fastest chopper."

"The smaller ones have landing skids. We could just hover and let you step aboard. I'm sorry sir, but we'll have to pick you up ashore. I'll fly south, find the first acceptable landing site and wait for you. Do you have a preference for which side of the river sir?"

"Use the left bank if you can. The enemy seems to be favoring the right."

"Uh – Secant – say again, enemy?"

"Affirmative. It's a long story. We'll need a place where we can safely beach the bow with a seven-foot draft. We don't have a dinghy, never needed one before."

"Begging your pardon, sir. You're towing a real nice looking inflatable with an outboard on it. Maybe you could use that." The other FBE pilots were right. The boss really was an idiot.

The big two-stroke outboard couldn't take much more if this. Gary needed to find a place to hide both boats and let Secant pass them. They had to do something to rescue Greg, if in fact he needed to be rescued at all. Dale would know if his son were involved with the FBE. His body language and actions would surely give him away. Besides, if they came to another lock and dam they'd lose their head start unless they got lucky again. Speaking of Lucky, his airplane would sure come in handy now.

It would be easy to hide his own boat by simply running up a tributary a hundred yards or so. The sailboat was the problem, with its fixed keel. Shallow water was out of the question. He powered on, listening to his misfiring engine, watching his temp gauge and looking for a miracle.

The small island was round, and high. A plan was forming in his mind as he hooked around below it, cutting the tortured two-stroke and extending the trolling motor. He saw Dale drop the small anchor he called a lunch hook as he pulled up alongside the sailboat, hearing it's little diesel puttering softly. "I'll go ashore and climb up to where I can see them coming and you can see my hand signals. Andrea – get in my boat. I'll keep you both directly across from them as they pass. They'll never see us."

"What good will that do?"

"We'll be behind them. We can use November Alpha to rescue your kid without exposing your slow boat. I still have one gun."

Dale smiled, but held his comment. If Gary only knew what resources Atropos held. At least the man wasn't entirely spineless after all. He asked Andrea to hail him when he was needed and went below to retrieve some equipment.

Lying prone on a flat place watching northward over a small ridge of exposed rock, Gary spotted the big military helicopter returning about half an hour later. If it were acting on behalf of the FBE it was too late to do anything anyway. If it saw them they would simply have to hope for the best. Law enforcement aircraft aren't supposed to be armed with airframe mounted weapons, and are forbidden to use deadly force against civilians. Of course that was a cold comfort after being shot at by the same agency just a couple hours earlier. Relief flooded over him as the thing roared over without any change of direction or altitude at all. As the noise subsided Gary returned his attention to watching for Secant.

There she was. The trawler had just come around the bend ahead of the forward barge of the tow she had locked through #36 with. Using the binoculars he could see Eldon Morris on the aft deck with the shotgunner. The man was still carrying the gleaming stainless weapon. The two seemed to be studying something trailing behind the trawler. Mystified, Gary watched as the two climbed over the stern rail and down out of sight about where he, Dale and his son had boarded. Perhaps young Greg had escaped using the inflatable dinghy. Maybe he'd gone overboard and the two were using Dale's dink to recapture him. Gary watched intently while preparing to scrabble down the bank to his boat if needs be. Would Andrea stay aboard with him this time?

As Secant adjusted her course to pass west of the mid-channel island, he could see Dale's dinghy, still in tow. The two men were hauling in her quarter-inch white nylon painter, drawing the rubber boat up close to the trawler. The big man handed off his gun and stepped in, immediately dropping to his knees for balance. He picked up and shook the gas tank and yanked the starter rope. A quick wisp of exhaust smoke appeared and stopped. The guy gave Morris a thumbs up as he returned to Secant's stern ladder. They intended to "borrow" the dingy all right, but not right away.

Captain Lucans had returned to his wheel and could plainly see where Gary's' binoculars were pointing. He had already begun to move the two boats slowly to keep them directly behind his line of sight and thus hidden from Secant. Gary's hand signals weren't needed except as a sort of confirmation. It worked perfectly. The trawler passed them so close that voices could be heard, but the FBE crew never noticed. Watching them plod southward, Gary saw the helicopter return and descend for a clearing on the outside of the bend a couple miles ahead. After a rush of activity on Secant, the two men boarded the dinghy and headed for the same clearing. As he lay still with his binoculars Captain Lucans climbed up to join him carrying a large gun of some sort. He proceeded to aim it at his own rubber boat. "What are you doing!?"

"Using the four-power PSO-1 for a telescope. I want to see too."

"What, Where did *that* come from?"

"Russia. Same as that chopper. I'll tell you about it later. Looks like your Eldon Morris is in a hurry. Any sign of Greg?"

"No, I was hoping he'd gotten away using that dinghy. He's probably still on the trawler."

"I agree. If I know my son, he's well hidden, but he won't be able to stay that way for long. On the other hand, those two that just left were the only ones worth worrying about. The rest probably won't hurt him. They'll just hold him for the boss, and he ain't coming back." Dale did something and the gun made a 'kerchunk-kerchunk sound.

You can't just - !"

"You know? You're right. This thing's only calibrated out to 1300 meters. By the way, it's a Soviet Dragunov SVD sniper rifle, 7.62 x 54R caliber. Ordinarily it's part of my keel ballast. Traded a 4-horse outboard for it in the Windward Islands three years ago. I only have a couple hundred rounds of ammunition for it."

"Got any more 'keel ballast' like that?"

"Yep. Look Gary, I'm only yankin' your chain. I'm not exactly itching for a gunfight with these people, but be realistic. Those aren't cops. What cops travel in a million dollar yacht? What cops shoot at you for no reason? If what you told me is true they kidnapped your daughter, and Andrea's too! Now they have Greg. If we were real crooks and they were legitimate law enforcement officers they'd have backup by now. That Morris fellow is pretty much on his own. He can't get any help because everyone hates him, even the lock operators."

"Someone gave him the boat and helicopter."

"Sure – and now he evidently wants our boats as well. Sorta makes you wonder who really owns M/v Secant, doesn't it? He must not have much interest in my little tender though. Look, he didn't even bother to beach it. It's drifting away. Think you could run it down for me with that speedboat of yours?"

Married couples who both serve as Federal Marshals are rare. Even rarer are the ones who work together on deep cover operations. Chuck and Rhonda Carver were such a couple.

They'd been infiltrating organized crime for so long that they'd made reputations for themselves within it. They usually moved seamlessly from one assignment to the next where they were always well received. Their criminal reputations had preceded them.

As part of the presidential investigation launched right after the election, they'd been placed in the FBE separately through the headquarters in the capitol. Eldon Morris had noticed them because both had been drummed out of the Navy for criminal activities. Both were qualified as coastal pilots. They had 'met' aboard M/v Secant and been inseparable ever since. Their nautical credentials were real. When Secant was under way they shared the watch schedule with the First Mate, Ann Winslow.

Both Chuck and Rhonda had been awakened when the stateroom door had opened, but they hadn't let the man know it. Neither recognized him. He'd only looked in, seen the 'sleeping' couple and gently eased the door shut. The boat had been stopped and there were sounds of unusual activity. Then they started moving again and the shooting had started. Chuck saw the same man who'd peeked in on them jump over the side and get picked up immediately by one of those overpowered fishing boats with a full length canvas convertible top that looked like it had started out as a trailering cover. A few minutes later the same boat blasted by without the soft top and circled around behind them. This was just the sort of thing he and Rhonda were afraid of: The public was starting to rise up against the despised agency. So far the raider had only committed an act of trespass, as far as they could tell, but the crew had responded with small arms fire.

Someone would be coming to muster them. The two got back in bed, but no one came. The helicopters' arrival a couple hours later gave them an excuse to get up early. No one mentioned the unusual events or even offered any explanation for the new inflatable yacht tender. After the Captain and his bodyguard Rocky left, only five people remained on board. The two trainees, Monique Vincente and Sheila Wells were unusually quiet and fully dressed, which probably meant they were armed. The First Mate seemed almost giddy, but that would be expected. Chuck observed that Ann was happiest when she was in charge. Rhonda felt that Ann was at her best when she had a man in her room, but her only choices had just left the ship. Chuck would be the only man aboard.

Standing down from her watch, Ann told them to split the next three watches any way they wanted, but to maintain maximum speed through the night. They needed to dock at Holden's Island by five on Saturday afternoon. Tomorrow.

Eldon Stewart Morris sat in the passenger cabin of the converted Russian Hind 24 troop transport helicopter wishing he could use it for what needed to be done. The thirteen detainees would all fit in it of course, but they couldn't be killed in it. The pilot couldn't be trusted, and couldn't be liquidated with the detainees either. Neither he nor Rocky could fly the thing. He would need Secant. He and Ann could manage her themselves. Monique, Sheila and Rhonda could be put ashore on the Island without arousing suspicion. Rocky would do the actual killing. He would probably enjoy doing Chuck as well. Early on the burly bodyguard had taken a dislike for the guy, probably because it had seemed so easy for him to scoop up Rhonda, the gorgeous new girl that had come aboard about the same time. For some reason, Eldon had never been comfortable with the man either. "Rocky, I'll have a special assignment for you tomorrow night. I think you'll find it to your liking."

Rocky just muttered "Sure, boss." He'd done 'special assignments' before. "We just gonna wait till the boat shows up tomorrow?"

"Well, not exactly. We've got a lot of work to do before." Rocky was the only person other than himself who knew the entire truth about the 'special detainees'. A few others knew a detail or two on a 'need to know' basis. Most of the prison staff had bought the military jurisdiction story. In a couple days it wouldn't matter.

After an hour in the dark Greg Lucans had found a light switch in his hiding place. He'd been sitting on a raised steel plate that served as the base for the entire crane. The area forward of the crane had once held an anchor windlass. Now it was an empty space with a long unused light switch. Greg could see the hawseholes where the anchor lines had passed through the hull. They had been fiberglassed over from the outside. Behind him was a two-foot drop to a catwalk over the bilges. No wonder the space had seemed so dank. The catwalk ended at a filthy bulkhead door maybe fifteen feet abaft. The engine room he had seen on the way in would be about there. The door opening would be between the two diesels forward. If he could open the door without being detected and was very, very careful, he might have the run of the ship. He might be able to make a break down the 'hallway', up the companionway and over the stern, but if his dad's dinghy was gone or swamped he'd be screwed.

Alone with her already dark thoughts, Andrea Sturm resented being sent out to retrieve Dales' little rubber boat while the two men argued over how to proceed back on Atropos. They were just like a couple of dogs, sniffing each other's butts. My gun is bigger than your gun. Who cared, anyway?

She was tying a small white rope from the front of the rubber raft to one of Gary's new cleats when she heard a voice behind her.

"Ahoy the bass boat! Are you a friend of Greg Lucans?"

"Uh, what? Do I know you?" The boat was peculiar looking, like nothing she'd ever seen before.

"Do you know Greg Lucans, Ma'am?"

"Maybe, who's asking?" Had this weird looking boat fished Greg out of the water?

"I'm John Walgren. Maybe he's mentioned me. Can I ask your name?"

"It's Andrea. Andrea Sturm. How did you recognize me?"

"Your boat registration number, 4535NA. It's been on the news lately. I know Alison Loch. So does Greg. Where are the rest of your people?"

Gary Loch and Dale Lucans went silent at the sight. November Alpha came into view accompanied by about the strangest looking craft either had ever seen. Hardly any longer than Gary's bass boat, it looked to be part trawler, part tugboat and part houseboat. It carried Dales' dink suspended between a pair of davits forward of the bow just ahead of a motorcycle lashed to the short foredeck. From there a low cabin ran back to a wheelhouse with inward slanting windshield glass. Only the aft four feet or so of the deck was open. The wheelhouse roof bristled with antennas. The 'big boat image' was nearly destroyed by a huge single outboard motor. Looking more closely, Dale spotted two more much smaller outboards. The thing moved well, despite it's ungainly appearance, at a speed Gary estimated at about 40 miles per hour. November Alpha porpoised on her skeg a bit in the effort to match it's speed. Subconsciously Gary willed Andrea to lower the nose-up trim.

"Ahoy the sailor Atropos! Rat Racer would like to offer assistance."

Side tied to Atropos and with four people in her wheel-house, Rat Racer didn't seem so large. Gary had known this was John Walgren – "Walgren Racing", as his daughter had called him, as soon as his boat had come into sight. Greg had described Rat Racer perfectly, inside and out.

Originally, she had been a deck boat, combining the large open deck of a pontoon boat with the speed and agility of a runabout. The superstructure had been added later, made of thin plywood covered with slick white rubber roofing membrane. Two bunks flanked a foot wide aisle in the front of the low cabin ahead of a sit-down height bathroom forward of the helm and an equally small chart table and navigation station to port. The 'bathroom' featured a porta-potty like the one Gary had.

What most surprised Gary and Dale was her electronics. Above her full instrument panel was a four-inch spherical compass – with an aircraft directional gyro set into its binnacle. Gary had never seen one of those in a boat before, and that was just the beginning. A depth sounder hung from the roof flanked by a marine VHF and a CB radio. At the lower right corner of the windshield a GPS receiver shared it's mounting with a stereo sound system. The opposite side of the wheelhouse held a pair of long-range short-wave radios and a TV. A VCR/DVD player occupied a slot under the chart table.

"Why didn't you hang that from the roof like your sounder?" Gary asked.

"Watch this, Mr. Loch." John unlatched and pulled out on a panel below the windshield and a two-burner range stove appeared. "It would fill up with cooking schmeg. You're sitting on the refrigerator."

Above the chart table at the sit-down nav station were a set of weather gauges. A barometer, thermometer and hygrometer. The chart table itself held a laptop computer. "How do you power all this, John?"

"That white box on the transom has a 12 horsepower garden tractor engine with two 80 amp car alternators in it. I can also charge my two 900 amp house batteries and the outboard's starting battery from shore power or from a windmill in a pinch. You may have noticed the three electric trolling motors. The two back there are fixed forward. The one at the bow is steerable from the helm wheel. I don't use that big outboard much except for towing or going upstream in a hurry. I can make six knots on the electrics alone, burning a gallon of gas every five hours with the twelve horse at a high idle. When you add in the current speed going downstream it works out to better than sixty miles per gallon. If I only need steerage way it's over a hundred." ·

"A hundred miles a gallon in a power boat. Impressive! What do you have for a water system?"

"Not much. Sink and shower are out on the aft deck. Not much privacy, just a pull-around curtain. I have a ten-gallon tank for drinking water in the prow under the foredeck. I filter and boil river water for cooking. You've seen my toilet. After dark the deck railing sometimes serves as a men's only facility, if you follow."

"Do you ever go out in salt water?"

"Nope, too top heavy and an almost flat bottom. We'd probably breach in the first three-foot breaker. I don't want to drown, Dale. I plan to live to the age of 104 and then be shot by a jealous husband."

John Walgren used that line a lot and usually got a good laugh from it. The effect fell short on these three who had been shot at recently and were in pursuit of the shooters. "Are you armed, John?"

"Only a sidearm. I've been teaching your son to use one. By the way, do you have a plan to get him back?"

"Sort of. I was going to do it alone. Planned to dock at the marina in Summerville and rent a car to go down river. I'd be ahead of Secant by about an hour when I reached the high bridge on Route 91. I'd line up as she approached, rappel down to her coach roof and capture the crew one at a time. The only crew left aboard are the nasty broad at the wheel and the two bikini babes. Once in control I would have run her hard aground, found Greg and started interrogating. Believe me, if they know where your girls are they would tell me."

"You missed at least two opponents. There was a couple sleeping in a stateroom about midship, starboard side upper. Probably the night shifts at the wheel. The guy looked formidable even in his sleep." There was a smugness in Gary's' voice.

"Do I detect a hint of friction between the three of you? You don't trust each other, do you?"

Gary spoke directly to Dale Lucans; "Why did Greg stay on that trawler? Why did he want us to help take down their spars?"

"He was trying to help you find out what you wanted to know. When all hell broke loose he was below, trying to disable their crane. He probably didn't know anything was wrong until the shooting started, he was cold, had your jacket on."

"He's wearing my jacket? My gun's in the pocket! The one I found at the tower site! John, did you say you've been teaching Greg to shoot?"

"Yeah – he's pretty good at it too. I brought one along for him, just in case. I left before the news broke of course. I was just going to intercept you and Greg to say hi before putting this boat on the hard for the winter. I keep its trailer in Summerville where my aunt and uncle lived. I inherited this boat from them."

"News? What news?"

"You don't know? You're kinda famous, Gary. The TV says a Hispanic woman impersonating a police officer kidnapped your young daughter. They say you're chasing her down river to Holden's Island, but it doesn't make much sense. It's almost as if they don't know the smog jail is there. To hear them tell it you'd think Holden's Island was deserted. When I saw the tape of your boat I recognized the cover on it as the work of Greg's dad, so I knew he was involved somehow."

Andrea reached for the switch on the overhead TV set. "OK?"

"Give me a second to turn on the power. See what you can accomplish with a little cooperation?"

The TV network news said nothing about the boat chase, but mentioned that the president had issued a statement of support to the family of recently kidnapped Alison Loch and an announcement that the Marshals Service was working with the Dunningsville police to return her safely home. John Walgren burned a DVD of the broadcast.

THE RESTITUTION

CHAPTER ELEVEN   Advantage

The plan was nothing more than a simple variation of what Dale Lucans had intended to do alone. After refueling at Summerville, Gary and Andrea dropped off Captain Lucans at the route 91 bridge just after sunset. John Walgren made arrangements with his friends at the marina to leave Atropos docked there for a few days before overtaking m/v Secant just above the bridge.

With the top gone and five hundred miles to cover, Gary Loch and Andrea Sturm had a long cold night ahead of them. Andrea lay feet forward in one of the sleeping bags trying to rest. Gary drove, crouched behind the little windshield wearing his leather jacket, John's full-face motorcycle helmet and the other sleeping bag. Running 25-MPH just inside the green can buoys in the light chop felt a lot like riding a horse in damp forty-degree weather. After an hour he was already anxious for Andrea to relieve him. Tomorrow wouldn't be much better. If only they could both get a couple hours of peaceful sleep before the fight started. He bumped the throttle up a little more.

Chuck Carver had the wheel, watching the bridge get closer. These high bridges would make ideal places to attack from. If the efforts displayed earlier were parts of a coordinated -.

Chuck saw the man just in time before turning on the searchlight. He was dressed in black, had a Russian Krinkov rifle strapped to his chest and held a coil of rappelling line. He flinched at the sight of the Krinkov. His training cried for him to stop the ship and confront him with the hailer but two things stopped him: first, he'd have to call in local law enforcement to make the actual arrest. Second, if he must face a high power rifle with nothing but a handgun he wanted to do it a close range.

The black-clad man started his rappel, smooth and well timed to deposit himself on the deck just forward of the crane. He would have made it, too. Chuck timed the man's descent and threw both screws into full reverse at the exact moment. The ship stopped dead in a third of its length. Unable to belay himself, Dale Lucans ran off the end of his line and fell in the water ten feet ahead of Secant's bow. Rhonda took over, holding Secant in position while Chuck went forward to investigate.

"Good evening sir. Nice night for a swim. I need to ask your intentions, of course." The man in the water said nothing. "I may not be who you think I am sir. Has someone you know been taken aboard this vessel against their will?" The swimmer shook his head in the affirmative. Chuck lowered his pistol and tossed him a life ring. "Do you have a boat nearby?" Another yes. "Stay there. I'll be about thirty seconds."

Dale Lucans was flabbergasted. A few seconds later the man flipped over the rail and entered the water with hardly a splash. "Let's move away from the ship a little, sir. She's going to pass under the bridge and drop an anchor. Can I take you into confidence sir?"

"Uh, yeah. Yes. What?"

"I'm not FBE. I'm from the Marshals Service. There is another Marshall aboard. We've been undercover for half a year. We think your family member is being held somewhere on Holden's Island other than the smog jail facility. Since Mister Morris went there in such a hurry we're afraid she's in mortal danger."

"We saw Morris leave your ship. Just him and that block headed bodyguard. Greg wasn't with them. He's still gotta be aboard. I'm trying to rescue him."

"Well that explains something. This Greg is what – your brother?"

"My son. Are you going to help me? I'm pretty sure he's still hiding on your ship. We came aboard this afternoon as a repair party. We were discovered and he didn't make it off with us."

"Well, that all fits. I take it you aren't who we expected. Call the Marshals Service in the capitol and give them the agent code CC-21. They'll confirm who I am and ask your location. Tell them I'm breaking cover now and will be contacting them en clair within the hour. Do as they tell you but don't lose that Krinkov. If I fail at this you might need it."

The man waved both arms and the crane boom swung out over the side and lowered its cargo hook. He grabbed it and was effortlessly lifted back over the rail and out of sight. A moment later the trawler started moving slowly downstream.

"I told you there was another man aboard." Rhonda said, her eyes twinkling. "Ann is so obvious. Maybe we can get her out of the way by charging her with CSC."

"You know – that's not a bad idea! The locals would take her off our hands that way. Otherwise we'd have to take her along and listen to her bitch and whine all the way to Holden's. Let's try to catch her in the act."

"What about Sheila and Monique? Eldon gave them guns you know."

"We'll take them first while Ann still has her pants down, so to speak."

Dale felt more than heard John Walgren approach him. He came in slowly, the big four stroke outboard idling. "What the hell just happened, Captain?"

"The two Gary saw sleeping are Federal Marshals. They're on our side. He gave me a message to deliver. Can I use your phone? Mine got wet."

The mention of an agent code got Dale transferred to a Marshals Service field coordinator. "Yes sir. His name is Charles Carver. His partner is Rhonda Carver. Your son is in capable hands. I'm sorry, but we won't be able to come for you until morning. Since we're the only law enforcement agency working this case we can't call in the locals to do it. They ask too many questions. Will you be OK until then?"

"OK? Sure will be, we don't really need any help. This boat might look a little strange, but it's fast and capable. Chuck and Rhonda Carver – husband and wife?"

"Yes they are."

The Carvers knew about the bilge catwalk that connected the engine room to the master stateroom. They'd both studied the plans for m/v Secant before starting the mission. Rhonda went to the stateroom door forward of the lower salon to wait and listen until Chuck signaled her by rapping twice on the other side of the deck under her feet. He turned off the ER lights before opening the catwalk entrance. He wasn't prepared for what he found.

Ann Winslow sat on the catwalk trussed up like a rib roast in the same black nylon webbing material that made up the outfit she wore. It was the harness of a dominatrix. Chuck had seen something similar in a stag movie when he was in college. That one had been made of leather, or maybe leatherette. The breasts were open in the same manner as her eyes in the mask. He couldn't help himself. He just stood there laughing until Rhonda came down. Greg Lucans was with her. Ann struggled with the binding, humiliated and enraged. "Is the victim willing to testify, Agent Carver?"

"Oh, I think we can talk him into it. We don't have to mention his weapon, do we?" Ann struggled and squealed.

"Dammit, Rot. You know I can't do that. Just consider yourself fortunate this is happening on a nearly deserted waterway instead of on Main Street somewhere. So far, the only folks reporting it have been lock operators and the like. Government employees. We tell them it's part of an undercover operation and they co-operate because we sign their paychecks and it makes 'em feel important. But sooner or later the media will get wind of it and figure out it's related to that debacle up in Dunningsville. Keeping it under wraps permanently is impossible. You need to turn this to advantage. Have the Marshals Service call in backup from every agency that can be of help. Rescue that girl, arrest Eldon Morris and disband the FBE once and for all. You've been promising that for months. Now is the time."

President Robert Owen Trayson glared over the top of his glasses at the chief of his political security staff. "Stop calling me Rot."

"Did you hear a word I said?"

The director of the federal Marshals Service cut in. "Stop it, you two. I know it's just the three of us, but at least we can be civil to one another. We're just starting to get the press to call the President "B.T." or Bob. We're a team here. Let's just stop saying "Rot" and "President Treason" in private, OK?"

"Yes, mother."

"What do you think, Gloria? Do I have a chance of turning this around?"

"Sure you can, but it'll cost you. Jim's right. It's time to shut down the FBE, and you know it, Bob. I'm frankly surprised you haven't done it already. Is it the money?"

"Of course it's the money. You know how I've been working on cutting back the social entitlement programs, and so far I haven't saved a nickel. If I shut Eldon down the funding is gone. The way I see it the programs need to go first or we run in deficit." I've already scaled back the military you know."

"You've obviously given this a lot of thought, Bob. Do you have a plan?"

"Yes I do. But it isn't going to be easy. The public doesn't know anything about the PESVI operation. We should be able to shut that down silently as long as the media doesn't get wind of it. The problem is Eldon himself. He's threatened from the start to go public if we try to rein him in. The man is a master of intimidation. I only know of one way to keep him quiet."

"You can't mean –"

"Of course not. At this point I am hoping this Loch fellow does it for us. Just what is his current status anyway, Gloria? Have your people located him yet?"

"Not exactly. He's headed south in a fast boat bound for Holden Island. We've spoken to at least one of his supporters though. We know he has at least three boats now, and at least half a dozen men, ah, people. At least one of them is a woman who's daughter disappeared while in Eldon's custody a few weeks ago. We don't have a name yet."

"Anything to add, Jim?"

"That guy certainly makes friends easily. His state, county and local police agencies are all standing by in his support. His machine shop is gathering firearms design data from the Internet in his absence. Admiral Sanders of NAS Lowreyville has requested your permission to offer him transportation. Speaking of Lowreyville, their municipal police department is raising funds to offer a reward for information leading to the safe return of his daughter. They have a little over twenty thousand so far, and it's only been three days."

"Time for a decision, people. I'm inclined to join his little circle of friends, but we can't do it publicly. Have your agents on Eldon's boat pick up the sailboat guy and head for Holden Island at top speed. With any luck, whatever is going to happen when Eldon meets Mister Loch will have already occurred by the time they arrive. The Carvers can help clean up the mess. Have Sanders stand by to provide air transport on short notice. He should move a couple of his choppers down near Eldon's island, but make sure he keeps it under wraps."

Rhonda Carver had no reason to dislike Sheila Wells or Monique Vincente, but couldn't trust them, either. At least not yet. Both of them had been hired by the FBE and assigned to the Passive Random Sampling Division, but neither had completed their training or been weapons qualified. Both had been armed when Rhonda had first confronted them. Now they were being offered a choice.

"Your boss is headed for prison. He's a kidnapper and a killer. He never intended to make either of you field agents. He just kept you as decorations. Didn't you ever wonder why he kept you dressed in bathing suits when the weather was in the forties? The way I see it, you each have a decision to make. If you feel you must remain loyal to Eldon Morris, I'll have to detain you. But if you'll help me I'll try to help you transfer to the Marshals Service. The pay and benefits are better, and the training will be real. What do you say, girls? It won't be that much of a change. As this ship's pilot, I outrank you. With Eldon gone and Ann Winslow already in jail, I'm in command here anyway. Chuck went on ahead with the owner of that overpowered houseboat that just left. The two civilians are with us to identify and possibly help rescue some of Eldon's kidnap victims. The older one is a licensed captain, but has no authority aboard this ship beyond what I delegate to him. Can I count on you?"

"What can we do?"

"Do we call you Captain?"

"If it's just us, call me Rhonda. If others are present, call me 'Ma'am'. With some luck, when this is over you might have to get used to calling me 'Special Agent Carver", but please don't start that yet. I'm still waiting to hear you both promise me your loyalty."

"You can count on me, Ma'am."

"Me too." It was especially difficult for Ms. Vincente. She'd tried for weeks to initiate a relationship with the soulless director in an attempt to curry his favor. He had never responded.

"Can we catch them, Mister Walgren?"

"I doubt it. This boat is fast, but it's no match for that bass boat. We both have to run the speed limit at least till daybreak because we can't see all the wing dams. After that we'll speed up, running just outside the channel. Problem is, Gary will too. Gary will be there two, maybe three hours ahead of us. Secant should make it several hours after we do. Make it about five o'clock tomorrow afternoon."

Chuck Carver was not impressed with 'Rat Racer'. In his opinion she was nothing but a small houseboat with a great big outboard. With no actual keel and a sort of flattened trihedral hull form combined with all that windage, she didn't really plane. The poor thing sort of skipped like a stone. Even worse, he felt almost blind. The windows were too small, too few and too far away from his eyes. Using his police credentials to justify exceeding the speed limit wouldn't make it any safer. It just made him personally responsible for collision avoidance. "Slow down a little, will ya? And turn off some of these gadgets. I can't see out for all the reflections from the dial lights and LEDs"

"Sorry, I guess I'm just used to it."

"Now there's something you don't see every day." Dennis Davis sat at his employer's desk, transfixed by the sight. He'd heard the helicopter long before seeing it, trying idly to identify it by sound. Now, forty feet away, landing on the manicured front lawn of Loch Tool and Die, it had his full attention. Ten feet above the flattening grass, three wheels popped from the bottom of it with a whirring servo sound that could be heard over the rotor blades through the window glass. It yawed back and forth almost ninety degrees each way before settling head on. Dennis considered himself fairly well acquainted with military aircraft. He'd never seen one of these before. Obviously an attack helicopter of some sort, the flat black machine had car-like doors on both sides. Just below and ahead of the forward doors on each side were small Gatling type machine guns. As the craft settled, the guns rotated forward, then lowered themselves following the contour of the rounded underbelly, ending up pointed into the same spot in the lawn below the nose. The effect was like the thing had an obscene pair of nine-fingered hands that folded themselves in prayer as it landed. Only after the motion had stopped did Dennis notice the man in the driver's seat. Lucky O'Connor. He didn't know the other man. Dennis tripped over his chair getting up.

"Mister Davis I presume? I'm Admiral Jason Sanders of Naval Air Station Lowreyville. I understand you know Mister O'Connor. Chief of Police Adamson said you might want in on this. Can you leave someone else in charge here?"

Dennis was still staring slack jawed at the aircraft on his lawn. "Uh, Huh?"

"This is the commanding officer of the Skycrane base. He's going to help us get Alison back! The President sent him!" Dennis just blinked at the chopper. "Don't even ask, Dennis. It's experimental, top secret or something. Can you come with us?"

Dennis snapped out of it. Of course! Airplanes are flown from the left seat, like cars. But helicopters normally have their primary flight controls on the right side, like a boat. "Dave – you're in charge. Let the guys leave at noon if they want. That's three hours from now. Saturday should be a day off anyway. Gary or I will call you first thing Monday morning." The idling turbine engines spooled up again as he got in behind Lucky. Dennis had been around a lot of aircraft turbine engines. Their exhaust tended to nauseate him a little. This one had no odor to it at all, but the air around it smelled somehow like a thunderstorm had just passed. "What does this thing run on? It doesn't smell like jet fuel, Admiral."

"Hydrogen, but don't tell anyone. Welcome aboard, Mister Davis. I hear you're a military aircraft buff."

"I guess so. Where are we going?"

"The President granted my request to offer assistance to your friend Gary Loch, but I'm restricted to only providing him with air transportation of a humanitarian nature. Medical evacuation, presumably. My command is not a medevac facility. We're set up to defend the shipping channel by presence and force. Most of our aircraft are ground attack fighters and heavy lifters. This little hydrogen fueled rotary wing coin fighter of the future is the closest I could find to an ambulance."

"Commanders of major Navy bases double as test pilots these days?"

"The service has changed a lot in recent years, Mister Davis. We used to pay civilian test pilots a fortune to wring out new designs as employees of the manufacturers. Your police chief tells me you're a tax conservative. You should understand this. We can't afford that anymore. Fifteen years ago, a man in my position would have resigned at fifty five and spent their last working years as a test pilot anyway. This way the taxpayers get double for their money. I'm test flying a fixed wing ground attack fighter these days. That one runs on hydrogen too. This helicopter was approved for production last winter. Now it's just waiting for funding. If it were really still experimental I sure wouldn't be carrying civilians in it."

"I thought they were still working on the technology for hydrogen powered vehicles. It's supposed to be a national priority. This 'vehicle' certainly works. Do you have hydrogen powered ground vehicles? Trucks?"

"Only in the labs and test tracks. Too much risk the public will get wind of them. It's easy to keep a military airplane secret. Nobody sees it up close – 'cept you two of course."

"I don't understand, sir. Why would the Navy want to keep practical hydrogen power a secret?"

Jason Norwood Sanders sat still for a second, exhaling slowly. "I've already told you too much. Just think about it for a moment. I'll give you a hint. It is not the Navy who wants the secrecy, and it has nothing to do with not educating a potential enemy." Dennis was dumbfounded.

Lucky O'Connor had been too preoccupied with the fate of his granddaughter to participate, but he got it anyway. "Money. Specifically motor fuel taxes."

"Bingo! Give Mister O'Connor a cee-gar."

Dennis slapped his forehead with the palm of his left hand. "OK, elemental hydrogen is easy to make and compress. People could make their own out of water and electricity if they had to. Half the cost of a gallon of gasoline is taxes. Think of the money they'd lose! Do they think they can keep this up forever?"

"Of course not. They are actually working on the technology. What they need are fuel cells, manufactured and marketed by the petroleum companies, of course. They turn hydrogen and oxygen back into water while releasing energy in the form of electricity. You couldn't do that in your back yard. Burning hydrogen in an internal combustion engine is just too easy. This machine can be converted to run on liquefied natural gas or even propane in a couple hours. A trained ground crew can have it running on conventional aviation fuel in a day. My guys could rig your car to run on hydrogen by Monday noon, but then they'd have to kill you. Speaking of which, I really do need you to keep this conversation to yourselves. If you leaked it I'd have to deny everything. You'd look like idiots and my career would be over."

"What's to keep us from putting homemade hydrogen in those fuel cells?"

"The buffers and additives they need to make the cells work. Actually there's a precedent. When the first cars were made, they ran on naphtha. There weren't any gas stations, of course, but naphtha was available everywhere as paint thinner. The engines knocked, but were built strong enough to take it. By the twenties, the fuel had been perfected with additives like tetraethyl lead to control the burn rate. The word 'octane' appeared, then the word 'gasoline'. It didn't take long for 'gasoline taxes' to be imposed. Naphtha was still available, of course. They called it 'white gas'. You can still buy it as fuel for camp stoves and lanterns. Hardly anybody uses it for paint thinner anymore, too flammable. It's still the main ingredient in gasoline. Ever hear of the two hundred mile per gallon carburetor?"

Lucky answered. "Yeah! It boiled the gas and fed it to the engine as a true vapor. They say it was patented."

"Yep, it was patented in 1936 and an improvement was added by the inventor in 1937. The test car managed to cover over two hundred miles on one precisely measured gallon of fuel. Trouble was, the fuel was naphtha. The additives in gasoline wouldn't boil to vapor, they just turned to gum in the boiling chamber and plugged it up. Water vapor was added to control the burning rate. The government couldn't allow the return to naphtha because they couldn't effectively tax it. The inventor skipped the country after his patent attorney was killed."

"Think of the improvements we could make on that concept today. If the water controlling the burn time were directly injected into the cylinders with computer accurate timing, the combustion heat would flash it to steam while the pistons were still high in the power stroke. Part naphtha engine, part steam engine. The waste heat would be turned into free power!"

"You know, Dennis – you're probably right! I never thought of that. And there's more – with hydrogen as the fuel you wouldn't have to carry a water supply. The exhaust is water vapor. Just condense and recycle it."

"Water doesn't cost anything to speak of."

"True, at least not in money, but it does involve a weight penalty. I tend to think in terms of aircraft. An exhaust condenser would weigh less than a full water tank. We're talking piston power though. Burning rates aren't a big problem with turbines."

Lucky was starting to lose interest again. "Alright, so hydrogen fuel presents more of a political problem than a technical one. It's nice to see the military doing something to contain its own costs though."

"Thanks for mentioning that, Mister O'Connor. It's something that's been bothering me for a long time. We live in a complex and hostile world. The armed forces and the law enforcement community are often all that keep our nation safe. Schools, libraries, the highway system, waterways like this one." He gestured to the Games River Shipping Canal below his feet. "All these things cost money. Lots of money. My command alone spent 162 million last year. I'm a big fan of President Trayson, and not because he signs my paycheck. My profession is tax supported, but I'm a conservative anyway. That's why I do extra duty in test flying without pay. I don't envy the president his problems with funding. He may be the most conservative president we've ever had, but he's stuck with five decades of social entitlements, most of them filled with waste, and an economy that can't maintain the tax base."

"That's why he hasn't dumped the Federal Bureau of Environment, isn't it?"

"Yes. And that's my point. He simply has to have the money it provides."

"So he keeps putting up with crooks like Morris?"

"I'm afraid so. He's already cut defense spending as much as he can. He's cut education, police, roads, research, government pensions. All that's left are the entitlement programs, but what can he do? Tell people who have paid in for fifty years that they can't retire? Deny the poor any medical treatment? Ignore disaster victims? What would you do in his place? I realize a lot of the problems were caused by the government itself, but you can't turn back time."

"It's too easy to speak freely when you're two thousand feet up in the company of others who both apparently think the same way and the conversation is already sworn to secrecy, but I'll give it a shot. What would I do? I'd do what Trayson says he'd like to do between his minced words: treat everything like an incentive or a disincentive. High taxes are a disincentive to business, so I'd lower the tax rates. That would be an incentive to growth, but not enough. If we want to generate enough tax money to fund things the way they are, we need to roll back the other disincentives, the regulatory ones. Of course that means losing the money that comes in through all those licensing bureaus. The FBE is only one of them. We can't just ignore the underlying problems, just get rid of the revenue generating functions. Taxes have to be simple. The more we want to receive, the more we have to pay. The public needs to understand that."

THE RESTITUTION

CHAPTER TWELVE *Good and Evil*

Landing the big Russian chopper at the airfield south of the complex had allowed Eldon Morris to return to his office all but unnoticed by the prison staff. Convenient as that was, he'd need the trawler when the time came to leave, and she was still a good ten hours out.

With any luck, no one would give M/V Secant a second look as she made her way south to the river's mouth and out into the gulf. She wouldn't be coming back, ever.

The left leaning government of the tiny gulf island nation of St. Somme' had no extradition agreements with any other countries. Its practice was to offer citizenship to any applicant able to deposit a significant amount of money in the St. Somme' Central Bank. Dual citizenships were the norm. Eldon Stewart Morris already owned land there. His new nation of residence would hardly be a secret, but would never be proven. A vessel as large and distinctive as Secant docked in the harbor at the capital city of Port Balfour would surely give him away, but she'd be on the bottom of the sea along with the unfortunate special detainees, Chuck and Rhonda, Ann Winslow and the two floozy agents. Rocky would be spared. In a place like St. Somme' it pays to have a good bodyguard.

Ten hours. Ann should be docking around five o'clock. He made a note to call Ann for an ETA at about noon, when he planned to wake up.

Chuck Carver checked his wristwatch as he woke up. He looked up and aft from the v-berth under the low foredeck and saw John Walgren's legs and lower torso at the wheel. "Where are we?"

"Good morning Agent Carver. We're still about two hundred miles north of Holden. Gary called. They're about two hours out and stopped to catch a little sleep before we go in. They want us to watch for 'em and wake them up when we get there. They tied up under a bridge. Shouldn't be that hard to spot."

"What do you mean 'go in'? It sounds like he plans to attack the prison."

"Oh, no, of course not. Morris won't be there. He'll have loaded the girls on his helicopter and taken them away from the river to shake us off his tail. I mean, what would *you* do in his position? No, Gary intends to land openly and find someone willing to say where they went. He can be very persuasive. He's going to have his father-in-law fly down in a private plane. We'll use that to pick up the trail again."

"That's nuts. He'll get himself killed. Does he realize his smiling face has been on national TV all week? The prison staff will make him in a minute. Will he listen to you? We gotta talk him out of this."

"You're the Federal Marshal, order him to stand down. Arrest Morris yourself. You have all the evidence you need to convict him."

"I can't do that. We have orders to observe only. We're supposed to gather evidence to be used only after the FBE is disbanded. I can't take any forcible action at all."

"What? Who issued your orders?"

"President Trayson himself."

Rhonda Carver heard a phone ringing. Muted, as if it were in a box or something. She followed the sound and found Ann Winslow's cell phone in the storage compartment below the compass binnacle. She answered it on the fourth ring.

"Uh, hello."

"Ann, this is Eldon. Listen carefully. I need to know the exact time you'll dock at the facility. We'll refuel, take on cargo and passengers and depart again immediately. Do you understand?"

Rhonda was thinking fast. Eldon would surely recognize her voice. "Oh, Eldon, a lot's happened. We got hit again! Those same people and a few more dropped down on us from a bridge. They shot Ann! Chuck got a couple of them before they cornered him and put him overboard. The girls were great. If it weren't for them I'd be dead. I can be on the island at about five, maybe five thirty. Will that be OK?"

"That will be fine. Is my ship damaged? It sounds like you've been through hell – Rhonda, is it? Were there any civilian witnesses, apart from the raiders?"

"Not that I know of." She felt a sharp but light bump, as if something had struck the hull. Whatever it was, it hadn't hit the propellers. "I wanted to ask you if I should call in the local cops but my communications are out. The antennas are all broken off. I didn't know about this phone till it rang. It was under the compass. I'd never put anything that generates a magnetic field there myself, so I never thought to check."

"Rhonda, what ever you do, don't alert the local police. Just be here at five this afternoon. Are Sheila and Monique the only crew you still have?"

"Yes, sir."

"Have them start removing anything on the foredeck between the crane and the anchor windlass. We'll be installing something new there later tonight."

After the call ended Eldon Morris sat down behind his desk thinking of Rhonda Carver. She'd taken the loss of her lover well. Gracefully, even. That spoke volumes on her loyalty to the bureau and himself. He was lucky to have her. Maybe he could use her on the way out to St. Somme as well. Too bad she had to die.

The talk of politics had died down aboard Jason Sanders' prototype helicopter. Racing down the river valley at fifteen hundred feet, all six eyes were straining for a glimpse of M/V Secant. Sanders spotted her, well ahead. As they passed overhead Sanders and Lucky O'Connor both noticed something strange: An empty boat, maybe fifteen feet long with an outboard and an open walk through windshield was sinking, stern first, about a quarter mile behind. It lay almost exactly in the middle of Secant's wake. If the two had collided, Secant clearly had no intention of offering aid. The sinking craft was empty, and no swimmers or life jackets were in the water. Weird. Admiral Sanders radioed the Coast Guard lifesaving station for the region and gave the coordinates.

Dorothy Spence happened upon a bit of luck. The guard who ordinarily took the G block prisoners their breakfast and noon meal on Saturday left his post in mid afternoon with stomach flu. Dorothy was called in early. She'd resolved to break the rules today and actually speak with James. It could be done early, long before the regular meal. They'd have time for an actual conversation. She wanted to know why he and the others in her care were being held and somehow believed he'd be honest with her. As she palmed the key to cell #1 she realized that if she hadn't been called in two hours early she may well have lost her courage. Alone in the wide hallway, Dorothy sat cross-legged on the floor, her eyes level with the food tray slot. Once she hesitated, then she pushed the slot door all the way in. "James?"

James Riad felt the hair on his neck stand up. A chill coursed through him as, just for a moment, he thought he'd been caught in the act. He had no time to conceal what he was doing. As soon as they came in they'd see, and he'd be -.

"James – it's me – Dorothy. Can we talk?"

Dorothy, the woman that part of his apparatus was intended to snare. The woman he so regretted needing to terrify. The only person to offer him any true human contact in well over a year. Dorothy wanted to talk to him willingly. In fact, she was initiating it. "Just a moment, my friend." Maybe he wouldn't have to do it.

She had seen his eyes before, under very different circumstances. As he sat down on the other side of the door, she saw his upper body, then his face. He wore a business suit, of all things. The same one he was arrested in. He'd saved it for this day, intended to escape in it. Dorothy didn't know that of course. The suit just added to the unreality of it. His face was dark. A suntan? How could - ? The file gave his race as Caucasian. Overall, he looked kind, gentle. It would be nice if he could touch her. "Why are you here, James?"

"I'm being very honest, Dorothy, please believe me. I have no idea why I'm here. By the way, where is here?"

"You don't know where you are?"

"At first, I thought I'd been abducted by terrorists and taken out of the country. I'm the chief financial officer at Northwest Aerospace. The head bookkeeper. We make things for the military, but all I know are the profits and losses, not the secrets. For the first few months I expected to be tortured for information. When I was first taken they kept ranting about beryllium copper, a kind of metal. I'd been trying to get Northwest to stop using it. Too expensive. They called it a pollutant."

"This is the Smog Jail. Most of the prisoners here are treated better than you people are. They mostly drove old cars or heated their homes with wood stoves, things like that. They usually stay just a few days waiting for their families to pay the fines and they walk out. Some of them enjoy the stay. It's pretty here. We were told that you people are short-term detainees under military jurisdiction, being held as terrorists. It just doesn't make sense. None of you ever leave, we never see any military people and most of you are young girls."

"Smog Jail? The one in Holden?"

"Yeah"

"I thought I was on the coast. I hear ship horns and bells. Never even thought of the river." And here James and Dorothy both missed an opportunity to save themselves a lot of trouble. James, like most of the public, thought the smog jail was in the city of Holden, a few miles north and on the west bank of the river. James still didn't know he was on an island with a busy shipping channel and massive security on one side and hungry alligators on the other.

"Boss, you gotta see dis." Rocky had been sleeping, stretched out on the couch in Eldon's inner office. The TV woke him up.

"This had better be good."

Ann Winslow was on the TV news. Dressed in a blanket, she was being hustled from a police cruiser into a building by a pair of uniformed officers. A curious crowd had formed, hoping for a glimpse of the lady being brought in wearing nothing but a harness costume. The grinning newsman was assuring his audience that the woman was not a prostitute. She was being charged with second degree criminal sexual conduct after attacking a man aboard a Yacht. Eldon recognized the black nylon straps dangling from the bottom of the blanket when the camera panned and zoomed in on them. The local officers had been assisted by the Federal Marshals Service.

This definitely didn't match what Rhonda Carver had told him. Rhonda had lied, either outright or under duress. Either way, Secant wasn't entirely under his control. "Rocky, I need you to take a fast boat up the river and intercept Secant. Use any means necessary to make sure it arrives here on time. Bring her back here yourself if you have to. If you have to scuttle the fast boat, so be it. Towing it back might slow you down. Monique might be able to drive it back for you." For some reason, Eldon favored tall, graceful Monique over her surfer babe counterpart Sheila. This way, if she were very lucky, she might survive.

How do two boats pass each other from opposite directions unnoticed on a river? It helps if the boats are small and the river is very wide.

Chuck Carver had decided to ride to Holden's Island with Gary and Andrea. He really didn't have a choice. His sense of duty didn't allow him to stand by and let the untrained civilian couple go into harms way alone. His position demanded he protect them. That left John Walgren alone on Rat Racer, and he was the only one to notice the oversize man driving an inboard water-ski boat north up the center of the channel at more than twice the speed limit. The trouble was, John had never seen Rocky Korozini. "Disgustingly rich fat creep thinks he owns the whole river. Bet that thing doesn't get four miles a gallon."

Rocky wasn't really quite as mindless as he seemed. Born Raul Cor Ade Sinin, He'd met Eldon Morris on a rusty former cargo ship chartered by a 'save the whales' organization. He'd caught Eldon's eye with his bravery, putting himself literally between the endangered baleen whales and the poachers' gas powered harpoons with nothing more than a little rubber blow-up boat. Eldon had taken the bright but socially unskilled non-practicing Muslim biology student under his wing. Eldon had thought up the name change and encouraged him to adopt a southern European accent and mannerisms. The result made him appear to be a thug. Young women, especially the whale saving kind, do love outlaws. Within a couple months of Eldon's entry into politics Rocky started doing things for him. Awful things. Things he could never be proud of. Things Allah would surely punish him for. Eldon soon became his employer, which made it easier. If he did these things under orders he was a soldier, not an evil man. In a warped but real way, it worked for him. Besides, Rocky Korozini was the soldier. To himself, he remained Raul Cor Ade Sinin.

Viewed from the ski boat, M/V Secant was huge, and if she were really under the control of people loyal to mister Loch, not easy to board. Hailing her was out of the question. He'd have to let her pass, then approach her from behind, where he'd be concealed from the wheelhouse, at least. Now he had a good reason to be thankful Eldon had never let him put a security camera back there. Tying up just above the propellers would be risky, but the sailboat's little rubber tender had survived it. Eldon was willing to write off the ski boat anyway.

He couldn't be certain Rhonda was loyal to the FBE. She may well have been forced to lie to Eldon, but the possibility existed she would give him up if she recognized him. He slowed down and took to the extreme east side of the channel to minimize the chance she would even notice. She was probably as familiar with the ski boat as he was. Most of Secant's crew used it from time to time for trips into the city of Holden. He'd have to look her over using binoculars. He'd never really been convinced the woman was what she appeared to be anyway. She had taken up with the other new hire helmsman almost as soon as they came aboard. They spent the first night on board together. That wasn't unusual in itself, but they had *stayed* together ever since. They seemed to anticipate each other's actions, finished each other's sentences. It was almost as if they'd come aboard as a team.

Rhonda was in the wheelhouse where she belonged. Two new men were on the deck, the ones who had offered to take down the crane and antennas for the trip under the stuck drawbridge. The young one who seemed to be in charge and the older man who had gotten away in the sailboat. There was no sign of the woman with the fishing boat or the man she'd rescued with it. Damn, that thing was fast. Probably faster even than the ski boat he was driving now. What really concerned Rocky were the two trainees. They were still armed. They wore slacks and sweaters with shoulder holsters over them in plain view. Their badges were still clipped to their waistbands, but they followed the men around like puppies. None of the five people he could see had any apparent fear of the others at all. This was not going to be easy.

For Commander Samuel D. Leary it was the unexpected fulfillment of a career-long dream, if under less than ideal conditions. To President Robert Trayson it was a deal with the devil.

Sam Leary had been on Trayson's carpet before. He'd served the last president in a cabinet level post under the Secretary of the Navy and held the rank of Admiral. Trayson had retained a few of his predecessor's military advisors, but not Leary. Shortly after the election he'd called him in, dismissed him from his duties and reassigned him to the duty he'd served before being brought to the capitol; commanding a defensively armed nuclear submarine. What better way to keep a politically ultra liberal military officer out of the public eye without wasting his considerable abilities?

Leary became one of the very few sub commanders to carry the rank and pay of an Admiral, but as a shipmaster, he was once again properly addressed as 'Captain Leary'. Convinced Trayson would be a one-term president, Leary served with pride and dedication, appreciating the fact he hadn't been simply fired. For his part, Trayson genuinely respected Sam Leary in spite of his liberalism. The man was well known as a man of his word. He rarely made promises, but when he did so, he always kept them.

"Sure, Rot. I can do it, but it'll cost you. When this is over you'll have to do a few things for me that you might not like."

"What things?"

"Fair enough. With Morris out of the way, I want you to transfer the functions of the FBE to the military and place it under my command. You can say it's to deal more effectively with the 'environmental emergency'. The media'll love that."

"You want Eldon's job."

"I want Eldon's boss's job. Eldon's not director anymore, remember?"

"What would you do differently?"

"Everything. We'd get rid of the entire passive sampling operation. That way you won't have to replace Eldon or explain his absence. If his West Coast kids want to keep their jobs, let them come here and work for me."

"No, that's not what I mean. How do you propose to match or improve on Eldon's revenue generating mechanism? We have to see at least that much money in order to pay for all your social entitlement programs. Even Eldon was losing ground. Those costs grow every year."

"Simple, we raise all the environmental permit fees and devise new ones. Make all the business owners pay based on their annual sales. Hell, Rot, we can do the same with drivers and homeowners!"

"Wait a minute, Sam. If we tax the businesses based on their sales they won't have any incentive to reduce their output of pollutants. Look at that machine shop in Dunningsville that started all this. They have no smokestacks, no coolant return, no chemical waste – they did that to avoid paying the fees and inspection charges. If they have to pay anyway, they'll go back to burning coal. It's cheaper."

"Not if we shut them down as soon as they hit the limits. Plug their chimneys, so to speak."

"You've just laid out a plan to bleed them for money and shut them down. How's that any different from what Eldon did?"

"Eldon just hit a few of them, incriminated them and cleaned them out. We'd charge them all equally, or at least evenly."

"What you propose is nothing but another layer of taxes, Sam. I'd never be re-elected. I'd have sold out the conservative business community that put me in office and destroyed untold thousands of jobs."

"You won't destroy any jobs, Bob. When the first few companies announce their intent to shut down we nationalize them. Keep them running under our own direction. Pay the employees more and tax them accordingly. The rest of the employers will get in line when they see a few of their kind crushed flat. They'll pay, believe me."

"And lay off more people to make up for it! Half of our general public is impoverished as it is, and you know what that means. Hundreds of thousands more people on public assistance. Where are you going to find the means to pay for that? It's a cycle, Sam. The more you tax, the more you pay out in entitlements. The more you pay, the more you have to tax."

"Please, spare me the sob story. I've seen your grand plan. Institutionalized extortion, kidnapping and murder. That Loch fellow is a good illustration. He was one of your faithful supporters. Your picture hangs in his office. You're having him killed.

Look, Rot. We don't need to have this conversation at all. Liberals and conservatives have been bickering like this for at least a century now and always will. It's real simple; Make the FBE a part of the Navy, put me in command and I'll do this. Otherwise, we never had this conversation. Now, where are those overflight photos of Holden Island?"

Gary Loch wasn't conflicted anymore. Being accompanied by an armed federal Marshal made all the difference in the world. Special agent Carver had actually asked permission to come along! The plan was to anchor near the east bank of the river about a half-mile north of the island and observe for an hour or so while appearing to be fishermen. Gary and Andrea were both feeling rested after their three hour nap. Agent Carver seemed worried, but Gary had decided that was just part of his nature.

They stopped at a private marina in the city of Holden and bought eighteen gallons of gasoline. The trip back home would require far more fuel running against the current and the prevailing wind. Gary was considering having Lucky fly him back so he could bring down the truck and trailer. He was tired of running long distances in the boat. Besides, that way he might be back at the shop Monday morning. Where was Lucky, by the way? He'd said he was on the way down by air. The cell phone had made his plane sound strange.

Carver had asked for a careful recon of the entire island before anchoring to watch the harbor. He'd spent a lot of time there and wanted to know if any changes were being made to the routine. He obviously wasn't convinced the girls had been moved off the island, and seemed to believe Alison and Diane weren't the only captives. He kept cautioning Gary about his overconfidence. Gary listened politely. Gary's plan was to stay along the West Bank, coasting with the current and playing at fishing while Andrea steered the boat with the electric motor. Chuck Carver would conceal himself below the low gunwale at Gary's feet and glass the place with his binoculars. They'd round the southern tip of the island close in, and then run north along it's east shore just outside the green channel markers about two hundred feet from the island with Carver seated in a fishing chair facing it.

"That's odd"

"Huh?"

"See that, Gary? The top row of windows have been covered with siding that doesn't match, and a small new window was installed in every third patch."

"I see it, OK. Why?"

"It looks like they abandoned the top floor for a while, then started using it for something else. I've been on this rock off and on for six months and never noticed that before. That building is the main detention center. This is the first time I've seen the back side of it, the water side. Rhonda and I were sent here primarily to find out if Morris was confining prisoners at his own discretion without due process. We could never spot a suitable location. That could be it, hiding under our noses."

Gary had a small fish on. As he reeled it up to the boat to release it, a seven foot long alligator exploded out of the water and took it, lure, line, pole and all, and disappeared with a powerful flick of it's tail, splashing all of them with the murky water. "That's why I've never seen that building from this side before."

"What gave you the idea Morris was keeping illegal prisoners in the first place, Agent Carver?"

"Well Miss Sturm, a man by the name of James Riad was abducted from his office at a big defense contractor a couple years ago during a routine FBE inspection and re-licensing. He's never been found. We were always interested in him. He's an immigrant from a country we're not on good terms with, so we used to run an investigation on him every year. We saw so much of him he became friends with some of our top people in the capitol. Nobody believes he defected. He was just a bean counter – Chief Financial Officer."

"You think Mister Morris grabbed him?"

"And then hid him away someplace or killed him when he found out he and his company were Trayson supporters. The persistent rumors of 'special detainees' clinched it for us, but we were about to give up on this semi-tropical Heap 'o Creeps until you folks showed up."

South of the main campus they pulled out of the shallows into more open water closer to the island, partly to avoid any more encounters with the local marine life. The airfield had the usual two armed guards, neither of whom ever moved too far from the rickety little line shack. It probably had a coffeepot in it. Two people, a man and a woman, were drag racing down the mile-long runway on lawn mowers. Carver said the girl was one of the pilots. He didn't think he'd ever seen her adversary before. Several aircraft lined the northern end of the runway. The big former Soviet Hind 24, a white business jet, two helicopters that looked like the kind traffic reporters would use, three private planes not unlike Lucky O'Connor's and something that seemed completely out of place. At first Gary took it for part of an airplane. Long, low to the ground, no wings, and just part of a tail – no. It was another helicopter, black and sinister looking. It had gimbaled machineguns on each side, drawn together under its nose. What kind of a prison would be guarded by something like that? It looked like it was praying. As Gary gawked at it the man on the mower glanced at him, and did a double take. Leaning way back in his seat he came to a stop and started waving both arms over his head smiling broadly. It was Dennis Davis.

"The Dolts? They don't know anything. They make good coffee though. I doubt if their guns are loaded. I sure wouldn't trust 'em with live ammo. When we landed I just asked them where to park. They haven't asked us a single question. Cover me, willya? I'm gonna go ask 'em for a restroom."

"What if one of them -?"

"Jumps me? Commander Sanders is in the 'airplane' as he calls it. See those Gatling guns? Three thousand rounds per minute – each. If he turns them on they point where he looks. 'Course the Dolts don't know that – yet."

"I've never seen one like that before, even in pictures. What is it anyway?"

"Something new. Runs on hydrogen. You're gonna love it. Don't ask Sanders too many questions."

"Sanders – Lowreyville?"

"Yep. Restroom, remember?"

"I'm next."

Chuck Carver just sat there in the partially beached boat, slack jawed. Gary had done exactly what he said he would. Motored right up to the island and asked the first person he saw if Eldon Morris had left the facility with his daughter. That person had been the female mower racer. She was the standby pilot, on duty since midnight yesterday, spending her weekly 48-hour single shift living in the small apartment in the back of the line shack. If Morris or one of the other bigshots had needed one of the helicopters, she would have flown it unless it was the Hind 24. Only Anatoly flew that. And that monstrosity would wake her up for sure. Eldon was still here somewhere.

"Want me to get someone to take you to him?"

"Nah, not right now."

She was glad. She'd been about to kick the Navy guy's butt at mower racing. Maybe he'd give her a peek in the warbird.

Twice she'd heard and felt something bump into the hull aft, and twice she'd ignored it. Now she cursed her own inattention. The port bridge door opened, and closed again before she realized it was the Captain's bodyguard Rocky. More than twice her size, three times her strength and a foot away, the 9mm pistol in her waistband had may as well been on the moon. He simply ran his enormous hand around her middle from her right side and took it. Now he had the gun and the physical advantage.

Oh well, it can't hurt to try. She let her startled look melt into a sort of play smile. "Damn, Rocky. You scared the piss out of me! Give me that back. How long you guys been back, anyway?"

She was wrong. It hurt plenty when he jerked her around, grabbed her unceremoniously by the front of her shirt and backhanded her across the face. His right hand probably weighed more than her head.

"Can it, bitch. We'll be having a little talk later, you and me. Meantime, I gotta take care of your new boyfriends and the cutie sisters. Bet I'll find 'em together, hmm? Paired off?"

"I don't know what you're talking about, Rocky. You hit me."

"I suppose you gonna tell me you don't know them sluts are keep'n company with those guys that made us look like morons the other day."

"Where?" Rhonda headed for the starboard door.

"Get your ass back here. I need you to stay right here. Hold sixteen knots, left of center in the marked channel. See this?"

"Yes, what is it?" Rhonda knew exactly what it was.

"It's a bomb. A grenade really, but with a control box. I made it a long time ago, back when I first noticed you weren't quite right. There's three ways it can go off. If you try to open either door from inside – boom. Use the radio or a cell phone – boom. I can set it off wit this if I hafta." He held up a garage door opener. "Of course it goes off if you touch it. I'll lock the doors from the outside just to be safe. Bye for now, Babe."

She'd only posted one lookout, on the bow. The idea was to spot submerged logs and the like before striking them. Sheila was supposed to be up there. Vaguely she remembered seeing the girl cup a hand over her crotch and walk knock kneed toward the women's head to port, grinning like an idiot at her. Rocky probably got her seconds later. If she was lucky he only tossed her overboard. No, wait a minute! Rocky thought she was partying with the new guys! He'd called them the cutie sisters. Sheila must have made it into the head before Rocky saw her. She'd be – there she was, at the port door. Rocky had just left by the other one. Rhonda motioned for her to get down. The poor thing just stood there with one eye cocked and half a smile on her face. "GET DOWN!"

She did it just in time. Rocky's face appeared at the door glass on the right an instant later. Rhonda's hand was frantically working the toggle switch that raised and lowered the crane boom. The last he knew, it wasn't working.

Sheila may have caught on slowly, but when she realized what was happening she acted effectively. She knew she had to find the others before the big thug did. Rhonda was somehow locked in the wheelhouse and had been disarmed. Monique had gone down to the salon to read, hoping one of the men would join her. Dale and Greg were both on the starboard rail the last she knew, watching for the next town and discussing ways to get back to their sailboat in Summerville.

Sheila felt the huge man's footfalls before she saw him lumber into the salon and grab her friend by the hair with a gun to her temple. He dragged her up the stairs to lock her in with Rhonda Carver and that, that – grenade? A grenade with wires coming out of it? Oh God. She broke into a dead run for the rail on the right side where the two men had been.

THE RESTITUTION

CHAPTER THIRTEEN   Rescue

Jason Sanders began to doubt the wisdom of inviting Mister Davis along with the far more level headed O'Connor. Lucky? The file said his given name was Roger. Roger O'Connor. Sort of like Gerry Barry or Phyllis Willis. No wonder he called himself Lucky. Dennis Davis was actually toying with the two armed guards, baiting them, daring them to confront him. They might not be the sharpest knives in the drawer, but the old M-16s were real enough, and he could tell they were fully loaded by the way the weapons balanced in their slings. An empty M-16 is very light in weight. Davis had way too much faith. Sure, if he got in trouble with the two goons he could bring the starboard minigun to bear on them in a second, but would they even notice? He certainly didn't want to actually fire the thing. It's aim wasn't really that precise. You sort of turned it on and walked the projectile stream onto whatever you wanted to destroy. It wasn't made for warning shots. Plow the lawn with it? He'd have a talk with Davis later.

Something was happening. Sanders thought he heard a phone ring. The guards looked at each other wide eyed and the tall one lurched into the line shack. The ringing stopped and the man came out with the phone in his hand, trailing cord. He turned it so his companion could hear too. Were they being ordered to check out the newcomers? He turned on the master switch and the arming toggle for the right Gatling. He felt it jerk a little in its gimbal mount.

The guns could be coupled to his line of vision, but didn't have to be. They could be controlled individually with coolie hat switches in the cyclic stick handle that controlled the aircraft in flight. The weapons officer in the left seat had more elaborate computer aiming capability, but much less aircraft control. If he'd left the weapon in line of vision mode it would already be trained on the guards. Dennis appeared in the doorway and the two men turned to face him. Jason slowly thumbed up his weapon. Dennis never lost his relaxed demeanor as he talked with the two agitated men. Presently he slapped one of them on the back and dogtrotted toward the machine spinning his index finger from the wrist as if telling the pilot to start the engine. "They think we work here. They're having an escape attempt and everyone has places they have to be. They assume we should be airborne. Might be a good idea. I'm going with Gary, if you don't mind. Gotta fill him in anyway, and find out what he's been up to. Where's Lucky?"

"He went over to talk with the gentlemen from the boat. You'd better send him back if he's coming with me."

The female pilot's name was Pam, and it was hard to shake her loose. The moment Dennis walked away from her she'd made straight for Lucky. All she wanted was a close look at the deadly looking black helo. She assumed that Lucky and Dennis were senior officers or manufacturers executives. The pilot wouldn't have any authority.

Dennis, Lucky, Gary, Andrea and Agent Carver needed to talk, and couldn't with her present. As soon as Dennis sent Lucky back to Sanders and asked if he could go with the boat she saw her chance. "That leaves the third seat empty! Can I ride with them?" She placed her hands together at the palms, just below her face. "Please?"

"You'll have to ask the pilot, Ma'am."

Lucky was strapping in when she ran up to the door on The Admiral's side. His answer to her excited question came as a complete surprise to Lucky.

"For liability reasons I've got to ask a bunch of questions. They'll sound weird enough to make you question my motives. Some will sound kinda personal, OK? If I ask something you honestly don't know, just say so. If you can not or will not answer, just walk away, alright? I bet you already figured out this airplane is part of a classified secret project. We're here to help, but we still have national security to think about. Ready?"

"Ready"

"What's your name?"

"Pam McCannis. Pamela Sue McCannis, sir."

"Licensed, rated and current helicopter pilot?"

"Yes sir. Commercial, 1300 hours total time."

"FBE agent or civil employee?"

"Neither. I work for Haslett Aviation. They lease these birds to the FBE with aircrew and ground support. All except for the Hind 24. They confiscated that last year. One of their own guys flies it. Quite well, I'm told."

"Married? Family to support?"

"Yes, no kids yet. You?"

"I'll ask the questions for now. Do you have an assigned duty station? This facility is at general quarters now, I understand"

"Well, I'm kinda supposed to stay here until someone needs a chopper, but that's always. Doesn't have anything to do with the escape. I suppose they might want me as a spotter."

"You could do that with us. You're in. Got any portable radios?" She shook her head yes. "Get us one. Grab one for the boat, too." Pam turned and ran to the line shack.

"Jump in the back, Lucky. I want her up here. She's going to show us how their whole security system works if we do our part. You didn't notice a weapon on her, did you?"

"I don't think so."

"I haven't either, and I'm still looking. Just in case, do you know how to use this?"

"Yeah, I used to have one like it. Turned it in."

"Listen. If she tries to get command of the airplane, just shoot her. Make sure the bullet goes out through a window without hitting anything important."

"You want me to shoot her? Just like that?"

"I don't *want* you to. I'm *ordering* you to shoot her if she attempts to take command of this helicopter. Do you know the difference between Command and Control? I intend to let her fly it if she wants to."

"I understand, but I'm glad you mentioned it. What if she manages to put you out of commission, Jason?"

"That would be a pretty good indication she was trying to take command, wouldn't it? Look, Lucky, this machine is top secret. It simply can not fall into the wrong hands. Do you see how much confidence I'm placing in you, sir? Show time, here she comes."

The tense, emotionally charged conversation had gone on for over an hour. Some of the other captives were beginning to notice it and were banging on their doors, wanting to be let in on it. Any human contact is precious to a person in solitary confinement.

"I have to go. They'll hear the racket and catch us. I'll be back with your meal and fresh clothes. Maybe we can talk later when I bring books."

The clothing exchange was to be his opportunity to snare her. It wouldn't be pleasant for her at all. "Dorothy – wait a minute. I can trust you, right? Really trust you?" Her eyes said he could. "I'm escaping. I've planned it for months. I'm set up to do it tonight and you were part of my plan from the start. I want to take these other people with me."

"You mean all this was just -?"

"Oh, no. Dorothy, believe me. All this is new. I never dreamed I'd actually meet you first, have you become my good friend. I was going to trap your hand in the meal slot, to bring your supervisor running with his keys. I've made an elaborate trap for him out of my bed frame. That's why you can't see it. With him helpless and you tied to this door, I could take his keys and weapon, release the rest of the captives and escape."

"A trap?"

"It won't hurt him. Just keep him from moving long enough for us to get away from here. I would have to gag both of you to keep you quiet, of course."

"Show me. I don't believe you." She felt used, but relieved, also. And more than a little suspicious about his true intentions, but still had no fear of the kindly, somewhat older man.

"It's too big and cumbersome to move to where you can see it. If you let me do this, you'll see it later. The snare for your hand won't injure you. I just didn't want to frighten you with it. That's why I'm telling you this."

"I have the key. I want to see it right now, so I can believe you."

"You have the KEY? Do you have all of them?"

"I was going to let you out, but I wanted to talk some more first. I wanted to take you home with me and let you leave from there. I had a plan too. I mean it, James. I have to see for myself. Scoot back, I'm coming in."

"Don't just rush in, Dorothy. The trap is set. Look closely and step around it carefully." The sound of a key in the lock made his head swim with anxiety.

She gasped at the sight of the trap as he took in the wonder of the wide open door. It was still recognizable as a set of bunk beds, but barely. The two spring bases, the kind made of little chain link wire sections with small springs all around in trampoline fashion stood upright beside the door. The two were hinged with a rope of twisted sheet fabric so the pair formed the shape of an open book. Someone entering in a hurry, looking at the hand caught in the meal slot would find themselves between them. Half the springs had been removed from their original positions and were now stretched across the hinge to snap the two halves together – as soon as the hapless supervisor tripped over the bar that propped them apart. A cord taken from mattress piping connected that bar, formerly an upright trim rail from the upper headboard, to another like it at the top of the trap. When either was tripped, both would go flying, though not far unless the cord broke. The man would be caught between the two bedsprings like the meat in a sandwich, unable to move.

She walked around it, marveling and relieved. A pile of leftover pieces and mattress stuffing filled the southeast corner of the cell. More of the bedsheet rope lay coiled on the floor. A food pan lay on the floor beside it, filled with water with a large piece of thin white cloth soaking in it. She saw a tiny homemade knife on the floor. Made of a bedframe part and sharpened on brick, it seemed too small to be intended as a weapon. She still felt no fear of James, although the trap gave her a new respect for him.

He offered her his hand, but she walked right into him. A hug was better than a handshake. It was a platonic hug, as if between a brother and sister. Both knew she would have to leave immediately. "Want to see the hand snare."

"Sure." She thought it was rhetorical. She'd be going with him, of course. Why snare her now? Besides, he wouldn't be able to - dread filled her. Someone was unlocking the passage door into the hallway. They would have already seen the open door.

Without a word, James pushed her away from the door and yanked the threadbare sheet from the pan of water and over his head, standing still, looking like a ghost. A soaking wet ghost from a Halloween party. The Captain of the Guard, as James had thought of him, was a smaller individual than he remembered from the two previous encounters, but the large canister of crowd-control pepper gas spray was the same. Unaimed, it spewed blinding, choking liquid as the bedspring trap snapped closed on Dorothy's supervisor. Almost closed, anyway. The guy was too thin and wiry for the trap to hold him effectively. His right arm was already out, flailing.

The wet sheet stopped most of the spray, but James still couldn't see very well through the tearing it caused, but he could see well enough through the wet fabric. He kicked the canister out of the exposed hand. Dorothy was gagging. He could hear her. Some of the other prisoners were screaming. Frantically, he held the bed frame halves together as the man struggled to get loose.

"I need your cuffs." There was no response. Dorothy was either in panic or sprayed. With the two pairs of handcuffs in pouches on her duty belt he could bind the trap shut and buy some time, but he couldn't let go and didn't have time to wait for her to recover. For that matter, he couldn't be sure she'd help him in a direct physical confrontation with her own boss, She'd worked for him a long time.

Open, the bed frames had been stable in their upright position. Closed, they lost most of their footprint, standing precariously like a closed book. The wrestling match tipped them over. First into the wall, then the bottom slipped out and the whole assembly fell flat to the floor. The guard bellowed in pain. At least that silenced the other prisoners. On top of the trap, holding it shut with his weight, James could see the man's cuff case, one of them at least. Risking broken fingers, he reached through the wire grid and unsnapped the case, extracting a pair of rusty, nickel plated cuffs. He snapped them onto the frame halves about waist high, one to each as the guard squirmed and cursed.

Dorothy had been squarely sprayed. She sat against the wall with her eyes tightly closed against the pain. She knew from the minimal training she'd received that rubbing her eyes or washing them with water could only make it worse. Only time would relieve it, so she waited. They were caught. Mild mannered James couldn't possibly contain Butch in that contraption very long. She would be fired for sure. Could she be arrested for breaking lockup rules? She jumped when he touched her.

"Lean forward, Dorothy. I need your handcuffs."

She let an eye open just a little. It was James. Butch lay flat on his back, trussed up in bed parts. A rag was stuffed in his mouth to keep him quiet. James was dangerous after all. A wave of new fear washed over her. "What do you want my cuffs for?"

"To keep him from getting loose. I've got to get the others and get out of here. Are you coming with me?"

She smiled. She could open her eyes a little.

Butch's key ring had only five keys on it. The first one he tried fit the door next to his, but none of the rest fit the following door. He tried them all again before noticing something. His door and cell #2 had been locked with ordinary home or office type passage locks with the inner knobs replaced with cover plates and the screws reversed. This door had a deadbolt lock only. All down the hall it was the same. #4 and #5 had knobs, #6 had another deadbolt. Inexpensive house locks are sometimes sold in kits, Two entry sets and a deadbolt, all keyed alike. This place had obviously been cheaply built. He tried the key that had opened #2 again and it worked the deadbolt lock. It would fit his own as well, he knew.

Prisoners were peeking outside the doors he'd unlocked. His neighbor, a middle aged woman wearing the standard white prison uniform said she heard a siren the moment the door to her south had first opened. That would have been his door, when Dorothy first opened it. He looked at the casing of door number four, the one he'd just opened. It had a small button, like the one that turns on the light in a refrigerator. The man inside was asleep, and didn't look healthy at all. Drawn and emaciated, he didn't look like he could even walk. The dark haired young girl from #3 scooted past James and took the old black man's hand, kneeling at his bedside. "Monroe, it's me, Diane. This man is going to help us escape from here! Can you stand?" It was obvious they'd been communicating somehow.

James was running down the hall for cell #5 when the shooting started. Three men with carbines had burst in through the passage into the cellblock hallway. The first fired at him as he flattened himself against the wall and missed. James heard the sonic crack as the bullet passed a foot from his head. The second shooter evidently tried to shoot around his colleague. His bullet buried itself in the East wall across from Dorothy, who had retrieved her supervisor's pepper spray canister and was now soaking the attackers with it as they fired. All three stopped shooting and started moaning and crying. The facility was on alert now. WE'LL BE BACK FOR YOU! He could hear blended cheers and protests from down the long hallway. Time had run out.

Dorothy was the only one who knew where to go, and she could barely see. She kept a hand on James' shoulder and kept her eyes closed most of the time, like a blind woman. She still held the gas canister at the ready. James Riad had taken the pistol Butch had carried and put it in his inner suit coat pocket. He'd armed himself with one of the carbines, as had Rose Wellington, the woman with such good hearing. Diane, the old guy's guardian angel had the third carbine, but just slung it over her shoulder, not knowing what else to do with it. She just didn't want it shooting at her anymore. James asked Rose to empty Diane's' chamber, but leave her loaded magazine in place. He was glad she knew what he was talking about.

"Turn here."

At this point there was no reason to doubt Dorothy Spence. She'd already risked her own life while saving theirs. They turned, and entered the stairway at the south end of the building. They'd be visible from the outside through the floor to ceiling windows on three sides. "Hurry".

"We have to get behind the prison building. It's our only chance."

James wanted to believe her, but it made no sense. Three more guards were rushing them. James Riad was fed up. Deliberately, he raised the old surplus M-2, snapped the selector to full automatic and cut them down. He'd used six rounds so far. The gun's last owner had fired one. The magazine held thirty. If the idiot had fully loaded it he had twenty-three rounds left. Better stop playing with full auto. Back in his family's country, long ago, he'd trained with the M-2 carbine. He doubted these guys had ever fired them. He was fairly sure they didn't even know they were full auto machineguns. He was going to die here. He'd take enough of these creeps with him to make sure his passing didn't stay a secret like the last two years of his life had. First, he had to get these people to safety. For the time being, that meant following Dorothy Spence.

Jason Sanders listened to the portable radio the girl had provided, hoping he'd hear the prison security chatter. All he heard was civil aviation. The handheld was a typical 360 channel aircraft Comm transceiver, It even had a sticker on it saying "Property of Haslett Aviation". Oh, well. He could still use it to contact Gary Loch. It was set to the air to air 'multicom' channel, 122.9. The other one probably was as well. He turned off his intercom mike so Pam the passenger couldn't hear. "November Alpha from Hotel X-Ray. Got me Gary?"

"Ah, yeah! November Alpha, ah, what hotel?"

"Relax Gary. Call me 'Hotel X-Ray' or just Jason, OK? I've got their girl pilot aboard. I'm going to try to learn all I can about their response to a jailbreak. She's pretty cooperative. I don't think she likes her job very much, and she thinks we're here to help

then went into a climbing turn to the southeast that astounded his passengers even though both were experienced pilots. It was more of a turning climb. A two G acceleration – upward, followed by a zero G rollout and a 300 MPH diving pass perpendicular to the direction from the runners to the boat, crossing between them and their pursuers. Hopefully, both sides would assume he was an FBE aircraft. The runners would try to escape at a right angle and the FBE and prison guards wouldn't shoot at them.

James Riad turned to face the menacing aircraft, telling Dorothy to get the others into the small stand of trees by the bank and conceal themselves. He knew what would happen. He'd be targeted as it broke out of the turn. From that instant on, the port Gatling would be locked on him. He'd have only one chance to take out the weapons officer, just before he hit the firing nib. The armor tub would protect the crew from weapons far more potent than his puny little M-2 USC, but the windows, including the windshields, were soft. Plain acrylic, just like a Piper Cub. He'd denied funding for ballistic glazing in the prototypes because of the cost. The engineers said it wouldn't make a significant difference weight and balance wise. Just before he fired his virtually hopeless final burst, he realized three things at once. The Gattling were not part of the original design at all, but the rocket pods were. Secondly, the guns were not aimed at him. The port side Gatling was aimed down and forward to the right, under the nose. The other one pointed up and away, nearly endangering the rotor disk, unless it was synchronized to shoot between the blades. That would be a neat trick with two guns, nine barrels and seven blades. The machine was *his*. Northwest designed and built it. He'd approved the purchase of every part, and it would be undergoing its final testing now. No wonder it hadn't fired on them. It was here for a rescue. Dorothy had mentioned a plan, but not elaborated. He jerked the gun down and windmilled his arms, laughing almost hysterically.

"What's he up to, Jas – I mean, Admiral Sanders?"

"He evidently wants to make friends. Surrendering possibly?" He was stuck. The runner obviously expected him to land and pick him up. The FBE shooters expected the runner to lay down his stolen rifle and surrender to them. He couldn't confront the FBE because of his civilian passengers – not to mention his orders from the President. He was forbidden to enter the fight or transport any illegal weapons, meaning any firearm in civilian use.

Humanitarian aid only. "November Alpha – have you made contact?"

"I've got all but one. The rest think he's sacrificing himself to buy time. He doesn't know we're here. Can you pick him up?"

"Negative. I have passengers and no armor."

Dorothy Spence broke away and ran for James, arms waving over her head, the tear gas canister still in her hand. "COME WITH ME. PLEASE! THE BOAT!"

Boat? James saw his helicopter climb away at the same moment. He turned around. Boat? He heard a single gunshot behind him, saw Dorothy crumple silently with a look of horrible pain on her face. He spun and fired out his remaining 23 rounds in one long burst before running to her. The finest woman he'd ever known was gone. The bullet had entered her neck just below the chin and blown out her cervical spine.

"I don't have time to unload my riders but maybe I could make them lie on the floor below the windows. I'd be over weight, but it would probably work as long as I don't get hit myself. Pam can fly this thing out if I do."

"No need, Hotel. We have him. One of the ladies bought it though."

Andrea Sturm could hear them coming through the dense growth. They were no longer making any attempt at silence. Gary had predicted they'd be overloaded. That would make the boat difficult to trim at high speed. She sat at the helm with her right foot on the trolling motor controller, her hand on the power tilt switch for the big motor and her eyes on it's ignition key. People starting clambering aboard over the stern, almost swamping it. Gary was barking orders.

"Get him to the front and make him comfortable. You too. Chuck and Dennis – help guide us out of here. I'm gonna need both of you back here with rifles. They'll be shooting at us, people. You in front – pass back that gun, OK? The rest of you lie flat on the deck. Be the smallest possible target."

Young, dark haired Diane sat up from kneeling over the exhausted old black man. She grasped the unfamiliar weapon and turned, handing it around the small tinted windshield – to her astounded mother.

THE RESTITUTION

CHAPTER FOURTEEN   The Race

Andrea handled the severely overburdened bass boat expertly at first, despite being overwhelmed with joy at the completely unexpected rescue of her daughter. She had done it. Days had become weeks as she'd depleted her meager resources. Then she'd met Gary and -. Gary still hadn't found his girl, Alison.

She knew she should be ashamed of herself, carrying on like this. She'd dropped the ball, and Gary had taken over for her, cutting back their speed. He'd said something about being conspicuous and getting them caught. He wanted everyone to stay low. Andrea couldn't do it. She couldn't take her eyes and mind from her daughter Diane.

Diane couldn't take her eyes and mind from the old black man. She'd first noticed the moaning and the incoherent voice coming from outside her cell almost as soon as she'd been brought in. Diane was a certified nursing assistant. It didn't take long to determine her neighbor was an elderly untreated diabetic. She pleaded with the hands that brought her food to check on him, to get him on an appropriate diet. The jerk wouldn't even acknowledge her. For weeks she'd been talking with him by shouting, coaching him on what to eat and what to discard, assuming his meal was identical to her own. It was obvious he'd done this on his own until he lost the ability or the will. For the last few days he'd fallen silent, only moaning. Diane's life saving effort had become a deathwatch. Now she had hope again. She had a chance to save him. She loved her mother more than ever, was completely awed at the lengths she'd gone to, but she was busy. She kept telling Agent Carver she wanted to go along when they took him to a hospital. Andrea fought back the urge to just take her daughter home and hug her. Diane was a big girl. A woman who saved lives and was good at it.

The anchorage they'd selected earlier wouldn't do. It was too close, too visible. Sanders had suggested this island a few miles north, just above the town of Holden. A sand bar, really. It had a ring of trees at its center surrounding the dry bed of what must be a pond of water when the river was high. Now, with the river at it's lowest, it was a good spot to hide a helicopter for a short time. He'd noticed it on the way down yesterday.

Exhausted, Gary Loch had slept through the night, as had Chuck Carver and John Walgren. They'd posted a lookout for Rat Racer and hailed him in about 9PM. His V-berth provided comfortable space for Monroe Jenkins, the diabetic, and Lucky, the other 'old guy'. Jenkins was rail thin, emaciated, and in a semi-permanent state of shock. The Admiral and his new female co-pilot had flown him out at first light for emergency medical attention at NAS Lowreyville. There hadn't been room for Andrea's daughter. They had only enough pressurized hydrogen fuel to make it one-way with a tiny reserve.

Carver had been calling the shots. He'd prevented Gary and Dennis from taking the carbines and blazing ashore to save Alison by a combination of logic and authority. The alert had been raised. Morris couldn't kill his captives now, he needed them as hostages. If he were raided his only recourse would be to leave under their cover. He'd move them as soon as he could, but the big Russian helicopter wouldn't be doing it. It's only pilot was another plant from the Marshals Service, and he'd been extracted. He'd flown himself out, actually, and was now on the ground at Lowreyville being debriefed. Morris didn't even *have* the Hind 24 anymore. That only left M/V Secant, with her planted pilot. Yes, Rocky the bodyguard had taken it over, but he probably still didn't know who Rhonda really was. He'd probably be holding Dale and Greg Lucans prisoner. "Let him board Secant with his captives. He can only make sixteen Knots and has 300 miles to go. That'll take him until midnight or later. My people have hostage rescue experts, and they're already on it. All we have to do is wait and not let the media know about it. He won't suspect a thing until he's looking down the bore of a Marshal's shotgun."

But the morning had brought a different story. The Marshals Service wouldn't be doing anything. When Carver finally got through to his field coordinator he'd been told his orders remained the same. "Observe only. Amass evidence for use after the Bureau is disbanded. Do not take hostile action."

Gary Loch was livid, and Chuck Carver was seriously worried for the safety of his wife. James Riad had recovered somewhat from the loss of Dorothy Spence, but would always remember the woman who had died because she believed in him.

This Eldon Stewart Morris would pay. He'd pay with his worthless life. "Look – they leave the dock!" In his grief, some of his childhood phrasing had returned.

"What do you say, Agent Carver? Still want to stop me?"

"No, I'm going." Agent Carver looked up from John Walgren's powerful little 80 x 600 Schmidt-Cassegrain type telescope. "Something's seriously wrong. Rhonda hasn't left the wheelhouse once since the sun came up. I think she's locked in. She can't go that long without a trip to the head. I'd think she'd break a window before going on the floor. She looks awful."

Dennis was going. Gary knew he would. James Riad was a surprise. "I must go. I promised the others I would come back for them, just as Dorothy promised me."

"But James, You've just escaped after two years as a captive. You need to rest."

"I need to keep my word, and I need my true name. I am Selim Sherif al Riad. I used the name James to avoid being seen as a terrorist. Now terrorists bring their filth to me. Terrorists with names you see as ordinary. I am not confused any longer. I have this weapon and I know how it is used." He had only one 30 round magazine, the one from Diane Sturm's M-2. Rose Wellington offered hers to Agent Carver, but he declined it. At contact range he preferred his handgun. Besides, he had five 15 round magazines for it. 75 total to the carbines' 30. Dennis accepted it gladly, and Agent Carver didn't object.

"Are you certain, Butch? You've been through hell."

"Pretty sure. A big one, seven-foot at least was dragging away Dorothy, the one I shot, by the time we got there. The spot where their footprints went in the water was all tore up with gator sign. The black helicopter didn't go anywhere near there and the only people around were on the fishin' boat we saw before it started, clear over near the other bank. Jimbo saw them guys almost git et by a gator too. Yep, gators et 'em all right, sure as you're born. But I got a real bad feelin'. That chopper didn't come from nowhere. I think that girl pilot y'all can't find had it hid down at the airport somewheres. I bet she was in cahoots with my ol' Dorothy Spence. You ain't seed the last of it, I'm thinkin, they musta seed ya take 'em all aboard. Take me along. I want them bitches bad."

"How'd they do it anyway?"

"With a big 'ol bear trap made outa a bed. Hurt me sumpin awful."

"OK. Get your deer rifle and come on aboard. I'll have them set up a stateroom for you." It might be good to have a real marksman aboard. He'd drown with the rest of them.

Gary's bass boat hugged the east bank of the river as it passed Holden's Island. No point in inviting gunfire from the smog jail staff. The Marshals and the local police could mop them up later. As it happened, no one fired on them at all. They weren't so hostile with their boss gone. The guards at the airfield actually waved at them.

Gary and John Walgren had inherited the two handheld aviation radios. Pam had said they should leave them set on 122.9 because nobody would be surprised to hear a running conversation there. They should just keep using callsigns. November Alpha was good. Rat Racer became Romeo Romeo.

"What's the plan, Alpha?"

"We're gonna harass them into running aground on one of these sand bars. Mrs. Carver is at the wheel, as far as we know. She'll let it happen as soon as she figures out what we're up to, so we don't have to keep it a secret. If Eldon figures it out he'll take over himself. That would be even better. He's a crappy helmsman."

"What should we do?"

"Just stay back. We'll be passing Secant in a bit. We'll do a little scouting for a good bar just outside the green can buoys where the channel is narrow. You just keep an eye on that trawler and don't let them know who you are, OK?"

"You bet, Alpha. Your best girl says be careful."

"Romeo Romeo has Andrea aboard? What about young Diane?"

"Negative, Alpha. Diane left with the others. The Marshals pilot came back with the Russian 'copter. That thing sure is big. They're being taken to Lowreyville, courtesy Admiral Sanders. Romeo is three up. Andrea, your father-in law and myself. Sanders is coming back himself. Says he's got some useful information from your town cop, Albert Adamson. If I understood right, he's bringing him down here along with one of his people. I told him we'd be on 122.9."

After more than a week of solitude, this was a change, at least. Alison had learned that several of the others had been locked up alone for well over a year! If she had heard that before they'd been dragged out and forced on this ship she would have lost her mind. This arrangement must be temporary.

Nine people, seven women and two men, shared what amounted to a small public rest room. They were packed in standing, with no room to even sit down. The space was smaller than an elevator.

Still, something about it was familiar. The sound? It was the sound of a ship under way, of course, but last time she hadn't known that. The brass meal slot fitting was just like the one in her cell. As soon as the door had slammed shut one of the two men had apologized in advance and urinated in the toilet while surrounded by women he didn't know. Said he couldn't wait any longer. One of them followed his lead as soon as he finished. Now, three hours later, the partial roll of toilet paper was gone. What if someone had to - ? Lord, Alison hoped she wouldn't be the first.

Someone started asking questions. Why had the others been locked up? Where were they? Was the FBE involved in every one of their situations? That turned into bedlam as all the pent-up hunger to know poured out. No one was answering.

"It's time." They'd dropped back about a quarter mile behind Secant. Gary throttled up smoothly to keep the bow from rising too much. With four men aboard, the boat would only make about sixty-five MPH, but that probably seemed supersonic to Eldon Morris if he happened to see them flash past.

Dennis Davis, like the others, was studying every detail of the trawler. "What's on the foredeck, just ahead of the crane mast?"

"Don't know. Was anything there before?"

"That's where we stacked parts for the tower. If he's hauling tower parts now, he's going the wrong way. Can you see if my wife's still on the bridge?" The object had a khaki colored canvas tarp over it. The same kind of tarp Gary had seen covering tower segments on the government owned island above Fairport.

"The Pilot's a woman. What's your wife look like, Chuck?"

"Alpha November – do you copy Romeo Romeo?"

"Go ahead, Lucky."

"Say your position?"

"We're about ten miles ahead. May have found what we're looking for. Will advise when we make our move."

"Romeo's clear. Standing by."

"OK, Lucky. You get to use the airplane radio from now on. Andrea and I'll just watch." John Walgren was showing his sense of humor.

They waited under the low branches at the east bank. It would be a game of chicken, pitting the nineteen-foot fishing boat against the 67-foot ocean-going power yacht. The sand bar lay submerged about four feet down, midway between two widely spaced channel markers at a bend in the river. Gary knew that when the helmsman saw them coming straight for them from about three points off the port bow the natural reaction would be a quick turn to the right. It would only take a second to drive the cumbersome trawler hard aground where they'd be easy rifle targets. All Secant carried were shotguns and pistols. Surrender would be Eldon and Rocky's only option.

"GO!" The bass boat exploded out of the weeds headed straight at the trawler. Gary and Dennis sat in the two bucket seats, elbows on the gunwales like a couple kids in a convertible. Selim 'James' Riad lay in the bow, his carbine aimed straight forward. Charles Carver rode in the high fishing chair just forward of the motor with Gary's binoculars. He saw his wife, her face a mask of terror. Just below her. In front of the crane mast he saw Rocky. He seemed to be sitting on something. A motorcycle? His feet were apart, his hands spinning cranks attached to a boxlike apparatus that was part of what he sat astride. At the center of his chest was a pair of round things, like the lenses of a big pair of binoculars, looking straight at him. A flash – smoke. "DECK GUN!!"

Gary tried to turn away too late. The water erupted in two or three places directly in front of them. Then he saw the nose of his boat become a wall of water and felt himself shoot over it, tumbling in mid-air. He caught an image of Dennis, also airborne, folding his knees up in front of himself and crossing his arms over his face. He did the same. Then he hit the water and everything stopped.

He was aware of someone else in the water with him, trying to push his head under. He naturally fought it, flailing his arms without effect. Fingers found his face, pinching his nose shut. With consciousness returning, he slowly realized the person wasn't trying to drown him, it was a lifesaving effort. He stopped fighting. He couldn't breathe. Gary blacked out again.

"I got them sumbitches aright, Mister Morris. Got em good. Not many knows ya gotta shoot under 'em when they's under the water. Muh pappy showed me how to shoot 'gators!"

"How many'd you get, Butch?"

"Both them rascals, Mister Morris."

Rocky had said he thought there'd been three. "You did well, Butch"

"Thank ya, sir! Kin ah shoot that big machine gun now?"

"Maybe later." Eldon had seen small body parts floating as they'd passed through the wreckage.

"November Alpha, do you copy Rat racer?" Lucky stopped in mid transmission. 'November Alpha' was off the air. Pieces of his son-in law's fishing boat were floating in the wake on both sides of the big trawler.

"Move in slow, John." The largest piece was the center section of the hull. It floated right side up and level, but very low in the water. Both windshields were still attached and unbroken. Water filled the space between them giving the appearance of two gunwales floating in formation. The rear portion was being left behind. Still attached to the heavy motor by wiring and control cables, it fought the current like an oversize spinning lure as the rest drifted downstream, as if it were still doggedly pursuing M/V Secant. All that remained of the front third of the vessel were fragments.

From Rat Racer's stubby foredeck, Lucky O'Connor saw movement. Someone was trying to crawl onto the flooded deck between the windshields. Andrea saw it too. "John – look there." Her voice was almost a whisper. John had switched to electric power, on batteries. Lucky could hear the three little trolling thrusters whirring', sometimes in unison, sometimes singly as John approached, matching speed with the wreck. Secant was just disappearing around the bend half a mile ahead.

"Hand me a boat hook." It was Gary, trying to hold on with one bleeding hand while holding Chuck Carver's head above water with the other. "I got him! Andrea – I need a hand here."

Gary was OK. Scratches and a superficial cut on his left forearm. Special Agent Charles Carver was not. At first he seemed intact, but unconscious. Then Lucky noticed the blood. And the small, round holes in his shirt. His issue ballistic vest was made to protect against pistol and shotgun fire, not Butch's deer rifle. Its efficiency was also reduced when it was wet. Butch thought he'd shot both men. He'd actually shot one of them twice. At least Carver hadn't suffered. Both bullets had pierced his heart.

Rat Racer lurched as Dennis Davis pulled himself up over the side onto the aft deck. "Are they OK? I tried to get to Mister Riad but he's all in pieces. Think we should recover some of the bigger ones for his family or something?"

"Good morning. Federal Marshals Service. How may I direct your call?"

"Agent Code CC-21."

" Thank you sir."

"Field Operations, Thompson."

"Mister Carver is dead, sir. They have Rhonda, his wife and partner."

"Slow down sir. What is your name again?"

"Loch. Gary Loch. And I'm not speaking too rapidly. This phone battery is about dead. Did you understand what I just told you Mr. Thompson?"

"Yes - CC-21 is dead, RC-21 is compromised."

"That would be a way to put it. Another man was killed. I understand you have been looking for him for some time. James Riad? Otherwise known as Selim al Riad? They both died saving the lives of others, including mine."

"What is your location, sir?"

"Missacantata River below Holden's Island, in pursuit of Eldon Stewart Morris, supposedly of the FBE. He has my daughter, a couple of my friends, Mrs. Carver and several others aboard his yacht as hostages. He murdered Carver and Riad with a mounted automatic deck cannon. Two of us survived when he blasted my boat out of the water. We need all the help you can give us." There was a long pause. Gary tapped on the cell phone, trying to wake up its fading battery. "Correction. Carver was murdered after the boat was destroyed. Sniper fire from Secant's deck."

"Ah, they. Carver was ordered to stand down earlier today. Office of the president. National security – He shouldn't-."

"Bullshit. That asshole has his WIFE! My daughter! Several others. He's headed for open water. Look, sir. We can PROVE all this."

"How?"

"We got three others out with Riad. We –". Gary nipped it. Suddenly he realized he was not talking to a friend.

"Other hostages? Rescued? Where are they, sir?"

Gary said nothing. He slowly pressed the 'end' button.

Andrea Sturm was the first to notice they were all falling apart. Gary had been angry before making the call to Chuck's superiors in the capitol. Now he was depressed nearly to tears. He sat on the foredeck watching over Chuck Carver's lifeless body, more or less incapacitated. His friend Dennis was asleep on John's v-berth. John Walgren sat easily at the wheel of his odd little boat, trailing behind Secant and slowing whenever he could see her clearly, speeding up when he couldn't see her at all. The young man wasn't really involved at all, just out for an adventure. She was sure he'd never put himself in harms way. The only one who still seemed to have his wits was Lucky O'Connor. He had John's tool kit out, making up a cord to power the one remaining airplane radio from Rat Racer's impressive electrical system. It's own battery was fading and he didn't want to risk missing Admiral Sanders. Was he planning to talk him into helping? The small helicopter was very well armed. Or did he only want him to remove the bodies? Agent Carver had been enough. The ghastly sight of Riad's head, shoulder and left arm was too much. They all were avoiding looking at it. At least it wasn't bleeding all over the aft deck anymore. She knew they were wasting time. They had no plan, and they'd be in the open ocean in thirteen hours.

"November Alpha, November Alpha. Do you read Hotel X-Ray, over?"

"November Alpha, November Alpha. From Hotel X." The voice was faint, indistinct, and distant.

"Hotel X-ray, Hotel X-Ray, Hotel X-Ray. Rat Racer responding for November Alpha, 75 miles south of Holden, over."

"Craft responding for November Alpha, Hotel X-ray will catch up in about twenty minutes. Say your type please?"

"We're a houseboat, sir. A small, white houseboat. We'll try to spot an island or a clearing for you."

Lucky'd heard it correctly. Dunningsville Police Chief Al Adamson had flown down with Sanders in the hydrogen chopper. So had, of all people Paul DuPont, the young man who owned the car that started this whole mess. Gary and Dennis couldn't imagine why the chief would want him here.

"An attempt was made on Paul's life last Thursday. When he went home from his new job in the courthouse a woman was waiting for him. I'll let him tell you the rest."

"Well, Mr. Loch, she had a gun. A handgun like a cop would carry, but she was almost naked and hysterical, not making any sense. I tried to quiet her down, but it just made her worse, you know, crazier. Then she started telling me how someone named Eldon was next. How she'd get him on the river. She said she'd shoot me, but then she took it back. I tried to get her to put her clothes back on. When I handed them to her, she shot at me and missed. I ran out and called 911 from the neighbors' house. She was gone when they got there."

"I'm sorry that happened to you, but what does that have to do with us?"

"Let me, OK Paul? We ran a profile on his attacker and got a recent hit from a small West Coast town. Some people reported hearing a single gunshot in an apartment building out there. The local police found a man named Bud O'Brien dead from a single GSW, 9MM. He turned out to be an FBE agent, assigned to escort another agent who had been sequestered after a duty related shooting. You guessed it, Annamaria Albarran. He'd been shot in her apartment, and she was gone without a trace. The report filed by the crime scene people out there describes a situation similar to what happened to Paul here. Now for the spooky part. It happened again yesterday morning, something similar at least, up north of here below Summerville. A young woman of the same description stole a boat at gunpoint while partially clothed, saying she was 'commandeering' it to 'get Eldon'. She took it south, and the Coast Guard found it half an hour later on a tip from the Admiral here."

"What the hell?"

"It's true Gary. Lucky saw it too. It was sinking when we spotted it, not a quarter mile behind Secant. The coast guard says it was scuttled. Holes chopped in the bottom with a hatchet."

"You think that nut job is on Secant with my daughter, Mrs. Carver and Dale & Greg Lucans, don't you?"

"It looks that way. I'm sorry, Mr. Loch."

"But I'll bet you still won't help us directly, will you?"

"You know very well I can't violate my orders, sir. I'm a naval officer under direct orders from the President. All I can do is provide you transportation of a humanitarian nature. I can't engage another vessel under the same command, and I can't transport or supply weapons for you. I'm already stretching those orders to the breaking point."

"Why would he allow you to do all you have, but not let you take over? The Marshals are in the same position. Ordinarily the government takes control of situations like this and makes civilians like us stand aside."

"I feel he's conflicted. He sympathizes with you, but he desperately needs the cash the FBE brings in. I hate to say it, but I'm afraid he wants you made comfortable until Morris kills you."

"You're a great judge of character, Admiral Sanders. I've been told I'm pretty good at it too. I can think of someone else who's conflicted."

"You're quite right, of course. Look, Gary, If you have any ideas I'm all ears. Just don't expect me to knowingly violate my orders."

The frustration of it was painful. Gary knew that if the helicopter's firepower were brought to bear on M/V Secant, Morris would not put up a fight. The Admiral wouldn't be willing to bring them the guns from Atropos either, and Gary wasn't sure he should even mention them. They were, after all, illegal in civilian hands. But the word 'knowingly' had given him an idea. "How much weight did you say your Skycrane can carry?"

THE RESTITUTION

CHAPTER FIFTEEN Flight

Finally at the wheel of his own boat again, Captain Dale Lucans tried without much success to plan the next day or two. Judith was coming down to join them for the rest of the run to the gulf. He'd been hoping she would, but there was one small problem. Small in places, at least.

Sheila Wells had possibly saved their lives when she herded them to the stern of Eldon's yacht and onto the inboard ski boat being towed there. They'd untied the powerful red and black boat from Secant's transom cleat and dropped its anchor. That had given him time to hot-wire the ignition and starter. By the time they headed back upstream toward Summerville the trawler was too far down river to hear them.

Summerville was where Judith had originally planned to meet them, but Dale needed to get Sheila off his boat first. Cop or not, she was a very attractive woman, and a little too old to pass off as being of interest to Greg. A little too sophisticated. She wore an expensive looking white cowl-neck sweater over a string bikini that could probably be laundered in a cereal bowl. Whenever she bent over you saw three things: the first was her agency-issue 9mm in its shoulder holster. The others had been provided by nature, and were barely contained by the bikini top. Judith would never understand. He'd told his wife they had a female federal officer aboard who needed to go to Holden, he just didn't want Judith to see her. He couldn't even ask Sheila to change clothes. She was wearing what she escaped in. The girl wanted to be taken to her headquarters on the island. That would do it. He and Greg would just motor the five miles back upstream to the city of Holden and pick Judith up at the public marina.

Greg sat on the bow pulpit with his lower legs dangling over the water. His dad and the pretty agent from the yacht obviously thought it was over. Maybe he should too. The Marshals Service had taken over. Eldon Morris should be under arrest along with that musclehead bodyguard. Alison and the other girl had no doubt been rescued. Alison's dad might be in a little trouble with the law, but John would be heading back upstream and watching for him. School would be re-opening in another week or so. What was this, anyway? Sunday? That was why he wanted the bow watch, to catch a ride back to school with John. So why was he so worried about Alison Maye Loch? He could catch up with her later, after things settled down, right? Well, no, not exactly. He missed Alison Loch. He wanted to see her *now*.

With the Captain steering the ship and his son idly watching the river ahead, Sheila Wells was doing the only thing the FBE had ever trained her for. Observing her surroundings. All of her surroundings, including the sky. "Captain Lucans – what do you make of this?"

"I don't know, agent Wells. Some kind of airplane I guess."

"But how can it stay in exactly the same spot like that? It's getting bigger!"

Dale watched more carefully. "You're right, Sheila. Whatever it is, it's heading straight toward us and coming downhill. If it doesn't change course it could hit us."

"Hit us? An airplane?"

"Or a helicopter or something. Don't take your eyes off it. If it gets close enough to identify let me know, especially if it's something your agency uses."

"Dale! It's turning!"

The dull black helicopter circled them once and came alongside, hovering just above the water. Its fuselage aft of the doors said 'Marines' in large, dull gray letters along with some numbers and the word 'experimental' in smaller print. The man at the controls held up his hand with all five fingers splayed, then closed his fist and opened two fingers, like a victory sign. Capt. Lucans selected channel seven on his VHF. "Marine aircraft, this is the sailing vessel Atropos. Ah, can we help you?"

The familiar voice of Gary Loch came back. "I was hoping you'd say that."

There were lots of preparations to be made and everything needed to be done as much as possible out of the public eye. Andy Boone, the Marshals Service pilot who had been embedded in the FBE under the name Anatoly volunteered to come back with the Russian Hind 24, but they decided it wasn't up to what they had in mind. Not enough external load capacity. Only a Skycrane would do. Still, Andy and his Hind served as a first-class people mover.

The real work fell mostly to Dale, Greg, Gary and Dennis Davis. Right here, halfway between Summerville and Holden was as good a place as any. With Atropos securely anchored facing the current, they set about lowering the temporary short mast and installing – stepping – the real one, all 62 feet of it. The bottom ten feet would extend down into the keel. Ordinarily it would need to be put up in sections using a gin pole with one of them dangling from a rope in a bosun's chair. The Hind made lifting it vertical and lowering it in place an easy ten minute job. Most of the standing rigging was already attached, so the adjustments were almost complete within a couple hours. Dale took Gary aft and pulled a cap off a fitting in the deck behind of the steering wheel. "I'd been planning to do this later, after shaking down the rest. We might be able to use the extra speed, and we'll have enough crew for it."

"Both masts? We'll be a real schooner, like a pirate ship! Arrgh!"

"Not exactly. Technically, we'll be a Marconi rigged yawl. A schooner has the shorter mast in front. If the short one were in back but ahead of the rudderpost she'd be a ketch. I wanted to do it that way, but the mizzen would interfere with the mainmast backstays. Give me a hand, Gary. We won't need the helicopter for this. We just drop in a silver coin for luck and stand up the short mast. That makes it a mizzen. Its mainsail becomes a spanker or jigger. Cool, huh?"

"Whatcha gonna do with the little jib you had up before?"

"I was going to store it. Got a better idea?"

"Would it do any good to put it up between the main mast and the staysail – that's what you called the front jib, isn't it?"

"You know – it just might. It might be tough to handle though, and we sure wouldn't want it tangled up with the stays if we had to maneuver in a fight. Let's try it another day."

Jason Sanders had not made the rank of Admiral by blindly following the rules. His superiors had always valued his ability to think outside the usual boundaries and get others to follow his lead. No one ever doubted his loyalty.

He knew he was overstepping this time. He was stretching a direct presidential order to the point where it was only held together by the weakest of semantic technicalities. He'd be tried for this. An Admiral facing a Captain's Mast. He wouldn't be imprisoned or discharged dishonorably because his action would be seen favorably by the public, but his career was over. President Trayson would see to that. He'd be very, very lucky if he received a Lieutenant Commander's pension.

Alone this time in the experimental HX-34 attack helicopter, he was leading the far slower HE-64E Skycrane by almost an hour when he arrived back at the work site. It was early evening in mid October and the daylight was beginning to fade. A few lights had been turned on.

The sight brought a lump to Sanders' throat. He'd been worrying about his pension, worrying if he were doing the right thing. Doubting himself. The sailing vessel Atropos had been transformed. What just a few hours ago had been an unfinished little white boat with a tiny comical sail had become a man-'o-war. Centuries ago, the people, the oppressed public, had built sturdy little ships like this and used them to throw off the chains of a government bent on fleecing them of what they'd worked so hard for. This was like a trip through time. It was the eighteenth century again. These people, ordinary, untrained civilians, were going to take this sleek little fiberglass warship up against the lead element of a government gone wrong, or at least a part of one. Pride filled Admiral Jason Sanders. He was proud to know these people. Proud to be helping them, though in such a small way. They weren't just trying to get a daughter back from a madman; they were taking back their way of life – and making history.

To hell with communications procedure. "Gary – you still on onetwentytwo nine?"

"Yep. Glad to see you, sir."

"Is the south end of the island you're tied up to clear enough for me"

"Yes, nothing on or over it. We've been saving it for you."

Lowreyville's intelligence section had generated some satellite and overflight imagery for them. Secant could be seen about 50 miles above the mouth of the delta. A close-up caught the double barrel machine cannon. They'd identified it as a relic from World War Two. Intended for patrol boats protecting homefront harbors, it used relatively short-range 50mm ammunition with explosive projectiles that traveled at low speeds, about 350 feet per second. Dennis recognized the characteristics immediately. "It's a grenade launcher, not a gun!"

"Right again, Mr. Davis. The ammunition is quite a bit like what they used in the Vietnam era M-79 but bigger, not interchangeable with it. There's more. One of them was taken to Holden Island back when it was an ordnance test facility to run trials on an improved round that detonated itself 500 yards from the muzzle if it didn't hit anything. It was supposed to make it safer to use 'in town', as it were. The records show that the weapon and 100 rounds of the test ammo were delivered to the island and disappeared there. 90 rounds were used in testing. Nine groups of ten rounds each. Morris must have found it with the ten unfired shells. How many did you say he used to sink your fishing boat?"

Gary looked at Dennis and Chuck Carver. "I saw at least two or three hit the water before we blew up, but I wasn't counting."

"If we'd been hit on the nose like that with an M-79, We'd all be toast. Old, weak charges?"

"Right yet again, Mr. Davis." The Admiral was beginning to like the slightly obnoxious walking Vietnam encyclopedia again.

They'd decided that four men would take Atropos out to engage Secant. Captain Lucans was master of the vessel. His son Greg had a personal interest in the rescue, Gary's daughter Alison. Dennis Davis had been involved from the start and Gary's involvement was obvious. The number four wasn't arbitrary. It would take exactly four to properly handle the sailboat. Any more would slow her down. Lucky and Andrea were still with John Walgren on Rat Racer, shadowing the trawler. Chief Adamson and the seemingly reformed Paul DuPont were with them as well. Sheila Wells wanted to be taken back to Summerville so she could refuel the ski boat and take it back to Holden's Island. Sanders didn't want to risk having her leak what she knew to Morris or any of his faithful in the FBE. Claiming short fuel for his helicopter, he insisted on taking her all the way back up to NAS Lowreyville, and the prospect didn't upset her at all. Everyone else would ride down with Andy Boone in the old Russian Hind 24. Everyone but Captain Lucans, who tingled with excitement. He'd seen every situation imaginable in forty years of sailing. He'd been around both horns, through the Red Sea and the Panama Canal, circumnavigated the world twice, been boarded by pirates and lived through a sinking. But he had never done anything to compare with this. His wife would think he'd finally lost his mind. He'd called her earlier, asked her to get a motel in Holden. He'd see her in a day or two. Something important had come up.

Dale stood watching from the pulpit as the monster came into sight. Nothing but lights and noise, really. He could hear The Admiral on the beach with a small handheld radio.

"Weightlifter, this is Command, over."

"Command, go ahead."

"Do you have the island? You are 500 yards north of it, over."

"Roger, Command. Island in sight. I see a white masthead light just beyond it. That the object, sir?"

"Pass left of the island and come around to heading three five zero. Nose to the land. Descend to four hundred feet. Kill your anticollision lights below five hundred. Liftreel lights --- Now. Enter HOGE directly above the masthead light."

"Hover Out of Ground Effect established, transferring directional to liftreel operator."

Standing on the deck in the hurricane gale coming from the double row of blinding lights directly above him, Dale Lucans saw two thin wire ropes dropping. One came almost perfectly to his hand. It was oily. As he'd been shown, he twisted the big eye splice over itself and settled it around the lifting bitt just forward of the newly stepped mizzenmast, bringing the loops up behind the crossbar so it couldn't come loose. That would become very important. Then he ran forward and made the bow lifting line fast the same way. He felt a jolt as the reel operator took up the slack, and then the gale became something way beyond his experience. For just a moment he regretted doing it as his deck pitched down in front and the island seemed to come at him. Then the wind calmed a little and the tiny island slid smoothly under his keel. He could see Jason and the girl still on the beach. The woman was waving to him, the naval officer saluting.

Now this was new. The forward motion was unexpected. He realized his anticipation had been for the part where he and almost nine tons of sailboat were lifted out of the water and taken high above it. He wasn't prepared for the feeling of flight. The blast of wind from above gradually became a gale over the bows.

Sand that had been stray footprints pelted him, and bits of paper blew out of hiding places. A bobber flew past his head and was gone. The radio Jason had clipped to his jacket spoke. "Are you with me sir?"

Dale fumbled for the push to talk button. "Yeah, I guess." He had to cup his hand in front of his mouth in order to talk.

"How's your ride? Any swaying fore and aft?"

"Not really, but she seems to be fishtailing a little. How fast are we going?"

"About one hundred miles per hour, sir. We can't go much faster without risking a pitch oscillation – swaying forward and backward. That would be very bad. We can live with a little side to side motion, it's easy for the pilot to damp out. The fishtailing is only a problem from a comfort standpoint. You might want to try trimming it out with your rudder."

Dale had thought of that himself but didn't act on it for fear of looking ridiculous. Hey – the lift reel operator suggested it! He'd been standing in the companionway. He could reach the wheel with one hand for balance and get behind it without making a fool of himself. He was already connected to the lifeline and he was wearing the parachute Jason had provided. It worked! The rudder was quite large, easily the size of one on a medium sized airplane, and he was going fast enough to make it effective in air.

"Careful sir. Not too much of that. You're pulling us off course."

As if in a dream, Dale Lucans flew his sailboat. He could see the river below twisting and turning. He was flying straight to the gulf. Over towns and cities, farms and forests. This was the essence of childhood fantasy. A sailing ship in flight. Half a mile high at a hundred miles an hour, dripping water on the world. He pinched himself by looking up. The bright lights were off now, only the anticollision lights were on. He watched the huge rotor hub for a moment, realizing he could follow the motion of each of the six blade roots individually in the Moonlight. How was that possible? He remembered a little bit of aeronautical engineering from freshman science. A propeller cannot turn so fast that the blade tips become supersonic without losing its effectiveness. Helicopter rotors were probably the same, and these were so long that it wouldn't take very many RPM to do it.

"Should I have my nav lights on?"

"Not unless you want to send a lot of nice folks to their eye doctors. Don't worry about colliding with an airplane or anything.

The rest of your team has your eight – ah, 'scuse me, two points abaft your port beam."

Dale looked carefully and there they were, bathed in red cabin light, watching him through the windows of the Hind 24. Standing at the helm, braced against the wind. Flying his sailboat in a tight formation with two giant helicopters.

THE RESTITUTION

CHAPTER SIXTEEN Engagement

The air was a lot warmer out in the gulf, but the men were soaking wet. The regulations say no one rides an external load, but transporting Atropos empty would have meant launching her into a twenty-knot wind and four-foot seas with no helmsman. Getting the rest of the crew aboard had been tough enough even with Dale holding her steady under diesel power. The crew transfer had taken half an hour.

The Captain seated them around his chart table. Gary noticed the folding segment that concealed a sewing machine. "Gentlemen – Secant will be arriving in this general vicinity in about three hours. Do any of you have any knowledge of naval combat?" Gary and Dennis said no. Greg didn't bother. "OK, let's not get bogged down. Secant just entered open water. They have no idea we're here already, right on the line to St. Somme' where the Admiral's intelligence people say Morris owns property. He won't recognize us at first because we have too many masts. Even that bozo can count to two, but our advantage of surprise won't last long. He also won't expect us to be able to outrun him, but we will as long as we don't make one basic mistake."

"The heading from the river mouth to Balfour harbor is south. Our 20 knot wind is from the west." Lucans took a black ink marker and drew a big circle on his perfect white table top, then drew crosshair lines through it, labeling the extensions N, S, E, & W, then he drew in a boat shape at the center, pointed south. "Gentlemen, this is very important." With a flourish, he added a big blue arrow across it from west to East and scrawled the word 'wind'. "We must never allow ourselves to get downwind of him. If Morris has an ounce of brains he'd turn west and leave us in his wake. We can outrun him easily with a 20-knot crosswind, we can almost match him using both motor and sail running downwind, but upwind we're screwed. He'll naturally want to hold his southern heading, but if we push him, well, he has basic provisions for several months and enough fuel to get halfway around the world. Now, any questions before we consider our tactics?"

Well read as he was, Dennis was clueless about sailing. "It's obvious we can't sail upwind, but how come we go fastest in a crosswind?"

"Think of it this way. Our best move going downwind is to extend the sails straight out to the sides so the wind just pushes us along, 'wing and wing' as they call it. Our speed is the wind speed less what we lose in water friction resistance, which is considerable. That's why we need engine power as well to match Secant's 16 knots. Sailing with a crosswind is better because we can set the sails almost across the wind line so they trap the air and force it off astern. It sort of squirts us forward. You'll see what I mean when we hoist sail for some practice."

"I have a question, Dale."

"Let's hear it Gary."

"Why are you doing this for me? I mean, you have nothing to gain. You got Greg back on your own, and now both of you are at risk again. Why?"

"Why did you come back to get us?"

"We thought they were holding you along with Rhonda Carver. We knew they'd reach open water, so we needed your boat"

"There's your answer, Gary. You'd do the same for us. Besides, those clowns are trashing my country too."

Gary was amazed by the power. The clumsy, overweight motorboat feeling was gone. The three sails were *huge*, especially the front two. The whole boat seemed alive to him, alive and willful. Dale was in his element now as well, controlling it. Gary was aware the man had intended to sail alone, and it humbled him. The three enormous white triangles above bulged and strained against their rigging. The raw power something he could feel under his feet. The deck was pitched over crazily, and the madman at the wheel was still barking for them to haul in more sheet. "Closer on the wind!" The two stainless steel electric winches were in almost constant use.

"Coming downwind, Mister Davis!" Dale snapped into a hard left turn. The heel disappeared for a second as the main boom swung across the deck, missing Dennis by a foot or less, Both booms jolted to a controlled stop as Atropos pitched over the other way. Gary had been on the 'up' side, ten feet above the water surface. Now he was leeward, and almost level with it. "How fast, Captain?"

"Twenty four knots. Eight over Secant's best. Coming about again, people. Then we'll try another upwind turn."

"Let's celebrate, my friend. A nice 12 year-old Scotch, perhaps?"

Rocky took the little pint bottle, downed about a third of it without any noticeable effect and handed it back to his boss.

"You have another unpleasant task tonight, but for now – we can relax." Eldon Morris took a shot from the bottle. Yesterday's events had unnerved him. He'd sent Rocky out to take lives before, but he'd never watched it done. One of the dead had been Rhonda's friend, the other helmsman. Someone he'd trusted. Eldon genuinely hoped she didn't know. She'd be gone herself very soon. No point in adding to her misery. The Scotch would soothe him.

Eldon had changed his mind about keeping Butch the sharpshooter alive and taking him along to St. Somme'. One cold-blooded killer would be quite enough. When the time came to call customs at Balfour Harbor he intended to report only two people aboard, Rocky and himself. He tried to count the ones who had to die tonight: Butch the bloodthirsty guard, Rhonda Carver, Monique, and nine prisoners. Rocky had prepared a proper manifest of the prisoners. Eldon didn't recognize some of the names; they'd been brought in too recently. One of the escapees names eluded him too: Diane something.

Eldon didn't know it yet but Rocky was going to make a pitch for keeping Monique alive, at least for a while. He'd been entertaining himself with her for two days and was becoming fond of her. Eldon thought she was in the brig with the prisoners.

Rhonda presented a special problem. He needed her to operate the ship. If Rocky did her with the others he'd have to take over. Rocky's helmsman skills were very limited. If she was spared, but saw or heard what was happening, she might do something foolish and the bomb would wreck his wheelhouse. Rocky would just have to disarm it and watch her himself.

But, no! If Rocky were guarding Rhonda, who would dispose of the prisoners and traitors? Problems, problems, problems. If he waited until just before making landfall in St. Somme' Rocky would have to put a dozen weighted bodies overboard in broad daylight. Maybe he needed Butch after all. Eldon praised himself for always thinking ahead.

"Mister Morris, Y'all wanta have a look here?"

"What do you see, Butch?"

"A pirate ship or sumpthin'. It's got one 'o them black flags with a skull head on it. A couple of 'em got guns."

"Let me see that." Rocky took the man's hunting rifle. He'd been using the big nine-power variable scope sight as a 'lookin' glass'. Sure enough, the yawl's mainmast flew the skull and crossbones at its peak. A man on the bow held a military rifle of some sort.

"Sailing vessel approaching trawler Secant, identify!" There was no response.

"Sailboat approaching Secant, identify yourself and say your intentions. You are armed and flying inappropriate colors!" Nothing.

The vessel wasn't really behaving in a threatening way. Eldon had noticed it earlier, running downwind. He'd dismissed her as a coastal cruiser staying just out of sight of land to make it seem more like open water. He estimated their courses would intersect a couple miles ahead and expected Rhonda to slow down to let them pass safely. The sailboat did have the right of way. Pirate flags were commonly sold as novelties. The man with the rifle could just be fishing. They might even have made out the outline of Eldon's own deck cannon and took *him* for a pirate.

The sailboat made a turn to the south, parallel to their own course, and a chill ran down Eldon's spine. The man with the gun was gone now, and the craft was pulling ahead. He relaxed a little, but then the boat slowed, matching their speed maybe a thousand yards out, broad on their starboard beam. Directly alongside. Eldon Morris began to worry again. Boats in the open ocean don't just turn 90 degrees and pace another vessel for no reason. "Rocky, uncover the deck gun. You never can tell."

"Good. He's starting to spook. Next he'll threaten us. I'm closing on him a little. About 750 yards should do it. Get ready to release that line, Gary! And let's put Lowreyville's intelligence section on our Christmas list!"

The line Gary Loch held was part of the rigging for the small sail at the back. It held the lower back corner of the rear sail out to the end of its boom, where it ran through a pulley, then forward along the foot of the sail to the small 'mizzen' mast. Even though it wrapped around the lifting bitt, the large post-and-crossarm cleat the helicopter had made such spectacular use of, forming a figure eight across it, Gary needed strength to hold it against the wind. He sat with his feet braced.

"Vessel approaching trawler Secant! Pull away or we will take defensive measures!" Dale had put the VHF audio on the deck speakers.

"Time to make it happen. Ready, gentlemen."

"Trawler Secant, Trawler Secant. Prepare to be boarded. You will not be harmed if you do as we say. Heave to and muster your crew on deck away from your gun. The helmsman may remain in her wheelhouse. Comply or be destroyed!"

A puff of smoke appeared at Secant's gun. "Easy, Gary. It's probably over the bow. Sure enough, the shell burst between the boats and well ahead of both of them.

Dale spun the wheel to bring the bow around to close the distance as his son called out. "One! 650 yards, Dad!" Greg was good at judging distance.

Another puff of smoke and bang from Secant's gun. Greg could see Rocky sitting at the gun through John's telescope.

Gary forced himself to keep his eyes open. He'd faced that deck gun before with disastrous results. The shell exploded directly between the ships and about a football field out. He heard a few small fragments hit the boat as he released what Dale had called the 'spanker clew outhaul halyard'. The rope zipped off its tackle as the proud sail collapsed to flutter from the mast like a flag. Gary heard cheering from the trawler's deck. They thought they'd made a damaging hit and crippled their antagonist. Belatedly, Greg yelled "two".

Dale took aim with his Dragunov and shattered the window of what had been Chuck and Rhonda's cabin. The 7.62 x 54R bullet went through the room and blew out the window on the other side. "That'll piss em off."

Smoke-smoke-smoke – Boom-boom-boom. Three more angry little black clouds exploded between themselves and Rocky's deck gun. He'd bought it; convinced he was hitting them. He had no idea the projectiles were made to self-distruct at 500 yards range. Greg sounded off. "Three - four - five! Only one or two left!"

Dale took careful aim again over his cockpit coaming. He had no desire to kill anyone. The idea was to force Rocky to waste the last of his grenade rounds. He followed the motion of the boat under him, aware the other vessel was moving also. CRACK! The sound was unmistakable, the whipcrack of a high-speed bullet passing near his head.

"Down! Sniper!" Greg had seen the third man on deck wrap a turn of sling around his forearm and raise his gun. "He's almost halfway back, dad. Almost to the window you shot out."

Dale swept the Russian semiautomatic back along Secant's rail. There he was. His hunting rifle was held upward as the pudgy, oily looking Eldon Morris pointed out something to him. The rifle came on line again, directly at him.

This shot was Dale's. Eldon's hand was still on the gaunt looking man's shoulder as Dale's heavy bullet smashed through his head after shattering all the lenses in his scope sight and his right eye. Eldon ran forward, shaking his hands in front of himself as if they were on fire, turned short and disappeared down the salon steps. "He went below, dad. Is he after the prisoners?"

"I don't think so."

"We're getting close to 500 yards." They saw and heard another shot from the deck gun. The shell detonated about fifteen feet above the water maybe twenty feet out. Grenade fragments pelted the side and deck. One of them tore a shallow channel across Gary's right leg just above the knee, ugly but superficial. No one else was hit. Greg at the telescope saw Rocky stand up and throw open the Ammo box that fed the gun. The man slammed it shut and ran for the wheelhouse.

"Was that what I think it was, Greg?"

"I think he's out all right, But what's he up to now?"

Rocky opened the door with a key and immediately flew back across the deck in a cloud of white smoke or – fire extinguisher powder! Rhonda didn't stop there. A moment later she landed the red canister across his face like a baseball bat. Rocky went down and stayed. Greg saw her bend down and take two pistols from his belt.

"Rhonda of Secant – Do you read Dale of Atropos? Over."

"Atropos, Roger. You're a welcome sight. I think the cannon's empty."

"Affirmative, Rhonda. Be careful, Eldon just went below."

"I'm going after him. If you're boarding you can back me up. If there's nothing else I'm charging him with kidnapping me."

"That's good, but you have at least nine more victims, probably locked in what used to be a ladies room. Good luck. We'll be aboard in about five."

The wheelhouse fire bottle weighed a good fifteen pounds. The force of the impact had changed the whole shape of Rocky's face. He was bleeding from his nose, mouth and both ears. His slimeball of a boss would be next. She'd seen Rocky blow the tiny boat carrying her husband out of the water on Eldon's orders. She'd seen him complimenting the rodent-like guard for the way he'd picked off the survivors. This was personal. Most people in Rhonda Carver's position would feel their sense of purpose had died with the one they loved. Rhonda did not. Her new purpose was to squash Eldon Morris like the parasitic insect he was.

The guard with the hunting rifle lay sprawled on the deck halfway back along the deck. Both his legs were out over the water, one on each side of a stanchion. A blob of blood and tissue had slid down the white superstructure behind where he'd been sitting, and Eldon had stepped in it. The bloody left footprints lead away from the body and down the salon steps. The voice on the radio had said he'd gone below. Growing fainter with each step, the footprints gave out in the carpeted lower salon, heading aft toward the centerline passage.

There was no sign of him here. She heard the prisoners in the 'brig'. They were banging on the door, begging to be let out. They'd be safer inside, and wouldn't get in the way.

Rhonda banged on the outside of the brig door. "I'm special agent Rhonda Carver of the Federal Marshals Service. I don't have the key yet, but you'll be safe in there for a little while longer. More help is on the way!"

She knew Eldon carried a gun, but it was very small, a .22 or .25 'vest pocket' pistol. No match for her .40 or Rocky's forty-five. She checked both guns before continuing. Her forty was as she normally carried it. The 12 round magazine was full and the chamber was loaded. She wished she had her two spare magazines and considered going back to search Rocky for them. Rocky's .45 was an old single action government model semiauto. Rhonda didn't care for guns meant to be carried 'cocked and locked', with their hammer back and the safety on. This time she'd make an exception. She needed the security of a second weapon and more shots. With her own pistol in her waistband, she pinched back it's slide enough to see the shiny brass chambered cartridge, then buttoned out the magazine to check it as well. The two bottom witness holes in the seven round mag were empty. Had he fired it? She hadn't heard any pistol shots. Maybe he carried it short loaded to keep the spring from taking a set. Maybe six was his lucky number or something.

With the prisoners quiet and her ears adapting to the silence, Rhonda noticed a new sound. A woman was trying to get her attention with her mouth either taped or being held shut. Had Eldon separated one of his captives from the others for use as a human shield? The sound came from the forward stateroom to port, Rocky's room. Rhonda kicked in the light door, a pistol in each hand.

"Is he in here?"

Monique, tied to the bed by her wrists and ankles, shook her head side to side. Her body had been covered with a light sheet. Rhonda peeled the tape back and started untying her. "Rocky do this?"

"Yeah. The pig has no idea how to treat a lady". Monique would be OK. "I think I heard him in the men's room across from the brig. I thought he was coming back again."

"That would be Eldon. Rocky won't be doing much at all. I stove in his face with a fire extinguisher a minute ago. You might have heard the thud when his ugly ass hit the deck. I've gotta get Eldon now. You up to helping me?"

"Yeah, sure. Rocky took my gun though. I don't know where he put it." Monique was wrapping herself in the sheet toga fashion.

"You might want to dress better. My help are all men."

"Just as soon as I can, Agent Carver."

"OK. Here, take my gun. I have Rocky's. Mine's just like yours, right? Department issue?"

With the other woman behind her, Rhonda bashed the door open. Eldon Morris sat on the toilet, frantically washing bits of Butch's head off his hands and face in the sink basin in front of him. He had wet his pants. How could she stomp him now? The man was pathetic, and besides, a witness was present. "Eldon Stewart Morris, You are under arrest." The rights statement could wait until they returned to territorial waters.

Monique turned and leveled her pistol as a man came down the salon stairs carrying a rifle that looked something like an AK-47, only bigger. "Don't shoot him! He's with the good guys."

From the first contact it had taken less than thirty minutes to gain control of the much larger M/V Secant and her Captain. Rocky Korozini succumbed to his fractured skull as Dennis began to administer first aid. Gary released the nine prisoners with a key from Rocky's pocket. The tiny 'brig' smelled terrible. Using it to confine Eldon Morris was Monique's idea. The horrified little creep squealed like a pig when he was locked inside with that reeking, overflowing head.

The open deck was like Heaven for the prisoners; particularly the ones who had been confined the longest. Three of them had to be carried out.

Now Gary Loch understood why Andrea Sturm had been so ineffective immediately after the rescue of her daughter on Saturday. Now it was his turn to be overwhelmed with relief. At least he wouldn't be expected to drive either of the boats back to land. All that mattered was that he had his little girl back.

"Oh, I am so sorry, daddy. It's all because of those guns. It wasn't John and Greg's fault, honestly! That awful Ross guy started it. Greg just –"

"You still think this all happened because of that party in Fort Miller, don't you?"

"Yes – didn't it?"

"It's a very long story. I think there's someone here you'll want to see, Al." He caught Dale Lucans' eye. Can you send your son over, Captain?"

Greg Lucans had been rehearsing what he'd say to her. She had no idea he was here. No reason to think he even remembered her.

"We wouldn't have been able to do it without Greg and his dad. Your friend John Walgren is with us too, on the mainland with his own boat." He saw his daughter's eyes go narrow "OK, on the *river* on the mainland."

Alison Loch was overcome. Greg had come through again, this time with her dad and some much bigger guns. She slowly stood to go to him, but his face turned away at the last moment and he pointed out across the water. "What the Hell is that?"

"What the Hell was that?" As soon as he asked, he knew. Among all the hundreds of details over the past few days, he'd forgotten one. A minor but important detail. One that now jeopardized the entire mission. The barely audible 'hiss-boom' sound was a yellow smoke flare being launched to warn any ships in the area that a submarine was surfacing among them. In peacetime, it's a matter of normal procedure. Commander Sam Leary had forgotten. Now his prey had been warned. He made a snap decision to ignore it. The vessels were in perfect position and if the satellite data was correct he had only a few minutes before Jason Sanders arrived.

Using a torpedo would have been so simple. He could have remained submerged, and told the crew it was a practice launch, a secret mission, an accident, anything. The problem was, even the least expensive torpedo cost twice as much as his house. Everyone wants an accounting when a torpedo is launched. Shells for the forward deck gun were a dime a dozen by military standards, but he had to do it himself.

Before clearing the pens, Captain Leary had ordered all six forward deck cameras removed for inspection. The crew would be blind to what he did. He'd put it up to individual training if anyone asked. Only the President and himself needed to know.

His boat, the Herbert N Willston, was one of the very few remaining Nuclear Attack Submarines. Its location was nearly always a secret. Only a handful of his staff officers knew their position at any given time. His orders were unknown to even his second in command. His task was simple: sink the FBE utility vessel Secant and the private sailing vessel Atropos in international waters. There must be no survivors, no distress messages, no witnesses and no flotsam. Speed is essential. Finding and destroying them together was ideal.

"Oh Lord no. It can't be. CAST OFF ATROPOS! DO IT NOW! GET THE BOATS AS FAR APART AS POSSIBLE!"

"What's the matter, Dale?"

"That's a submarine surfacing flare! A sub is coming up RIGHT HERE! We just got everything we need to destroy their second largest money-grubbing operation. What do you suppose they intend to do, congratulate us?"

"We don't know –"

" And we don't want to find out. RHONDA! Get that thing moving! Try to get on the other side of it."

Gary was still a little addled. "Other side of what?"

"OF THAT!" An enormous black steel whale shape burst up a couple hundred yards east of where the two boats were starting to separate. A lone man emerged from a hatch on the thing's sail and started down a short ladder toward a four-barrel deck gun forward.

Gary Loch suddenly became aware of what was happening. He'd handed off the Dragunov to Dennis, who was in the wheelhouse with Rhonda Carver. The sniper's .30-06 stood against the rail a few feet away. He dove for it and checked it's five round magazine. Three remained. The scope was useless but he could see the post and notch iron sights under it. He lined up on the man and waited.

The gunner reached the weapon controls. This was nothing like the hand cranked antique Rocky had used. The thing spun around so fast Gary was amazed the man wasn't thrown off. As he came around the muzzles lowered. They obviously didn't want to talk. His intent must be to either take out the trawler's engines or to tear up the waterline and sink them. A shield of curved steel protected the gunner from return small-arms fire. Even his feet rested up behind it. Gary had no shot, and Secant was about to be blasted out from under him. A shot rang out from Atropos, then two more. Dale and his Dragunov. The man jumped down to take cover behind the mount. His hand shot for the firing nib.

A ragged roar followed. In the space of little more than a second, twenty or so 25mm high explosive anti-ship projectiles tore into Secant's wake. The trawler was no longer where it was when Commander Leary sighted on it. To compensate, he'd have to take the controls again.

Gary knew what the man would do. It was human nature. The gun spun again to come to bear on the sparkling white sailboat that had fired on him.

When Dale had fired, he'd aimed for the deck gun controls, not the gunner. Gary did not have that option. Lacking Dale's marksmanship and telescopic sight, He needed to aim where he had the largest target: The gunner's center of mass. He squeezed off the shot. The man turned and gave him what he saw as a dirty look, then fired his cannon.

This wasn't good. Dale Lucans had hit the gun's control box squarely, but it had no effect. Most of the box was an equalizing chamber that kept it from being crushed by sea pressure. The actual controller only filled the top inch or so of it. Instead of disabling the weapon he'd brought it down upon himself.

The awful roar came. Dale could hear and feel the hits, just below his feet. The boat moved sideways in the water on it's own, away from the gun. He could hear people below deck screaming. Vaguely, he could hear another similar gun being fired from behind. He turned his head instinctively, but saw nothing. After a second that seemed like hours the fusillade ended.

Gary tried to remember how many people had been aboard the sailboat. Monique Vincente had gone over to clean up after her ordeal with Rocky. A few of the prisoners had gone just to be away from the trawler. Dennis and Greg were still safely with him, but that wouldn't save them for long. "RHONDA! STAY AHEAD OF THAT GUN!" He raced for the wheelhouse as the big gun slowly turned.

What Dale Lucans had attempted, Gary had achieved by accident. His poorly aimed bullet had missed the gunner entirely but had entered the control box just below the top and destroyed the servo driver for the gun carriage. The gunner was reduced to hand cranking it now, and not as effectively as Rocky had managed.

Gary had a buzzing sound in his ears. Kinda like the one he'd get when he'd lose a bid for work at his shop, only louder. It kept growing until –

"Look! Jason's back!"

Rhonda had no knowledge of any Jason. The helicopter was the same color as the submarine. "Give me that. If you won't do it I will!

"He's the good guys, Rhonda. Just watch."

"You want the landing, Pam?"

"Landing? What landing?"

"I asked you if you were sure you wanted to do this. It's too late to back out now. We're going to land right on their missile deck, right in front of the gun."

"But he'll *shoot* us.'

"No he won't. He won't be able to."

Pam McCannis approached from behind the gun and swung around to face the submarine head on. "Set us down over the last one, Pam." The machine settled and Sanders reached over to shut down the hydrogen turbines. "If this works out, we'll be riding back almost to shore with them. If he won't be convinced we're all toast. Are you ready for this?"

"Yes sir, I am." She set the switch to transfer control of the Gatling guns to her helmet sensors. The horrid things would follow her every gaze. Jason Sanders opened the door and stepped out onto the closed hydraulic door over a 30 kiloton warhead, stepped down to the deck and walked calmly up to the cannon.

"Hello Sam."

"Good morning, Jason"

"You can still walk away from this you know."

"I have to do this, and I can't leave witnesses. You do understand that, don't you."

"I understand, but it doesn't have to be that way. Will you hear me out?"

Leary was still cranking, slowly bringing the gun to the trawler. "What's to hear? You can't stop me."

"I can, and if need be I will. Stop moving that weapon. You look like a fool."

"If I give the word, my people will open the doors under your airplane. It'll be thrown in the water like a toy. Then what are you going to do, shoot me with your sidearm?"

"Bullshit, Sam. Opening that door is part of the irrevocable launch sequence. If you do that, the bird will jam in the tube long enough to burn out the bottom of your pressure vessel with it's backblast. You, Pam, your whole crew and I'll be killed. You're here to silence everyone who knows about this FBE garbage, aren't you? Did you volunteer or did Trayson recruit you for it?"

"The President assigned me."

"Verbally, I imagine. He assigned me to help protect the hostages Eldon Morris was holding."

"I'm not aware of any hostages. Morris was escaping with billions in stolen securities."

"That's possible, but he was holding about a dozen prisoners illegally, for his own various reasons. Most of them were on that trawler, about to be murdered. The sailboat's part of a rescue effort. So am I."

186

"Why would Trayson be on both sides?"

"He was conflicted, but he's not anymore. He made his decision when he sent you out. He tried to recall me. Look, the man's a conservative. Maybe reactionary would be a better term. He despises Morris, the FBE and everything like them. He just needs the money because he can't eliminate the social spending programs. It was difficult for him, but the money won."

"So you're here contrary to a presidential order."

"True. I'm refusing an order I know to be wrong. You're following an order you know to be wrong. Do the Nuremberg trials come to mind?" Admiral Leary had no answer. It was time to close. "Look, Sam, you can't win this way. Secant can make circles around you all day; you'll never get on her. If you keep trying, you'll bring your twenty-five close enough to my helo for Pam to feel the need to wreck your day with her miniguns. I know why you didn't just torpedo them. It was the paperwork! Does your crew even know what you're up to? By the way, your H.E.A.S. ammunition probably won't be any more effective against Secant than it was on Atropos."

"You mentioned walking away from this. What do you have in mind?"

"All you have to do is be the first to see the error of what you're doing. Don't make us stop you. You won't regret it, Sam. This is gonna be headline news tonight. The President is finished. He can't lie to the people any longer. That has to be music to your ears, I'm well aware of your own politics. I'm saving the best for after this is over. What do you say, Sam? Is it over?"

There was a long pause. Samuel Leary sighed and started turning the elevation crank, raising the barrels high above the horizon. Well above Secant, well above the helicopter on his deck. "It's over. Have your people check the sailboat. What information were you holding back, Jason? Has Trayson already resigned?"

"Nope. I already have three of the FBE's illegal prisoners stashed safely back at Lowreyville, just begging to come forward. You couldn't have gotten them all, because they aren't all here. I was just giving you time, and enough information to end it yourself. I knew you would. Politics be damned, you're a fine officer. I want to see you get out of this with your honor and your command intact. It'll mean a lot when the public sees that it ended as soon as we came face to face as equals and compared mission profiles. If anyone has anything to answer for, it's me."

THE RESTITUTION

CHAPTER SEVENTEEN   The People

"A little further aft, if you please, gentlemen. Pay off about a foot of the forward springline and take it up astern." Secant's deck was too high for this. The bow of the surfaced Herbert N. Willston had been almost the perfect height. In consideration of the fact that he'd done the damage himself, Commander Leary had permitted it. He also ordered his ballast adjusted to fine-tune the match, provided a few tools, and men to handle the spring and breast lines. Dale would run the saw himself, then drill the flange holes using the sub's deck as a scaffold. The other side was finished already. A few of the men had the courage to tease the old man about using a nuclear submarine that cost 400 million as a bosun's chair for a 38-foot sailboat. He took it in stride.

Earlier, when Captain Lucans had gone below to survey the damage, he expected near total destruction. His little boat had taken a direct hit from a state-of-the-art antiship / antiaircraft weapon firing 'High Explosive Anti Ship' ammunition at point blank range. What he found set him laughing.

The gun's four reciprocating barrels, spaced ten inches apart on center both horizontally and vertically, were arranged to converge at fifteen hundred meters, about a mile downrange. Sensors calculated the target's size by machine vision and automatically swept it with devastating fire for maximum effect. The high explosive projectiles were made to detonate milliseconds after penetrating a substantial object, again for maximum effect. Atropos was not a substantial object. The twenty-eight rounds, each an inch in diameter and five inches long had passed through the fiberglass sailboat hull without noticing it. They'd self destructed in mid-air almost three miles away. No automatic sweep had occurred either, with Gary Loch's 30-06 bullet lodged in the servo driver.

Each side of his salon had four ragged cloverleaf shaped holes arranged in a ten-inch square just below the lower overhead level. His chart table was littered with fiberglass fragments. The five former prisoners, just getting up off the cabin sole where Dale had told them to lay, thought he'd lost his mind. Still chuckling, he went aft to a lazerette and removed one of two rectangular portholes, still in it's shipping carton. He scuffed some of the splinters off his table with the edge of the box and opened it, removing the sheet of installation instructions and a cutout template. Dale tried it on both sides. The template covered all the holes easily.

"What's so funny?"

He shifted the paper template forward a few inches. "I was planning to put them about here."

Rhonda Carver identified one of the abductees as Melinda Hoskin, another defense contractor executive. Her situation had never been recognized. The Marshals Service had been investigating her case as a defection. Rhonda and the two naval officers agreed it would be best if Jason Sanders took Ms. Hoskin to Lowreyville immediately. She was obviously not a traitor, but it would take time to remove the warrants against her. No good could come from exposing her to arrest.

No one wanted to stay on M/V Secant for the four-hour ride north to the public marina at Marebaeu, twenty miles above the river mouth, where the former prisoners were to be taken into temporary protective custody by the Federal Marshals. Rhonda had declined Admiral Leary's offer to provide a pilot. Secant was now government property under her care. She would do her duty despite her personal loss.

Dale was flattered that so many seemed to prefer his craft to a 67 foot luxury trawler, but he had concerns of his own; he'd never intended for Atropos to carry so many people. Twelve was the legal limit, and that many worried him, especially with the untested new windows. Sometimes called 'fish eyes', the leeward one would be under water at a good heel. "Listen up, all of you. Greg and I can take seven or eight of you, but not everybody. We'd be overloaded. Who wants to ride back with Mrs. Carver?"

"OK, I will, If my daughter is up to it. Dennis – How about it? We've stayed together this long."

"Oh, well – OK. I was hoping to get some more sailing time."

"Sorry dad. I want to stay with Alison if I can"

"Jeez, I should have seen that coming. That leaves room for you, Dennis. Still want to sail? I could use the help, and you're a good student."

With the 20-knot wind 2 points abaft her port beam, S/V Atropos was nothing but white sails on the horizon an hour later. Gary sat enjoying the view from Eldon's bridge chair. His daughter and Greg Lucans were below in the main salon. As close as the two seemed to be, he was beginning to worry about the passage aft and all the empty staterooms there.

"It's been quite a while. Maybe I'd better go check on our friend Morris. Will you take over for a few minutes? Just hold 355 degrees. Leave the throttles alone unless you see other traffic on a collision course from the right or ahead."

"Motor Vessel Secant, do you read Dale of Atropos, over"

"Secant roger. Go ahead Dale."

"We're within VHF range of Marebeau. Rat Racer has my wife aboard. John called her in Summerville and she drove on down. Tell Greg for me, huh?"

"Sure will. He's below. I still haven't been able to pry him away from my daughter."

"Ha Ha. One more thing. The marina's full of federal Marshals. They say we'll be under their protection until at least after President Trayson makes his address tonight. The TV news people think he may resign. John says he officially disbanded the FBE a couple hours ago and called it his last official act."

"Thanks, Dale. Let me know what you find out when you get there, will you? Secant is out and standing by."

Rhonda knocked on the brig door. "I'm going to let you out now, Mister Morris. I remind you, you're under arrest. We'll be docking in a couple hours and you'll be taken to jail for kidnapping, among other crimes. Oh, you no longer have a job. Your agency was disbanded." She opened the door, handcuffs in hand. The space was empty. Eldon Morris was gone.

Any of them could have let him out. With none of his cohorts remaining, Rhonda had left the key in the heavy lock outside the door. It was still there. She looked at Greg and Alison.

"We thought he was in there the whole time" Greg said. Alison shook her head in agreement. These two had no reason to let him out. Could the submarine crew have 'rescued' him somehow?

"I need to search the ship. He has to be here somewhere. You two come back up with me, you'll be safer with your dad."

"Safe? From that little creep?"

Rhonda opened the wheelhouse compartment she'd locked all the guns in except her own. They were all there. "Arm yourselves and lock the doors. I should be done clearing the boat in about ten minutes at most. If I'm not back in fifteen you'll have to assume something bad happened and act accordingly. If you leave here, disable any guns you aren't taking with you. If it were me, I'd chuck 'em overboard. Radio Atropos, tell Dale Lucans what happened and wish me luck."

"Where did you learn to rig a VHF antenna out of feedline wire like that Greg? It works perfectly."

"I helped John make his. It's made the same way, but it's strung up inside a piece of plastic pipe so it looks real and doesn't get wet in the rain."

"John Walgren also taught you about guns, didn't he?"

"Yeah, a little."

"Why don't you pick out one you like and familiarize yourself with it. Then you should call your dad."

The weapon Greg Lucans chose was Eldon's .25 ACP pocket automatic. It was smaller than the one John had been using to teach him but was by far the most similar. All it's stuff was in the same places. The safety selector, slide stop, magazine release – just as with the .380 John had taken from Ross Gofman, the hammer dropped harmlessly when you thumbed down the safety lever.

If Gary had known why Greg chose the .25 he'd have given him the .32 from his own pocket, the one Greg had already used after finding it in Gary's jacket pocket. "It's a little small, but there's not much chance you'll need it anyway. How about you, Honey?"

Alison tightened her fingers into little open-palm fists, closed her eyes and cringed visibly. This wasn't going to be easy.

Recapturing Eldon alone was the correct thing to do. As the only law enforcement agent aboard it was her responsibility. That was a good way to rationalize it. Rhonda was painfully aware that the need for it was probably her own fault. She'd been the last to leave the salon, and the area adjoining the improvised brig. Besides, none of the others had any reason to let him go. They all knew he was responsible for what had happened to them, but none except Monique Vincente knew him well enough to feel any need to either help or hurt him. Monique had been the first to join the sailboat. There was only one explanation: she had forgotten to lock the door. She clearly remembered closing him in, but could not remember actually turning the key. Had the others noticed? Were they just being nice about it? Rhonda walked aft down the centerline passage, around the engine room stairwell, to the stern companionway. Nothing. The accumulation of dust was still undisturbed on the knob for the door that never opened. Eldon always said the lock was jammed, and the aft stateroom on the port side wasn't needed anyway. Always suspicious, Rhonda and Chuck had checked it almost daily for months. This time it would be different. After checking the engine compartment, both bilges and the windlass catwalk she was going to force it open. Maybe Gary and Greg could help.

"I've got to use the restroom. Bad timing, huh?"

"Well, when you gotta go -. You better go with her, Greg. Use the private head in the captain's cabin. It's just below the helm. I'll be able to hear you."

"Daddy!"

"You know, if anything goes wrong I'll hear if you yell for me. We really don't know what that man is capable of." Alison turned slightly red. "And take that little baby gun along. See if you can familiarize Alison with it. When you come back I'll start showing you two how to keep this tub on course for the river mouth."

Greg held his comment. He was a passable helmsman himself. At least as competent as Gary Loch. He just wanted to stay near Alison.

Was it a noise? Maybe a vibration, more felt than heard. A sort of a thud, like something had fallen on the deck somewhere toward the back. It happened again, while Gary was listening for it. Definitely well back, not near where the kids were, directly below him. The kids would be back soon, they'd instinctively watch for collision hazards. He'd seen no other vessels since Atropos disappeared over the horizon, and the autopilot was on. He'd only be gone a minute.

He stayed on the main deck to port, past where Butch the sniper had died. No activity on the stern, Gary went down the companionway there, as they'd done when they first came aboard. Still nothing. He began to wonder why he hadn't seen Rhonda yet.

Coming quietly forward in the centerline passage, he noticed the engine compartment door was ajar, but the light wasn't on.

This was not like Rhonda Carver. Rhonda was meticulously careful. She wouldn't go stumbling around in the dark between two running diesel engines without any backup if she had any choice. Leaving doors open wasn't her style either. Gary searched for a light switch, hearing a sizzling sound, like someone was cooking on a griddle. The smell matched too, but the burgers were probably spoiled. He tried to remember seeing a galley. He'd only looked down here once, just for a moment.

What he found was a flashlight. The old military anglehead kind, in a clip on the wall. He turned it on and almost retched.

Rhonda lay face down between the engines. One of her Achilles tendons had been cut to the bone behind her ankle, probably by someone reaching through between the metal stair treads from behind. That would be why and how she ended up face down at the foot of the steps where the back of her head had been split open lengthwise. By what? A sword? An axe maybe? Whoever did this was definitely not Eldon Stewart Morris. Rhonda's body was on top of him. Most of him anyway. He was face up, in a manner that made it look like Rhonda had two heads, one of which was male, chubby, and on backwards. Smaller pieces of Eldon Morris were scattered all over the bright white compartment and the pale grey diesels. A ghastly blob evidently ejected from his ample middle was jammed between the starboard engine and it's hot exhaust manifold, sizzling. This was not the work of anyone human.

Disgust and grief snapped into raw terror as an indistinct shape loomed up from beyond the other engine, just outside of his flashlight beam. Startled and horrified, Gary's whole body jerked back instinctively. His left hand struck the ladder rail hard enough to make him loose his grip on the flashlight. It bounced off something and landed on the middle of Rhonda's back, still lit. He only saw it for an instant. Dark, smooth, somehow slippery looking. Slimy? His mind was playing tricks on him. Standing motionless, he was too stunned to pick up the flashlight, let alone move out of the backlit entranceway. The thing in the darkness would have a perfect view of his outline. As the knowledge of his disadvantaged position dragged itself out of his petrified brain, he sensed motion and something flying at him. He lurched sideways as an enormous meat cleaver flew past him and clattered off the railing. The only place for him to go was into the space aft of the engine to his right, the one not cooking part of Eldon Morris. The footing here was uneven. He reached out with his right hand to steady himself and remembered he was carrying a gun in it.

He had two guns, actually. The one he held so ineffectively one-handed was Rocky's stainless shotgun, loaded with six rounds of 12-gauge buckshot. His eyesight and sanity returning, Gary took a proper two hand grip and racked the first shell into it's chamber. The 'clack-chunk' sound drove his adversary to action. An arm appeared. Slim and smooth looking in the darkness, it unlatched the bulkhead door at the front of the compartment as a deafening gunshot and muzzle flash filled the space between them. Like a camera flash, the sudden light burned the image of carnage into his eyes. A cannibal's butchershop. The door slammed closed and Gary was alone again, surrounded by gore. He picked up the flashlight.

Now what? She had gone – She? Yes. The shape had been unmistakably female. Athletic and agile as a cat. She'd gone forward, onto the catwalk Greg and Dale had described to him. It led forward over the bilge to the mechanism for the cargo crane, an unused anchor windlass compartment and a trap door in the Captain's cabin sole. Alison! She and Greg Lucans had been there a couple minutes ago, using the head. Whoever the apparition was, he had only seconds to stop her.

Instinct demanded that he follow, but with the first glimmer of clarity since the encounter with this ghost had begun, he realized he had no chance of catching her. He'd never seen the catwalk. She evidently lived there. He'd be better off going the other way. Up the ladder, he bolted forward up the centerline passage, across the length of the main salon and simply jumped the three steps up to the mezzanine level captain's cabin entrance. He crashed through it in a dead run.

In light, the murderer had form and substance. She was covered in blood as if she'd been crawling around among the remains of her victims. Swimming in them. She was otherwise attractive. Maybe five foot ten, she had the shape of a lifeguard if not a beauty queen. Her teeth appeared perfect, as did her eyes, the only parts not blood smeared. Her hair was a little past shoulder length, spiking out at weird angles, caked with blood. The features were vaguely Indian looking, or maybe Hispanic. At first, Gary thought she was nude. She was wearing a two piece bathing suit, or possibly underwear. Hard to tell with all the blood. She was ranting and cackling like a lunatic in several languages. Like a lunatic? She clearly was truly a lunatic. Way beyond worldly help, she needed to be stopped, permanently. Gary started to bring his shotgun up.

The crazed woman was faster. She pivoted in an instant, taking her gun off Greg, who'd gotten himself between her and the bathroom door, and had it aimed squarely at Gary's head before he got the shotgun even half raised. In two long steps she had her pistol pressed tight against his forehead.

"I hope Hell agrees with you, Mister Morris."

"I'm not Mister Morris. You already took care of Mister Morris and saved us the trouble. Why did you kill the woman, Rhonda Carver? She didn't do anything to you. She's one of us. We came to rescue you! Don't you remember? We let all of you out of the brig and locked Mister Morris in there. You let him out, didn't you?"

"You are Morris. He is Morris." She spun the weapon back at Greg Lucans, and brought it back so fast Gary had no chance to react. "You are Morris. You'll die! Then Morris! MorrisMorris-Morris"

Inches in front of his face, Gary Loch saw the thumb of her right hand push up the gun's decocking safety lever.

The head door opened. Alison only intended to give the little .25 back to Greg. There was no time. Gary's little girl had the position. She could see the bloody gun's hammer starting to move back. She had to get close because she didn't know how to aim.

POP! The tiny pistol sounded like a toy. The blood-soaked woman's perfect eyes flashed with a split second of clarity. POP POP POP! The life drained out of her eyes leaving them dead again. She lowered the FBE issue pistol and collapsed on the floor at Gary's feet, face up. Alison just stood there. She pushed the thing into her dad's hands and started to cry.

"You saved my life. Probably Greg's too. I guess being locked up alone for all that time drove her over the edge. Let's just hope none of the other hostages are that bad off. She killed Rhonda just a minute ago. I was too late. She killed Eldon Morris too."

"This lady wasn't one of us, Daddy. She's the crazy policewoman who took me away! She shot another policeman just for being nice to me!"

Moored offshore in the Yacht basin at Marebeau, M/V Secant was quarantined as a floating crime scene. The dead were all identified easily by fingerprints and photographs from the seized FBE employment records. Butch, Rocky and Rhonda had all died scarcely knowing what hit them. Eldon Morris had not been so fortunate. He'd essentially been dismembered alive with the huge cleaver using Secant's port engine, running and hot, as a chopping block.

Alison was right. The woman she shot was Annamaria Albarran. She'd come from the West Coast, murdering almost every man she'd come in contact with. Paul DuPont and the owner of the 16 foot runabout Lucky and Jason had seen sinking in Secants wake had been fortunate. Her killing spree had claimed ten lives, starting with Reinhold Hahnemann. Rhonda Carver had been her last victim, and the only woman. The two days Annamaria spent in the sweltering bilge with no food partly explained her appearance.

The Federal Marshals were great. They sought no charges against Gary or any of those who had helped him. Most of the casualties had died at the hands of FBE operatives. Only two were claimed by the rescuers, Butch and Annamaria. Not only were their deaths justified, both happened on the high sea, out of federal jurisdiction. All and all, a good report for everyone except the FBE passive sampling division, and President Robert Owen Trayson.

The presidential address to the nation was scheduled at 8PM standard time. John Walgren expected several folks would watch it with him, and he planned to burn a disk of it. He wasn't prepared for the crowd that gathered.

Gary, Alison, Dale & Greg Lucans and Dennis Davis were expected. Lucky, Andrea and her daughter Diane Sturm were already aboard, as was Dale's wife. That made ten. Too many people already for a twenty-foot houseboat with a five-inch TV. Then the others began showing up. When the helicopters landed, he knew they were in trouble. Admiral Sanders came screaming in with Pam McCannis *and her husband,* who they'd picked up from their front lawn in Holden. Next came Andy Boone, the Marshal who as 'Anatoly', had been planted as the Hind 24 pilot. He still had the huge FBE-owned chopper, and used it to bring down Rose

Wellington and Monroe Jenkins along with several of their family members who'd been reunited with them at Lowreyville. Mr. Jenkins was recovering rapidly thanks to the Naval Air Station medical staff. He was far more excited to see Diane Sturm than the president's address. He owed his life to her. He knew it, and his family knew it. Diane's mother was more proud than she would have believed possible.

The protective detail from the Marshals service had come to a decision. The former captives would all be taken to NAS Lowreyville for medical exams, psychological evaluations, counseling, and simply to be protected from the press for a few days. Their families would be offered transportation to join them

Decades earlier, the Marebeau public marina had been a formal yacht club. Bankrupt in the late '70s, its assets had been seized by the city for back taxes. Three features remained; the 50-foot flagpole with spreaders and gaff, the dining hall, and the last of its flag officers, Vice Commandant Charles Oberlin.

After the club faded away the 'Commodore' continued to show up promptly at 0800 to make colors. Now in his late eighties and a resident of an assisted living facility, the old man still walked the seven blocks each morning and evening in his double-breasted dark blue blazer and white cap, enduring the snickers of his fellow residents. First he'd hoist the ensign to the position of honor at the gaff head, step smartly back and salute it. Then he would raise the old yacht club burgee to the top of the mast and hoist his Vice Commandant flag to the right spreader. He had a box full of club burgees, but his last officer's flag was being reduced to tatters. The marina staff only needed to tend one hoist, the port spreader, and then only when storm signals were flown. Even though he was sort of a pathetic figure to most of them, they still respected him. They had another flag stored away to use after he was gone; a solid blue 'owner absent' flag.

The officer's flag caught the eye of Admiral Sanders as he landed in the boatyard. "You have a flag officer for a public marina?"

"It's a long story. Care to meet him? He just showed up to take down the flags. He'd love it if an Admiral was present. He's real old. A leftover from when this was a fancy yacht club. Guy was a sailor in the Second War. Sort of a hero actually, has a bunch of medals."

Commodore Oberlin took in the situation and offered a solution. "Use the club dining hall, It's got a TV and everything."

One of the marina dockhands ridiculed the idea. "That building hasn't been used in years. It's a mess."

"I beg your pardon, the facility is standing tall. I swept it out last week and the water hasn't been turned off for the winter yet. You people don't take very good care of it, but I do. Every once in a while the city rents it out for parties, you know."

"You swept it? How did you get a key?

"I've always had the key."

Admiral Sanders felt himself in awe of the old gentleman. He tried to see himself in thirty years, wondering if he'd have a fraction of his pride and dignity. "Would you care to inspect a prototype of our next combat helicopter, Mr. Oberlin? I'll have to ask for confidentiality until it's revealed to the public of course. We'll be landing on the foredeck of the nuclear attack submarine Herbert N. Willston and picking up her commander. The round trip should take about 25 minutes." Commodore Oberlin would have two Admirals assisting evening colors.

Someone had found a box of white tablecloths. Gary shared a table with Andrea Sturm. After mixing for a while, Dale Lucans and his wife joined them. Alison held Greg Lucans' hand at a table nearby. Diane Sturm was front and center, sitting with John Walgren, Monroe Jenkins and his two grown children.

Lucky O'Connor had left. He'd found a ride to the airport and was home in Carthage already with his wife Carla and his other granddaughter Heather. He'd been away long enough.

Dennis Davis had tried to attach himself to Andy Boone, trying to learn all he could about the fascinating Russian helicopter. Agent Boone had almost rudely ditched him. It took Dennis a while to realize why; the Marshals were officially in mourning for the loss of Chuck and Rhonda Carver. The black elastic strips around their badges were mourning bands. Andy was the only surviving member of the team sent to infiltrate the FBE. The Marshals were a protective detail, but their mood was somber, and it was rubbing off on the others, except for the former prisoners. Their tears were shed in joy and thankfulness.

Naval officers Jason Sanders and Samuel Leary stood at ease along the back wall with the old Commodore, quietly waiting for the President to make his announcement. All three knew history was about to be made.

"You know, Jason, I'm going to lose my command over this. I'm as much to blame as Trayson. Thank you for stopping me before I murdered these people. And thank you for coming to take me off my sub. If I have to be arrested, I'd rather it didn't happen in front of my men."

"I hope it doesn't come to that. These people not only forgive you, they accepted you into this, ah, party. I think the public will see it the same way." Admiral Sanders stopped and pointed at the TV.

"The President will begin his address any second now, Ladies and Gentlemen. Julie – what's your analysis of President Trayson's actions so far today?"

"Well, Nick, it definitely sounds like he intends to step down. In all his comments today both public and in private he's referred to his administration in the past tense. The helicopter gun camera footage we received from-" Jason and Sam Leary looked at each other, stunned.

"Ladies and Gentlemen, the President, Robert Owen Trayson."

"This will be my last address to you as your President. I have done something so shameful, so undeserving of your trust that I must resign effective immediately. I will leave you in the very capable hands of Vice President Harold Palmer after asking two things. First, if the people demand that I be punished for my recent actions, I ask him not to use his authority to pardon me. Secondly, I'd like to ask not only President Palmer, but also all the citizens of this great nation to face a problem we've all been avoiding for decades. You can no longer avoid it, and it will take all the strength and courage you can muster. Please, do it now. You need to come together and set a new course before any more tragedies like mine unfold. Only the determination of a handful of citizens and the intelligence of two of your naval officers prevented a disaster of my making from coming to pass."

"Last week I ordered the deaths, the brutal murders, of at least twenty people in order to protect the Federal Bureau of Environment, an agency of the government that you elected me to eliminate. Why would I do that? To protect the money the FBE brings in. Earlier this afternoon, as my last official act, I finally ordered the elimination of the FBE. Its many honest employees will be offered jobs in other state and federal agencies."

"Decades ago, we as a people made a commitment to protect the less fortunate among us with economic safety nets patterned broadly on our successful if now inadequately funded federal retirement savings program. The idea was a good one. Based on normal human generosity, we provided a subsistence income to those who fell into poverty so they could get back on their feet. Our model was held up for the world to see, and we were applauded. Unfortunately we ignored human nature."

"People, like the liquids of science, tend to seek the path of least resistance. To far too many of us, working in industry or commerce represents resistance. Folks began to 'qualify' for these benefits by either limiting their earned income, increasing the size of their families, or both. A term I have personally overused to describe what our safety net has become is 'entitlement programs', and we now have dozens of them, all started with the very best of intentions. If we choose as individuals or families to qualify, we can become entitled to free or subsidized food, housing, transportation, medical care, advanced education, clothing, and even cash to spend as we please. Please don't get too smug. Most of us do it to some extent. Have you paid back your college loans? Have you declared bankruptcy on a credit card? Do you know the balance left due to foreign lenders is added to our national debt?"

"As more and more of us became entitled, less and less have been left working and paying taxes to pay for all of it."

"The taxpayers, knowing they were about to become the voting minority, said 'enough' when they elected me president after sixteen years of politically liberal leadership. I promised to roll back taxes and eliminate the worst of the government's revenue enhancement schemes. That brings me to the FBE."

"The FBE came into being six years ago, charged with the daunting task of cleaning up the mess we've made of our priceless land, air and water resources. We conservatives saw it at the time as another entitlement program. One that gave away public funds by making jobs for cleanup workers. Oh, that it were so. The founder of the FBE was an environmentalist by the name of Eldon Stewart Morris. His vision was very different from his public position. Under his direction, the FBE became the second largest revenue-generating arm of the national government. All of you

200

know what he did. He sold permits to industry that allowed them to continue poisoning us, and just as bad, he began trapping businesses and individuals alike in violations of questionable administrative laws of his agencies' own making for the sole purpose of extracting enormous fines and restitution payments."

"The rationale was, taxes adversely affect a large group of voters more or less evenly. Fines and restitution settlements affect just a few, but ruin them in the process. You saw through it and gave me the opportunity to win the election by promising three things: lower taxes, the limiting of the FBE to its original mission, and the removal of Eldon Morris as FBE director. Finally, on this day I was able to deliver on two of these promises."

"As you may remember, my first act in office was to publicly fire Eldon Morris. That was a sham. Nothing but a shameless play on words. I did fire him as Director all right, but I immediately re-hired him to run the Random Passive Sampling Division. That's the section that does the trapping I mentioned earlier. He ran it profitably for two years. Oh Lord, was it profitable. Last year Eldon's crew of 100 agents accounted for 35 percent of our government income."

"Why would I allow such a thing, you ask? I needed the money. When I was elected I set myself a timeline. I expected to have forty percent of the entitlement programs de-funded by the end of my first year in office. My efforts failed. At the end of that first year, entitlements were up by seven percent and growing. People have become totally dependent on those programs. Our economy can't possibly assimilate seventy million new workers, and we've put up so many tax and regulatory barriers to growth that even if we repeal them all today, we wouldn't see a significant number of new employers for years, even if we curbed imports. Millions of our people would starve if I had my way. Pandora's box is open, ladies and gentlemen."

"Eldon made one real change as the chairman of the PRSD. Whenever he identified a potential new victim he ran their name by my re-election campaign staff. Wait." The President half covered his face with his hand. "I'm not being entirely truthful. He'd seek the approval of my Political Security staff. Here begins the part I had no knowledge of, not that it excuses me from the rightful blame."

"Thirteen times over the past two years, Eldon's people have jumped the gun and arrested someone they later learned my staff wished to protect. In order to keep my office from finding out about it, Eldon would illegally incarcerate them without due process. Without any process at all, in fact. Law enforcement suspected the FBE was involved in a couple of the cases, but mostly we assumed either common criminals or terrorists were responsible. In one case we announced that a lady had defected, taking secrets from her defense contractor employer to our enemies. To that woman, whose identity will be released after the investigation, I owe the most heartfelt apology."

"This travesty continued until two weeks ago when a young woman was arrested by two overzealous FBE agents, one of whom assassinated her own partner for reasons that are still not fully understood. Her family somehow picked up her trail and followed her to an FBE facility on Holden's Island in the Missacantata River. By that time the news media was picking up on it. The family launched a partially successful rescue effort last Saturday that won the freedom of at least three of the unfortunate prisoners and doomed Eldon's scheme. This office and the news media only learned of this today. The rescued prisoners did not include Miss Alison Loch, the daughter of Gary Loch who carried out the rescue effort."

"I had previously given clearance for the Naval Air Station at Lowreyville to assist local law enforcement in their effort to solve what the media was calling the Alison Loch affair. Admiral Jason Sanders, commanding, elected to provide this assistance personally, and give it directly to Gary Loch, since no one else was performing effectively. We should all be glad he took this unorthodox step."

"At this point Eldon Morris knew that it was only a short matter of time. He decided to run. Taking his remaining prisoners as hostages, he and a handful of co-conspirators stole an armed trawler from the FBE fleet and headed south for open water, apparently to seek refuge in a foreign country. We learned of this early, and assumed all thirteen prisoners were involved. Mister Loch and his people tried to get him to release the captives by coming alongside in a fishing boat and were blasted out of the water with a deck cannon. At least two people were killed including federal Marshal Charles Carver. We still are not sure exactly how he became involved. He may have joined with the Loch family because his own wife was one of the captives. Loch and his remaining supporters continued the chase into open water with a racing sailboat belonging to Dale and Judith Lucans of Hennison, a town on the Games River Northwest of Dunningsville where the Loch family lives. At this point I made the worst mistake of my life."

"I, too, thought all thirteen hostages and Eldon's entire gang were aboard the motor vessel Secant, the stolen trawler. I also assumed all of Alison Loch's would-be rescuers were aboard the sailboat Atropos. Thinking only of the billions in revenue that stood to be lost if the true nature of the FBE were revealed in the aftermath of a successful rescue, I ordered a nuclear attack Submarine operating in the area to intercept both vessels – and destroy them. I implied that they were both working for terrorists bent on debasing the economy by crippling the FBE."

"Fortunately, Admiral Sanders was monitoring the situation from a helicopter. The sub commander had, like Sanders, elected to perform his duty personally, no doubt to spare his crew the moral repercussions of such a dubious act. When Sanders saw the sub targeting the sailboat, he had his pilot land the machine on the sub, directly in front of it's deadly guns, giving himself time to reveal the truth and stop the attack in the nick of time."

"Now you know as much as I did. More will be revealed, as it becomes known. You also know the underlying problems, and know they won't be easy to fix. I gave it my best and it consumed me. Only you, the people can do it. Those of you who are receiving tax money will have to ask yourselves "Do I need this badly enough to sell out my country for it?" Those of you who are paying taxes need to ask yourself "Do I need this badly enough to starve out my neighbors to keep it?" Then we all need to come together and eliminate enough of our jungle of pointless regulations to allow real economic growth. We need to stop taxing our employers into desperation. If we can't do these things, we must recognize the true cost of all our entitlements and pay for them without complaint. Contrary to the common myth, the government can't just print more money. Money is what it is because we back it with our hard work. And that's true however we choose to spend it."

"In closing, let me ask that you to put your faith in President Palmer. If you decide to take the conservative path, he's your man. Harold is a better man than I, but he'll be starting with a big disadvantage. 35 percent of his revenue is gone. He'll have only three choices; either A, he gets you to approve the biggest tax hike in history, or B, he finds new ways to steal from you, or C, you allow him to make big cuts in entitlements. I doubt if he'll go for B. He's too good a man. Good night, and all my best."

Commodore Oberlin asked the two Admirals, neither in particular "Is that the way it really happened?"

Leary answered. "That – was pretty close."

Judith Lucans asked Gary Loch and her husband, neither in particular, almost the same question.

Gary Loch answered. "That – was pretty close."

Captain Dale Lucans suddenly looked old, tired. "Gary, I've been thinking. You really seemed to take to sailing. You and Andrea seemed to be happy on the water. Now your boat's gone. Would you like to have a bigger one? You have the resources for it. You have a good second in command for your company and your kids are grown." He took his wife's hand in both of his.

"What are you saying, Dale?"

"It's time for me to go ashore for the last time. All this has made me see that. I owe the rest of my life to Judith. Atropos has served her purpose, for me at least. Did I ever tell you what I named my first and second boats?"

"No, but I wondered. I couldn't even imagine where you got the name Atropos."

"Andrea tapped on Gary's hand. Let me try. Clotho, right? And Lachesis." Gary was stunned. Dale's smile changed to a smile of a different shape. She continued. "The Three Fates of Greek Myth. Clotho spun the thread of life. Lachesis measured the length of it. Atropos cut it. You expected to die on that boat, didn't you?"

Gary blinked. "All that from the word Atropos?"

Dale held up his hand, palm forward to stop him. "Yes, I did. And it almost happened yesterday. That was close enough. I'm going home. I know a broker down here who'll do the transfer paperwork. This marina would be a great place to make berth, and you can hire a captain until you get it down. What do you say, Gary? If you want her she's yours. I'll bet you and Andrea here could use a good extended vacation. She'll need a new name though. Just don't call her Clotho."

Maybeline Cohen-Brumbage considered herself to be the center of all social life at the Magnolia Shores Assisted Living

Centre. She'd felt superior to the others around her ever since she was a school girl. Fifty years ago she had been the 29 year old child bride of Commodore Nick Brumbage of the Marebeau Yacht Club, a man twenty years her senior. Maybeline never cared about the club at all, but enjoyed the status it gave her in the community. She also enjoyed Nick's considerable wealth.

The club's decline and bankruptcy provided her the low point of her life. She'd come to blame it on her husband's Vice Commodore, Charles Oberlin.

His daily walks to the dock with those ridiculous flags, wearing that moth-eaten old costume gave a focus to her resentment. She made it her purpose to humiliate him at every opportunity.

Each evening after dinner she would seat herself in the common area near the main entrance directly facing the TV and a dozen of her friends would join her. She considered them her entourage. Mr. Oberlin would have to pass behind her on his way in and out. Residents were not permitted to use any other doors to the outside. Sometimes she would insult him. Sometimes she would try to bait him into a conversation and get him to take a position so she could destroy it. Sometimes she simply ignored him. Her entourage would do the same. This had been such a time when he left. That had been a long time ago, and she was secretly beginning to worry. Ordinarily he'd be gone about an hour. He'd left at about a quarter after five. It was almost 10 PM now. They would lock the front door in half an hour. Where could he be?

Her entourage was extra large tonight. Someone had wanted to see a stupid Presidential address of some sort, thought it was important. A lot of them thought it was important. Hardly any of them were even listening to her anymore. The President was off by the time the news was tuned in, but the announcers were still talking about it, and kept it up for a good half hour. They were always talking about people Maybeline had never heard of. Why should anybody care? One of them actually shushed her! And the President wasn't even talking! The Vice President came on, and someone shushed her again!

All through the evening the TV kept on breaking into her programs to talk some more. About nine-thirty they broke in and showed a lot of people coming out of a building somewhere that looked a lot like the old yacht club dining hall. The woman reporter with the microphone just talked and talked as the folks came out. Three men came out last as a group. Two were in Navy dress uniforms, but the one in the middle was wearing a proper yachting jacket and hat. That caught her attention. Maybe it was someone she knew from the old days! Wouldn't that be grand? One of her friends involved with the President! She watched carefully, but the man never showed himself clearly. A secret mission?

Early in the evening they'd heard a helicopter flying low. Nursing home residents always notice helicopters. They heard another half an hour later, but neither landed to take anyone away to the hospital. This one was different, much louder, closer. Two police cars stopped in front of her picture window, blocking all five lanes and lighting up the space between them with their powerful spotlights, just as they did when the helicopter from Mercy Wood took away Mrs. Rubenstein a couple years ago.

But this one was no ambulance helicopter. Black and wicked looking, it screamed in fast, making a howling roar louder than anything Maybeline could remember. She noticed the indistinct military markings and two huge guns under it's nose that moved on their own. It landed between the police cars with the blades still spinning. The driver side front door opened and a man in a yacht club officer's uniform stepped out. Maybeline felt faint for a moment. He walked a few steps toward the building and then turned smartly to exchange salutes with the naval officers still in the machine. The man held the salute as they lifted off, then walked through the entrance as it darted out of sight blowing wind and grit through the open door.

"Charles?"

"Not tonight, May. I've had a long day."

One of the entourage asked if it had been storming.

Twenty miles below Esprit they started noticing bits of junk in the river. Pieces of shattered wood, bottles and cans, furniture. Five miles later the stuff had become so thick they were constantly jinking back and forth to avoid colliding with it. Five miles out, Nettie spotted a spare car tire with a cat riding on it. "Can we rescue her, John? Please?"

He changed course to intercept the surfing cat and Nettie tried reaching out for it. The terrified creature sprang for her hand from a couple feet away, clawing a row of bleeding gashes all the way up to her shoulder and across her back before she could react. By the time Nettie saw where it went, the little tiger was on the coach roof. It obviously wanted to be as far from the water as possible.

"Think you've made enough rescues for one day?"

"Bite me."

"That's Tabby's job."

Just before the town came into view they noticed some of the larger piles of flotsam were smoking. Then, rounding the last bend before the Esprit Narrows, they saw why.

The town of Esprit was gone. Nothing remained but the bridges, a few hundred smoldering foundations and the radio tower. The hillside was blackened almost to the ridgeline.

Across the river, Norwalk had suffered too. The water-front business district was devastated. Almost all the windows were broken. Smoke rose from a dozen small fires and several cars had been flipped over. Two coast guard boats rode at anchor a hundred yards offshore. "Did the explosions do that? From clear across the river?"

"No way, Nettie. Looks more like the riot spread across the bridge. See the looter's bodies? There – hanging from the lamppost in front of that big store. Either a looter that got caught or an owner who tried to defend himself and failed. Those coast guard boats are running a picket. No one gets in or out without being inspected. I'll bet the Army guard or the state patrol is doing the same thing on the highways just outside the city limits."